The Night Watchman

Fourth book in The Psychological Thrillers series

CHRIS SIMMS

Other novels by Chris Simms:

<u>The Psychological Thrillers</u>
Outside the White Lines
Pecking Order
Midnight Rambler
The Night Watchman

<u>The Supernatural Thrillers</u>
Sing Me To Sleep
Dead Gorgeous

<u>Jon Spicer Series</u>
Killing the Beasts
Shifting Skin
Savage Moon
Hell's Fire
The Edge
Cut Adrift
Sleeping Dogs
Death Games
Dark Angel

<u>DC Iona Khan Series</u>
Scratch Deeper
A Price To Pay

<u>DC Sean Blake Series</u>
Loose Tongues
Marked Men

Copyright © 2024 Chris Simms

The right of Chris Simms to be identified as the author of this work has been asserted by him in accordance with the Copyright, Designs and Patents Act 1988.

All rights reserved.

ISBN: 9798346970323

To The Big Kid
with a fearsome knowledge of guns.

PROLOGUE

Their nostrils widen, then narrow, widen, then narrow. They aren't in control of their breathing. Adrenaline is. Fight or flight. But this pair? They aren't in a position to fight. And they can't take flight, either. All they can do is lie there, air shunting in and out like they've just run their fastest race ever.

The movement of their nostrils – I know it's a bit bizarre, but stay with me on this – it reminds me of jellyfish propelling themselves through water. Of course, jellyfish don't make any sound. They're incredibly serene, actually. But it's that same…wafting motion. It takes me back to diving off the coast of Belize. Gorgeous, warm, aquamarine waters. Some of the best reefs in the world, over there. Up with the Gulf of Aqaba. And what's left of the Great Barrier. Absolutely beautiful.

Not like this dingy shithole of a house. Not like this vile couple of specimens. Two people who are worse, in my humble opinion, than anything spawned in the depths of the deepest ocean. Hey-ho. I've let them stew long enough. Time for work.

I slide off the chair and the scraping sound causes the one on the right – Luke is his name – to shrink back. I rip the tape off his eyes, then do his mate's. A few tearful blinks and they focus in on me. Luke has a look I've seen many times before. I think of it as the three Ds. Disbelief. Dismay. Dread. There they were, just another nice, normal day at work. Getting ready to spread their drugs across half of Manchester when, all of a sudden, this fucking nutter comes crashing through the door. And now they find themselves with their wrists and ankles bound, lying on the kitchen floor. Add to that a probable broken nose, split lips, cracked ribs. Pounding headaches. Blood building up behind their gags. Having to swallow half-congealed lumps of it back. That stomach churning aftertaste of copper. Nasty. And now they can see again, what's the bastard responsible for it all doing? Sitting there with a smile on his face and a knife in his hand.

I let the tension build, my eyes moving slowly from one to the other. The mate, Ads, I can tell he still thinks his situation isn't completely hopeless. He's wrong, but credit to him. Feisty bastard. Which means it's Luke. Yeah, he'll definitely crumble first. So I shift the blade to my other hand, go back on one knee and peel enough tape from Luke's lips so he can speak from the corner of his mouth. First thing to emerge is a long drool of blood. I wait for that to dwindle before speaking.

'Where's the kid?'

CHAPTER 1

9 days earlier.

Guy Haslam's footsteps bounced back at him as he paced slowly through what remained of the night. On either side were shipping containers, stacked six high. A canyon of sheer metal filled by shadow. This far in, it's always bastard cold, he thought, lifting his gaze as he pulled the zip of his jacket up. Pale clumps of cloud were showing against the dark sky.

From the direction of the terminal buildings, noises were carrying. Slams of car doors. High-pitched beeps as yard lads scanned themselves in. The clang of the electric gate. It wouldn't be long before the throaty roars of diesels began to erupt. It was his favourite part of the night shift; this, the sounds of life returning. Sometimes, during those long hours patrolling the deserted site, he was tempted to believe it wasn't just his family dying out, but the entire human race.

He reached an intersection in the maze-like arrangement, turned his torch on and swung it both ways. The door of a nearby container was slightly ajar. He walked over and, once at the base of the stack, raised the beam. The wire of the tamper-proof seal had been snipped. It was the fourth container up, about the same distance from the ground as the guttering on a house. How the hell did they scale up there in the pitch black? He'd never spotted a flicker of light or heard the scrape of a container door being opened.

Lowering the beam of his torch, he made a note of the compromised container's location: row 14, stack 126, column A, 4 high. Out beyond the far end of the aisle, a spike of bright orange was lancing the horizon. Sun. He strode gratefully towards it and soon emerged into the beginnings of a crisp new day.

To his right were train tracks where the first inbound service was soon due. A moveable gantry with a cabin suspended below it spanned the rails. Clambering up a ladder was Andy, one of the few day workers he'd warmed to since starting the job. His hand lifted in greeting.

'Yo, Guy!' the other man called down. 'Ready for your bed?'

'Ready for my bed,' he replied with a smile. 'Got the first rail-to-yard move, then?'

Andy touched a forefinger to his temple. 'Listen to you - using all the right lingo.'

'Getting there, mate. Slowly.'

'You take it easy.'

'And you.'

Once in the main building, he headed straight to the manager's office. Matthew Hughes, a kindly-looking man in his late fifties, was already at his desk, loosening the cap of a navy-blue flask. The windowsill behind him was filled by a row of potted plants, some with flowers just beginning to bud. 'Morning, Guy. Quiet night?'

'Yeah,' he nodded, placing his radio back on the charging rack. 'Though I just found another compromised container.'

'Whereabouts?'

Guy slid the report file from a shelf and removed a sheet. 'Empty storage. Same as all the others.'

'A reefer, was it?'

Reefer, Guy thought. Refrigerated unit. The ones with an internal cooling system for transporting perishable goods like food or flowers. 'Yup.'

The manager began pouring coffee into a mug. 'Only the one?'

'That's right. Not sure exactly when it happened. I patrolled that section twice. First at about...' He had to stop himself from saying oh-one-thirty-hours. 'Half-one in the morning. Second at –'

'Well, empty storage isn't anything to lose sleep over.' Hughes glanced up and smiled. 'Just jot the location down and I'll get one of the yard lads to re-secure it.' His attention went back to some paperwork.

The man's nonchalance struck Guy as bizarre. It was the same reaction each time. Since starting work at the freight terminal a fortnight ago, he'd come across a compromised container almost every night he'd been on duty. He took a seat at the little round meeting table and began to fill in the form. 'I tried to carry out a visual inspection of the perimeter fence yesterday evening. Before it got dark. Starting with the section that borders the road. But there's such a build-up of ground-level vegetation. Now we're getting into summer, that's only going to get worse. It makes it impossible to assess whether the security fence itself could have been–'

'I wouldn't get too concerned, Guy. Really.' Hughes turned in his seat and peered over the top of his precious plants. Across the tarmac, a section of fence was in view. 'If it's not laden containers that are being targeted, we don't consider it a problem. It's just youths. And if they want to get on site, they will.'

Guy almost shook his head. Someone just admitting defeat like that? It wasn't right. In fact, it was a bit pathetic.

But then he considered his own life. Who the fuck are you to talk? He wrote down the location of the container. 'That's me done until Sunday, then.'

'Oh – that reminds me. I realise you're now meant to be off for the next four nights, but we're short on Friday. Any chance you can cover that night for me and have Monday night off instead?'

'Come in on Friday?'

'Yes. And then off on Monday.'

Guy considered what else he might have on. Absolutely nothing, as usual. 'Yeah, I can do that.'

'Oh, that's much appreciated. Thanks.'

'No problem. See you Friday.'

'See you Friday.'

He'd hung up the company jacket in his locker and was shrugging on an old Craghoppers fleece when a voice spoke behind him.

'Reckon I've got it, Guy. Seriously, I do.'

Bollocks, he thought, instantly recognising the nasal whine. Nathan Fenton. A yard lad whose way of speaking hovered between friendliness and taking the piss. His eyes, though, were never warm.

'What's that, then?' Guy asked, shoving his security pass into the pocket of his trousers before turning round.

Nathan was somewhere in his late thirties. Bald head he kept scrupulously shaved. Little goatee-moustache thing encircling his thin lips. Another man stood alongside him, looking vaguely intrigued.

'My sister,' Nathan announced, 'she met this bloke who'd come back to the UK after working overseas. Turns out he'd tried to open a bar in Thailand with this local bird. Like a partnership thing, though he was also shagging her. Like you do. But their laws over there – if you're Western – don't let you own the property. Has to be in the Thai's name. So, once it's up and running like, all paid for by him, she and her family squeezed him out. They got the business, he ends up back in the UK. Broke.' Nathan let the comment hang. Long enough for his mate to look away in embarrassment.

'So what are you saying?' Guy asked, voice low.

Nathan immediately raised both palms, smiling his fake smile. 'Not saying you resorted to a Thai bride, mate!' He took a little step forward that was somehow ingratiating. 'Not that! But the foreign business venture – something along those lines, was it?'

Guy shook his head. 'Nice try, but way off.'

Nathan's grin stayed stuck on. 'Way off? Sure?' He cocked his head. 'So, you've not been working on the oil rigs. And it wasn't a mine or farm or something in Australia. And not Thailand or somewhere like that.' He used his shoulder to nudge his friend. 'We've got a dark horse here, Daz.' He pursed his lips in mock frustration. 'You leave it with me, Guy.'

'Happy to.' He shut his locker and walked directly at Nathan, who, at the last second, melted to the side.

'I'll get it one of these days!' Nathan called after him.

Doubt it, Guy said to himself.

CHAPTER 2

A walkway led from the terminal building to the staff car park. On the far side of the two-metre fence, the first trucks were queuing to get in. Most were carrying a shipping container. Guy scanned a few of the names: Cosco, OOCL, Sealand, Yang Ming. Others were just a cab with a driver sat at the wheel. Guy searched his head for the term. Skellies. Skeletal trailers. There to pick up a laden import container from the depot. After that, the driver would transport the container to where its contents were due. Usually, a retailer's warehouse or distribution centre. Once the contents had been tipped, the empty container was driven back to the depot.

From behind him, the rev of engines was being drowned out by a chorus of metallic whines and clanks: the six-seventeen train as it took the spur off the Manchester-Liverpool line to crawl into the freight terminal. Guy let himself through the pedestrian security gate, walked across the car park and out onto the service road. More trucks were lined up in a side lane. Some had been there overnight as the drivers caught up on sleep. Bits of rubbish were scattered along the verge of overgrown grass. Stuff jettisoned by the waiting lorry drivers: cans, bottles, foil food wrappers, burger cartons, wet wipes and worse.

Further along, the road rose as it passed over the Bridgewater Canal. Once at the midpoint, Guy turned to look back at the depot. Andy was already lowering the crane's spreader on to the end container of the now stationary train. Guy watched as the twist locks engaged at each corner and the container rose silently from the train's wagon into the air. Best job that, he said to himself. Playing giant Lego. One of the yard lads had already steered an RST to the transit area beside the rails. Large black letters down its massive arms spelled the word Hyster. The squat vehicle waited for the container to be lowered.

At the end of the service road, Guy checked both ways. Industrial units stretched off to his left, most enclosed by fences topped with razor wire. Signs attached to the chain-metal links made various pronouncements. No parking at any time. CCTV in operation. Beware guard dogs! It was a weird place, the edge of the city. Busy during the day, dead at night. But close enough to residential areas for it to attract thieves. He narrowed his eyes: three lads were loitering in a lay-by less than fifty metres off. They didn't look like they'd arrived for work early. Not proper work, anyway.

He turned right and, at the neighbouring buildings, ambled across empty parking spaces to a modest industrial unit in the corner of the courtyard. A small sign read 'Martyna's Bakery'. The bulk of her sales were direct to shops and restaurants, but she was also happy to serve anyone who dropped by. The smell reached him well before he got to the door. Fresh sourdough. It was all Martyna used, as had her dad in his bakery over in Poland. Guy had discovered the place within days of taking the job at the freight terminal. Now it was the only place he'd buy bread from.

The door grated slightly as he pushed it open. Wasn't

like that yesterday. He scanned the wicker baskets to see what she'd put out. Little square loaves of rye bread dotted with pumpkin seeds. Larger ones with a thick crust. Rolls of tiger bread. Cylindrical loaves coated in oats. A tray to the side held small squares of apple cake. Next to them, bumpy slices of something yellow.

'Guy, good morning!'

He returned her smile. Martyna had large round cheeks that, when she grinned, seemed to force her eyes back into her face. A row of impressively even teeth that Guy was certain had nothing to do with expensive dental work. Customary dusting of flour in her straight brown hair.

'Martyna, good to see you. How's things?'

She was brushing her hands on a blue and white apron. 'They are all fine. It was a little problem dropping Gabriela off earlier, but you know...'

'She OK?'

'Yes. She has a little sniffle. The child minder, she was concerned at first.'

Guy nodded. There weren't, apparently, many childminders in Manchester who were happy to take a kid at five in the morning. 'Sorted now, though?'

'Oh, yes. She was just being cautious. So, anything you like the look of?'

Guy let out a large sigh. 'The entire shop?'

Martyna laughed.

'What are these?' He pointed at the cylindrical ones covered in oats.

'Oh, it's wheeler bread. When you slice it, they're like wheels. Wheat and rye.'

'Sold.'

She took one from the basket and placed it in the slicing machine. 'Medium?'

'Thanks. And what's going on with your door?'

She sent a frown towards it. 'I think in the night, it's been kicked. I will call someone to come and –'

'Leave it with me. I'll sort it out.'

'No, you need to sleep!'

'I will. For a bit. You close up at three, right?'

'Yes, but–'

'I'll be here just before with my toolbox. It'll only be the bottom plate. Five-minute job.'

She pointed to the cake trays before turning to the coffee machine. 'You must have a slice of that one. By the apple tart.'

'The yellow ones? What are they?'

'Carpathian custard cake. It's special. You'll see.'

'Martyna, are you after turning me into a balloon?' he asked, plucking one out with some tongs and placing it in a little cardboard tray.

'A balloon? No, you visit the gym too much for that.'

'The gym?' Guy patted the swell of his stomach. 'I wish.' He thought about the shape he used to be in. It seemed a long time ago, but wasn't. Not really. 'What do I owe you?'

She placed his cappuccino on the counter, then bagged the cake and bread up. 'Two pounds.'

'Two pounds?'

'Two pounds.'

'Don't be silly. The coffee alone is more than that. And the cake...'

'Two pounds.' She crossed her arms. 'You fix my door, it's two pounds.'

'I can't pay you two pounds.'

'Then you don't pay me anything.'

He took the paper bag and drink off the counter, then whipped out a ten-pound note and slapped it down. 'See you at three!'

'Guy – your change!'

He waved a hand as he stepped out the door. Back on the road, he could see no sign of the lads from earlier. He continued towards Wharfside Way, a security fence to his right separating him from a vast, empty parking area. On its far side loomed Old Trafford. The sun had just cleared the football stadium's upper edge, beams of light playing through the criss-crossing white struts which rose from the rim of the massive stands.

Soon after turning off Wharfside Way, the Manchester Ship Canal came into view. Guy made a beeline for the tree-lined promenade that bordered it and plonked himself down on his usual bench. A couple of swans were making their way across the ruffled water. He breathed in the cool breeze, nodding at an early morning jogger passing by. A quick check of his watch. Twenty-five past six. So, mid-afternoon over in Brisbane. They were probably just about to have afternoon tea and cakes. To delay making the call, Guy took a sip of coffee and studied the troubled water's surface. How many times have I felt the underside of a RIB slapping against wavelets like that? Hunkered down in the prow of the vessel as it raced through the dead of night towards some foreign shore?

Or that time on a morning much like this. Chasing a couple of pirate skiffs across the Somali Sea, pursuing them right back to their base on Cape Guardafui. The look on their faces when we drove our RIB straight onto the beach. Them fleeing on foot, us shooting their skiffs full of holes and then burning their ramshackle base to the ground. Happy days. And look at my life now.

Come on, mate. Let's just get this done.

He placed his coffee on the bench, took out his phone and prised the back cover off. Tucked into the casing was a spare SIM card. He removed his own one from the device and slid the other in. Once the phone had settled down, he called the care home's number, knowing it would be his brother's name that showed at the other end.

'Lee, hello. It's Martin here.'

'Hi Martin. I was hoping to speak to my dad?'

'Right-o. I'm pretty sure he's awake. He managed a respectable bit of lunch earlier on.'

'Yeah? That's good. What did he have?'

'Shepherd's pie. A few spoonfuls.'

'Figures. He's always liked that.' He listened to the soft thump of the care home worker's footsteps. Occasionally, a low groan or cry of distress carried down the line. Guy flinched inwardly at the sounds. He imagined a long corridor with tiny rooms on either side. Occupants confined to their cots or slumped in armchairs. Drool-covered chins and dead-eyed stares. 'How's he been?' It was a question he hated to ask.

'Oh, you know. He was quite lucid earlier, actually. Mentioned someone called Guy. Is that his brother?'

'Really?' Guy looked up. 'His son. My brother.'

'Ah.'

'What... what did he say about him?'

'He got a bit agitated, to be honest. Where he was, what he was doing. Those kinds of question. Is he older or younger than you?'

'Guy? Older. Only by a year. He's a bit of a...a... restless spirit.'

'That would make sense. I'm not sure if he's ever phoned your dad.'

'No... he works abroad a lot. Once he's out of the country, contact is pretty tricky.'

'Oh – fair enough. Right, we're here. One moment.' The pitch of the man's voice changed. 'Harry? I've got Lee on the line.'

'Mmm?'

'Your son, Lee. He's phoning from England. Would you like a word?'

'Lee, did you say?'

'Here you go.' A momentary burst of noise. Like a car window being cracked open on the motorway. 'Whoops,' said Martin. 'Got it? You sure?'

'Hello?' His father's voice was wafer thin.

'Hi, Dad. It's Lee. How are you?'

'Oh, I'm fine, thank you very much.'

Guy could immediately tell his father had no idea who he was talking to. 'Have you been up to much today?'

'Tennis, this morning.'

Tennis? He's never even picked up a racket. 'Good for you.'

'Yes, I won both my rounds. Not sure who I'm up against tomorrow.'

'It's a tournament, is it?'

'Yes.'

'I'm sure you'll see them off. And I hear your lunch was nice. Shepherd's pie, wasn't it?'

'Lunch? No time for lunch. I could do with new plimsolls. Mine are wearing very thin on these courts. Are you the person to arrange that?'

Guy let his eyes close. Poor bastard. 'Yes. Size nine, isn't it?'

'Yes. I shall need them first thing in the morning.'

'Not a problem.'

'Great. Well, can you make arrangements with this person here? Good night.'

'Night.'

The care home assistant came back on the line. 'Lots of energy this afternoon. I think there was tennis on the TV earlier on.'

Guy opened his eyes. Had to wipe a tear away. Across the expanse of water, a tram was gliding into the gleaming development that was MediaCity. 'How about his physical health? Is it holding up?'

The thud of the man's footsteps had resumed. 'Well, you're aware of how this illness progresses?'

'Yes. As his mind deteriorates further, control of his major organs does, too. He's already had one stroke.'

'Lee, I'm not being evasive here. But, really, this is a conversation for the head nurse. Shall I book you a phone appointment?'

'I had a look at flights over. Within the next month.' He ran a hand through his short hair. 'Thing is, if I came, will he even know who I am? Will he even last that long?'

'This isn't something...really...as I said, the head nurse, she'll be the best person to –'

'Sorry, mate. That wasn't fair of me. Yes, the head nurse. Whenever she's free.'

'I'll book you a time.' The man sounded relieved.

'Perfect. Any idea when it's likely to be?'

'Not sure. But I'll make sure she's aware not to ring in the middle of the night for you.'

'It's OK – I'm a light sleeper. Cheers, Martin.'

'Thanks, Lee.'

He took a sip of his coffee. Half-cold. Shit. He gulped back the rest of it, grabbed hold of the paper bag, and got to his feet. A narrow footbridge arched over the ship canal, chest-high Perspex panels giving him a good view of the mud-coloured water below. On his left, the canal led in the direction of Liverpool. Funny, he thought. Less than seventy years ago, countless tons of freight were being carried along here every week. Now? The only things you ever saw on the water were rowing boats from the nearby club.

The bridge started to vibrate. Footsteps, rapidly approaching from behind. Next thing, a man in his early twenties brushed past. Tracksuit bottoms and trainers. Black baseball cap. Roadman's uniform. Would-be gangster. Guy could tell there was another, possibly two, still behind him. The one in front came to a stop, turned round and smiled. Nasty crooked teeth. Neck tattoo poking above the collar of his NorthFace top. 'Got a deal for you, my friend.'

CHAPTER 3

Guy's way was blocked. He glanced over his shoulder to see another man, also somewhere in his early twenties. He was bigger, heavier and with a straggling mass of unkempt hair. UnderArmour sweat top and baggy jeans. Guy took an immediate dislike to his slightly open mouth and piggy-eyes. His face had the suggestion of cruelty. Next to him was a much younger lad. Sixteen? That scowl of someone trying their best to look tough. So, Guy thought, the three I spotted earlier on. Wonder if they're the same ones who tried to bust into Martyna's bakery? Guy turned back to the man in front of him.

'Nice morning, hey?'

'It is,' Guy replied cautiously. 'What's up?'

'Nothing, bruv. Nothing. Just after a little chat.'

Guy stepped to the side and turned so his back was against the Perspex barrier. Now all three were in his eyeline. Better. He waited for someone to say something.

The one who'd overtaken him brushed a hand across his chin. A cluster of gold rings on his fingers. 'How's it going working at the freight terminal? Enjoying it?'

Guy gave a questioning tilt of his head.

The man grinned. 'We seen you coming out! Plenty of times now.'

'Yeah?'

'Come on,' the man said. 'Look at you: safety shoes, cargo trousers. Under that fleece, you're wearing a polo top. It'll have the Freight Master logo right here.' He lifted a hand and tapped a finger against his own chest. 'Am I right?'

No point denying it, Guy thought. He nodded.

'You work nights, right? You just done a Saturday – Tuesday. Now you're off until Sunday.'

Fair enough figuring out where I work, thought Guy. But knowing my shift pattern, too... 'What's this all about?'

'It's about this, bruv.' He slid a wedge of twenty-pound notes from the pocket of his tracksuit bottoms. 'Four hundred, cash. It's yours.'

'It's mine?' He gave an uncertain smile. 'Don't remember dropping it.'

The man's eyes cut to the other two. 'Likes a joke, this one!'

The younger one immediately grinned. On seeing no one else was, he quickly looked down. When his chin lifted, the sour look was back. Guy studied him for a second longer. You're too young for this type of crap. Just like I was.

'Four hundred,' the man repeated. 'For a twenty-four-hour loan of your security pass. This time tomorrow, you'll have it back.'

'Four hundred in cash? For my security pass?'

The man nodded. 'Easy money.'

'Why?'

'Hey – ask no questions and all that. Deal?'

Guy thought about the price of a plane ticket to Brisbane. 'I... I don't think so. Thanks, anyway.'

The man narrowed his eyes. 'You don't want the money?'

'I don't want the money, no.'

The straggly haired one on his left now spoke up. 'You've moved into a place on Farrant Road, haven't you? By Seedley Park.'

Guy tried to hide his shock. They've been following me and I hadn't even noticed. Not good. 'Why's that important?'

'Just saying, like.' He lifted a shoulder. Let it fall.

The other one held out the cash again. 'Four hundred! Easy money, bruv. Come on.'

Guy breathed in deeply through his nose. 'Listen, I appreciate the offer. But, no. I'm not interested.'

The bigger man stepped closer. A hand shot out and slapped Guy's bag. The paper ripped and slices of bread cascaded onto the walkway. The cake took a second longer to slide out. It hit the ground with a soggy little thud.

The one with the cash held it out again. 'We know where you live, you prick. Now, take the fucking money.'

Guy regarded the handles of the bag hanging from his fingers. The cake had landed soft side down. Was looking forward to that. 'I... listen, it's not even seven in the morning. I just want to go home and get some sleep here.'

'Then take the fucking money – or you'll be losing a lot more than some bread.'

He let his eyes drift across the three of them. The younger one tried to glare back, lips moving ever so slightly as he swallowed. Jesus, thought Guy. I could lift you up. Toss you straight over this barrier into the water. He addressed the older two. 'You say I'll lose a lot more than some bread.' He smiled grimly. 'Sorry lads, but I've got fuck all in my life worth losing.'

The three of them stared at him in silence. Finally, the one with the cash shook his head. 'You'll be changing your mind. Few more weeks in that job. You'll see.' He deliberately stepped on the slices of bread as he moved past. 'Come on, Ads. Leave the cunt.'

Ads, thought Guy. I'll remember that.

He watched the heavier man clear his throat and gob

out a lump of phlegm. It landed on Guy's shoe. Then the two of them set off back the way they'd come. The younger one continued staring at Guy with a baffled look. Then he spun round and hurried after the older pair.

Guy regarded his ruined bread and cake. There goes breakfast. He used a slice to wipe the phlegm off his shoe then started kicking it all under the gap of the Perspex barrier. The food dropped into the water below and, within seconds, the first seagulls were swooping in.

Guy saw the three of them were now on the promenade. The two older ones were busily talking into phones as they walked. The youngest one had trailed behind. His step faltered slightly as he glanced back to the footbridge. Guy held his gaze. You've got a choice, son, he wanted to call out. Don't follow those two. As if reading his thoughts, the lad raised a middle finger then jogged to catch them up.

Guy brushed crumbs from his fingers. His heart was still thudding in his chest. He watched the young lad with a sense of regret. Just like I was at his age. A cocky little shit. He continued over the bridge, eyes scanning the glossy buildings of MediaCity. A row of bars and restaurants formed the ground-level premises at the base of one of the highest towers. Upmarket places to catch the well-paid employees in the offices above. The one at the end of the row was undergoing some kind of refurbishment; its plate-glass windows obscured by chipboards as a steady stream of workmen filed in and out the open doors.

The talk with the care home assistant started replaying in his head. What the hell should I do? When he reached Eccles New Road, he found himself turning left rather than continuing straight on towards Seedley Park. A side road soon appeared. Really, Guy? You're doing this? He walked slowly down it and regarded the entry sign at the end. Weaste Cemetery. It would be the first time he'd returned since burying his younger brother three weeks before.

CHAPTER 4

He wandered down the cemetery's main avenue, the silence of the morning broken only by a solitary blackbird's trill. A few pink blossoms still clung to a nearby cherry tree. Funny, he thought. Didn't notice that on the day of Lee's funeral. His eyes swept several grandiose monuments. A tall, narrow obelisk with a pointed top. Next to it, a pale edifice that looked like someone had taken the tip of a cathedral's spire and jammed it into the ground. Figures at prayer were carved into its elaborate pillars. Didn't notice any of this, he thought.

He knew Lee was on the far side, in a section beyond the older ranks of graves. Guy picked his way carefully between them, not totally sure if he was going in the right direction. Headstones greened with age. He read the names where the lettering was still legible.

Percy Sheldon.
Emily Grant.
Dorothy Ridpath.
Wilfred Potter.

Up ahead, he spotted the newer section where Lee was buried. When choosing a headstone, he'd liked the York stone ones best. But they were so expensive. The cost of granite ones was lower, if it wasn't something fancy like Blue Pearl or Ruby Red. He'd opted for the cheapest: polished black, traditional round top, two feet six inches in height.

Guy came to a halt before the fresh grave. Should I have included a flower container, too? Even though it would have added nearly another two hundred to the bill. Lots of the nearby graves had flowers or other little ornaments. Vases or animals. The lack of anything on his brother's grave lent it an air of sadness.

Lee Haslam, aged 43. Taken from this world too soon.

Guy looked away as emotion welled up. 'This is so... fucked.' He crouched, bringing himself eye-level with his brother's name. 'What the hell am I supposed to do about dad? How do I tell him about you?'

A gentle breeze stirred the leaves on a row of birch trees at the cemetery's edge. Other than that, silence.

'I mean, if I fly over there – assuming he lives that long – you know what he'll say when it's me who turns up. "What are you doing here? Where's Lee? Why isn't Lee here?" You know he bloody will.' He plucked a blade of grass, rolled it between his forefinger and thumb. 'Should be me in that box, not you. You, the family success story.' He bowed his head. 'Bloody hell, Lee, why? Why did you go and do it?' He threw the bit of grass at the headstone. It touched the smooth surface and dropped to the ground. 'Idiot.'

He remained like that for a few more seconds, then raised himself back up and rotated his hips one way, then the other. Stretched his lower back. Really need to start doing some exercise, he thought with a last look at the grave. 'Don't worry, mate. I'll think of something. Not quite sure what, but I'll think of something.'

An engine started up as he walked back towards the entrance. Council worker in a green tabard, pushing a lawnmower along the verge. Guy waved a hand in greeting and the man nodded back. Traffic was now building on the main road. Commuters heading towards the city centre. Enough of a gap eventually opened to let him jog stiffly across. Soon, he had entered a cramped network of residential roads. It struck him as odd that two minutes' walk from the overpriced apartments of MediaCity and Salford Quays was some of the city's cheapest housing. What separated one world from another? Just a couple of main roads.

Twin tower blocks obscured a wide strip of sky directly ahead. Laidlow and Copmere. Or the Two Sisters, as they were known locally. At least, Guy thought with a shudder, you're not among the poor bastards consigned to live in them.

He took a right turn into Farrant Road. If any trees had ever lined the street, they were long gone. Bushes and plants, too. In fact, the only green he could see were the clusters of wheelie bins in every front yard. Most of the houses – including the one he lived in – had been turned into flats and bedsits. The gate to number twenty-three was missing. Someone had dumped a grease-stained cooker beside the front path. Guy checked the road behind him. No sign of his three friends. He fished his keys out and walked up to the front door.

The hall smelled of crap food, as usual. He used his foot to nudge aside a few cartons and crumpled bags, all of which bore the McDonald's logo. Worst thing to have happened in years, he thought. That place offering home deliveries. He wasn't sure what anyone else in the building did. He'd never so much as glimpsed most of them. Did they just sit in their rooms and order in food? The stair carpet had worn through to little more than bare mesh in places. On the first-floor landing, he slid his key into the nearest door and pushed it open. Home, sweet home.

A living-area which incorporated a bed, sofa, small table and galley kitchen. Two inner doors, one to a miniscule bathroom and one to a broom cupboard. One medium-sized window that looked down on a rear garden which hadn't been touched in months. Probably years.

What to do about breakfast? He checked the cupboard. Next to several tins of chickpeas, kidney beans and chopped tomatoes, was a big bag of oats. Porridge? There was milk in the tiny fridge. Porridge it was, then. Not your usual summer choice, he thought, but still a good option.

The best thing he'd done since moving in was to claim the microwave, oven and grill combi from Lee's apartment in Salford Quays. It was a very efficient way of preparing meals for one. The thing could defrost frozen portions, warm-up leftovers, bake bread, roast potatoes, grill meat. The old cooker was now just an extra store cupboard, the hob a handy work surface.

Once the oats and milk were warming through in the microwave, he crossed to the little store cupboard. Muffled sounds of talking descended from the ceiling. Laughter and applause. Telly was on, then. And would stay that way until about eleven that night. Soon, whoever lived below would start their first bout of coughing. The contents of his cupboard were immaculate. He'd affixed shelves to one side on which were lined various tins, bottles and sprays. A vacuum against the rear wall alongside a large umbrella, long-handled duster, mop and bucket. Tucked in next to them were the tall canvas cases that held his two fishing rods. One for fly-fishing, one for course-fishing, depending on whether it was a river, lake or the sea. High on the other wall were a series of hooks from which he'd hung bags that contained a one-man tent, camouflaged basha tarp and hammock. Next down was his dry bag. On the floor below that was a metal trunk with two heavy-duty padlocks. Though you couldn't tell at first glance, the thing was also bolted to the floorboards. On top of it were his hiking shoes, trainers and a toolbox. He lifted the toolbox out. It was one of the few things Simone had left behind when their marriage imploded. No doubt it had only been left because her new partner already had one. After all, she'd taken pretty much everything else. He placed it near the table, ready for when he headed back to Martyna's.

He checked the microwave timer. Still a minute to go. Over at the window, he looked down into the mini wilderness that was the garden. Odd: no sign of the birdfeeder he'd hung in the lower branches of an apple tree the previous week. Squirrels, maybe? That was annoying: it had just started to attract smaller birds. Bluetits, sparrows. One time, a bullfinch. The undergrowth was too long for him to see if it was lying beneath the branch. He'd have to go down and check after breakfast.

The microwave pinged. Sitting at the table, he sprinkled a pinch of salt on the porridge, followed by a splash of milk. 'Just right, Goldilocks, just right.' A habit so ingrained, he was barely conscious of muttering it. As he started eating, he mulled over what had been said earlier. It wasn't the first time they'd made the offer of cash, that was obvious. The one with all the money had even said, 'likes a joke, this one'. How many others had been approached leaving work? And his parting shot: 'You'll be changing your mind. Few more weeks in this job.'

He thought about the empty reefers whose doors were being forced open. No wonder there were so many if security passes were being loaned out. Apart from the main entrance, how many other access points were there for the site? He retrieved his iPad from the table and hesitated for a moment. Then, rather than open his browser, clicked on his emails.

Skimming straight over the latest batch of junk messages, his eyes stopped at the one which had recently appeared. It was from a private Facebook group he was still part of.

Bourneville – are you out there, mate?

Bourneville. Some clown decided Guy had a passing resemblance to the actor who played Jason Bourne. Until someone else pointed out Guy was a bit chubbier. Hence, Bourneville. Guy had tried to point out that the make of chocolate was actually spelled Bournville, but it was no good: the nickname had stuck.

He stared at the message for a moment longer, then dragged it across to the trashcan and dropped it in. After how everything had turned out, the thought of facing his former comrades – even over the internet – was just too much.

Next, he typed the postcode for the freight terminal into Google. Clicking on the map, he switched to satellite view and zoomed in. The gate at the far end, off Europa Way. The rail side one, beside the train tracks. Another into the adjoining trading estate, Orion. The terminal itself was massive. He zoomed out so Manchester United's stadium came into view. The thing could fit into the freight terminal six times over. And he was expected to cover the whole thing on his own? It was a joke.

Four hundred quid in cash. Guy tapped his spoon against the edge of the bowl. That was a lot of money. Which meant that whatever had been hidden inside the empty containers was worth a heck of a lot more. And it was coming in all the time. There was only one thing he could think of: drugs. What had taken his younger brother's life.

#

A narrow passageway blocked by wheelie-bins ran down the side of the house. After dragging a few aside, he was able to squeeze through. Despite the proximity of the bins, people had still dumped rubbish on the ground. Some of it was too big for the wheelie bins, including a couple of sofa cushions and the front wheel of a bike. Further down was a broken toaster with a used condom lying across it. People could be so rank.

The gate into the back garden couldn't be properly closed because of the ivy which hung from the fence. He edged through the gap. The first thing he saw was the birdfeeder lying on the remains of a bag of building sand. The hinged lid of the feeder was open and the thing was empty. Thieving squirrels. Or, once they'd pulled it from the branch, a hedgehog or badger.

He took the bag of birdseed from his pocket, refilled the feeder and then began high stepping across the mass of undergrowth. Once he'd got to the tree, he selected a sturdier branch with a steeper upward angle and hung the feeder from that. As he made his way back to the gate, he checked the windows of the ground-floor flat. As before, the curtains were firmly drawn. Dead flies, bits of crumpled paper and a comprehensive collection of empty Aldi's own vodka bottles were spread across the windowsills. For all anyone knows, he thought, the tenant could be a withered husk in there. Passed away years ago.

CHAPTER 5

'How did you like the custard cake?' asked Martyna, as she stacked empty wicker baskets into a pile.

Guy was kneeling at the base of her door, which he'd propped open with his toolbox. He'd detached the metal base plate and straightened out the buckled corner with his pliers and some tactical blows of a hammer. Now, plate back in place, he was putting a two-centimetre tamper-proof screw into the last of the holes he'd drilled through the metal. 'You know what, Martyna? This jogger stumbled into me on the footbridge over the Manchester Ship Canal. The bag tore and I lost the bloody lot.'

'No! These stupid joggers. They never look. I'm so sorry. Tomorrow, you come in and I'll have some more ready.'

'I'm off now until Friday night.' He placed the drill to one side and tested the base plate with his fingers. Would take a minor explosive charge to get that off.

'Saturday morning, then. I will make more for that day.'

'Well... if you insist.' He replaced his tools and snapped the lid shut. 'Sorted.'

'Thank you, Guy. It's very kind –' The door into the

bakery opened behind her and Gabriela appeared round the counter.

'Oh no,' Guy said in a dramatic voice. 'Here comes trouble. I really hope she doesn't try jumping on my back like she did last time.' Guy made a show of trying to get to his feet, groaning with the effort while one hand scrabbled uselessly at the door frame.

Gabriela took the cue and raced across the shop, her laugh of delight cutting off as she launched herself onto him. Pudgy arms enclosed his neck.

'Ooof!' Guy said, as he straightened up and began a high-knee trot across the car park, one hand lightly gripping her wrists so she couldn't slip. More laughter erupted. The little puffs of air tickled his ear.

Martyna called out from inside the building. 'Gabriela, you really must not –'

Guy whinnied as he traced a slow circle, which ended up back at the bakery's door.

Martyna was fighting to keep a straight face. 'I am so sorry. She is –'

'It's fine,' Guy answered, lowering himself to one knee. The little girl certainly wasn't shy; this was only the second time he'd met her.

'Again?' came a little clockwork voice.

'Gabriela! Off him, now. Off!'

Her arms loosened and her feet reconnected with the floor. 'That was fun.'

'I bet.' He grinned down at her. 'You need to get across to the beach at Scarborough. They still do rides there. On real donkeys.'

'Sca-bruh?'

'Scarborough. You can catch the –' He glanced at Martyna, realising she might not appreciate him planting the seed. 'It's not too far.'

'Mumma, can we go there?'

Guy grimaced in Martyna's direction before mouthing the word, sorry.

Martyna flicked the apology aside with her fingers. 'Maybe one day. When it's the holidays.'

'When is it the holidays?' Gabriela asked.

Time to make myself scarce, thought Guy, retrieving his toolbox. 'I'd better be off. See you soon, Martyna.' He ducked his head. 'And see you soon, trouble.'

'See you soon, trouble!'

'Thank you again, Guy.'

He gave a backward wave as he headed for the main road. At the main entrance to the freight terminal, four lorries were queuing to get through the Vehicle Booking System. Two with Maersk containers, one with Hapag-Lloyd and one empty skel. Beyond the barrier, three coloured lines led off across the tarmac: green to laden storage, blue to rail side and white to empty. At the far side of the site, all three lines then reconverged to be replaced by a single red line, which then led back to the exit barrier.

As he crossed the staff car park, he did a quick count of its spaces. Three rows, each with about twenty spaces. As usual, it was about three-quarters full. So, at any time, there were almost fifty staff on site. He held his pass to the touchpad and shouldered the side gate open as soon as the lock released.

He found Andy in the canteen, a cup of tea beside him, eyes on his phone as he brushed the screen with a forefinger. Guy placed his toolbox on the adjacent table and took a seat opposite him.

Andy glanced up. 'The fuck are you doing here? And why've you bought a toolbox in?'

'Sorting out something for a friend who's round the corner.'

'Very neighbourly of you. And now you've decided to pop into work because...'

Guy sat back, using the movement to glance either side. The nearest people were three tables away. 'Actually, I was hoping to catch you on your break. There's something I wanted to ask you about.'

Andy blinked. 'Yeah? What's that?'

Guy sat forward again and lowered his voice. 'Most nights I've worked here, an empty reefer or two has been broken into. What's that all about?'

Now the other man checked to see who might be in earshot. 'Who's breaking into them, you mean?'

'Who's breaking into them. Why they're breaking into them. How big the issue is.'

'You've let Hughes know about this?'

Guy could see the site manager in his head. The man's nonchalant smile. 'He doesn't seem to give a shit, if I'm honest. All he says is to make a note of the container's location on the report form. That's it.'

Andy nodded. 'No surprise.' He put his phone aside. 'So, no one's mentioned the collectors to you?'

'Collectors? No. What's that?'

'Who's that,' Andy corrected him. 'The collectors are kids, mainly. Teens, late teens. That sort of age. They're paid to get on site and retrieve... merchandise from specific containers. Pay is per kilo of how much they bring out.'

Per kilo, thought Guy. 'We're talking drugs here?'

Andy tapped the side of his nose in reply.

Guy shook his head. Fucking knew it. He thought of his brother, Lee. It had been a heroin overdose that had ended his life. Heroin. The high-flying media executive, sticking that shit into his veins. 'So, the collectors, they come...' He tried to map out the process in his mind, but the attempt just led to a mass of new questions springing up. The kids had to have been recruited by organised crime. Rumour had it there were three, possibly four, gangs who controlled the movement of drugs in the city. Who was currently in control of this particular racket, he had no idea.

His mind turned to the containers. He knew there were eight inbound and eight outbound rail services every day. Andy had previously told him each train carried about two hundred containers. So, around three thousand two hundred units arriving and leaving every day. A decent percentage of those would go into storage while the shipping line which owned them awaited a new order to come in. 'What's the... I mean how - how do these collectors know where to look? There are God-knows-how-many thousands of containers stacked up in empty storage.'

'That, my friend, is the million-dollar question,' Andy whispered. He checked his phone. 'Listen, my break is about to finish. Your shift starts at six, right?'

'I'm off now. For two nights, anyway.'

'Really? You live quite close, don't you? Walking distance?'

Guy nodded.

'Do you know The Three Flags?'

'Off Albion Way, near Salford Crescent?'

'That's the one.'

Jesus, thought Guy. It's still going? Back in the day, it certainly wasn't somewhere you went for a quiet pint. Fake timber frontage and mullioned windows. Separated from the neighbouring buildings by a grim expanse of asphalt. No vehicles ever parked there except old, knackered work vans. 'I do.'

'Want to meet there later for a couple of pints? Better than talking here.'

Guy wondered how long it had been since he'd ventured into any pub. The places, he'd come to learn, were best avoided. Too many nights ending in carnage of one type or another. 'Yeah – sounds good.'

Andy lifted his phone. 'What's your number? I'll give you a bell.'

Guy realised he still had Lee's SIM in his handset. And he needed to keep it there until the head nurse had rung. 'It's out of action while I'm moving providers. Just give me a time.'

'Eight?'

'Eight it is.'

Andy got to his feet. He started to move away from the table, but paused. 'You been approached, then?'

Guy tilted his head back to make eye contact. 'This morning, when I came off shift.'

'How many of them?'

'Three. Well, two. The third, I guess, was their little monkey who does the fetching.'

'Sounds about right. Eight o'clock?'

'See you then.' Guy looked at the cup of tea Andy had left behind. In a few hours' time, that won't be tea. It'll be a pint of beer. Be careful. You can have two. And that's only so you can find out what the hell's going on in this place.

CHAPTER 6

The lights were off in Martyna's place when it came into view. He diverted across to the entrance and checked the front door. Solid. Though, he thought, she could do with a motion-sensor light above it. All the other units in the little courtyard had one – which made hers the easiest option.

As he continued back towards Salford Quays, he mulled over what Andy had said. Collectors. He pictured the young lad from that morning. For someone like him, climbing the stacks of shipping containers would be relatively easy. A pair of pliers would cut the security seal. Slide the door's bolt and he'd be in. Within minutes, he'd be scuttling back out with a rucksack full of packages for delivering... where? Whoever was next in the chain. Up the packages would go until they reached the man at the top. A modern-day Fagin, no doubt living in a big house far away from here. The thought of it made Guy kick out at a coffee cup lying on the pavement.

He'd reached the side of the ship canal when his phone buzzed. Had to be the nursing home over in Australia. He was able to sit on his usual bench. 'Hello?'

'Is that Mr Lee Haslam?' A soft female voice with that

Aussy twang. She sounded older than him. Maybe in her fifties?

'Yes, speaking.'

'Are you able to talk, Mr Haslam? It's Vanessa Powell, head nurse at Brookfield House.'

'Yup, thanks for calling.'

'That's fine. I gather you wanted an update on your father's health?'

'Yes. Please.'

'He's really not very well, Mr Haslam. In fact, we've noticed his condition has been deteriorating quite fast.'

Guy tried to swallow but wasn't quite successful. A cough struggled its way clear of his throat. 'Sorry. Deteriorating quite fast?'

'Yes. His circulation is starting to fail. And he's been having some trouble with his breathing.'

'OK.'

'The last thing I want to do is pressure you. But you know how keen he's been to see you. How often he's been asking.'

'Yeah, I realise. And I've been looking at flights over –'

'That's good. I think you should try to get here as quickly as you can.'

'As quickly as...how long has he got left?'

'It's so very hard to say, Mr Haslam. But his intake of food and fluids is decreasing every day. On that basis alone...'

Across the water, he could see people inside MediaCity's bars and restaurants. Most would be in their twenties and thirties. This sort of conversation not even on their horizons. 'Are we talking days? Weeks?'

'Weeks.'

He wanted to ask how many, but it felt too much like haggling. 'Not a month, though?'

'I don't think it will be that long. Sorry.'

'Right. I... I'm worried he might not even know who I am. Earlier, on the phone, he didn't have a clue.'

'With a phone call, it's only your voice. But you in person, that's different.'

Guy jiggled his knee up and down. 'Actually, I've got a brother who – currently – is a lot closer to Australia. But there's... they have a bad history, him and my dad. I know this sounds odd, but we look very similar. Sound similar. What if he was able to visit instead? Would dad even know?'

'Sorry – you're suggesting your brother visits?'

'Yes, but pretending to be me.'

'Why... I'm not sure I'm following you here. Why do that?'

'They fell out. Back when me and Guy were teenagers. The two of them were always rowing. Guy was...' He realised he was rolling his hand over and over as he searched for the right words. 'They just aggravated each other. Neither would back down. You know... pride and that. Thing is, Guy really regrets it now, and I think –'

'Mr Haslam? Lee?'

'Sorry. I didn't mean to go on.'

'It's not that. But what you're suggesting is not... I haven't experienced that.'

'Of course. But could it work?'

'Will your father be able to tell the difference between you and your brother? Is that what you're asking?'

'Yes.'

'I really don't think this is something I should –'

'No, you're right. I realise. But... does he even know who you are? From day to day? Does he even remember who he is?'

'Dementia is such a cruel disease. What it does to a person can make their behaviour very erratic. But is your father still in there? Sometimes, he is, yes. What you're asking me, though, isn't something I can offer an opinion on. As a professional.'

'OK. I understand.'

'Perhaps discuss it with Guy? It could be the final

opportunity for them both. Him and your father. For a reconciliation. But, whatever the two of you decide, you need to make a decision as soon as you can.'

'We will. And sorry to put you on the spot like that, but I'm just trying –'

'Really, it's not a problem. These are times we can never prepare for.'

'Thanks. I'll let you go. Thanks for calling.'

'My pleasure. Let's speak again, soon.'

'Yes. Bye.'

He cradled the phone in both hands. Christ, he thought. What a mess. What she'd said about their last chance. Might the old man actually want to see me? Could we even end up... end up...' He saw himself at the bedside, leaning forward, feeling the clasp of his father's arms. He pushed the thought from his head. Wasn't going to happen. No way. Lights from the bars were now catching on the rippling water. Glints of red and yellow springing from side to side. The sound of laughter drifted across. Come on Guy, he said to himself. No use sitting here moping.

When he reached the plaza before the BBC's offices, he found himself going to the right rather than heading straight across. This way took him towards the row of restaurants and bars. He peered through plate-glass windows. The shiny, happy crowd, he thought, clocking the massed bottles and glasses on the tables. People like my brother. The excited hand gestures and animated expressions.

A bloke – not much over thirty – glanced to his side and their gazes touched. A micro-exchange of information in the blink of an eye. Then the man turned back to his colleagues and his smile lifted again. Guy took in the man's neat hair and fitted shirt. The slim waist and tight trousers. What had he seen, looking out? An older bloke in saggy jeans and a sweatshirt, carrying a toolbox. Probably thought I'm here to mend an extractor fan or unblock a toilet. Or, he thought, looking to the final bar with its boarded-up windows, I'm working on that one.

Lights were on inside and the inner and outer doors were open. Carpets were down and two women were directing a bloke who was hanging something from the ceiling. The sign was also now up at the front. Reverie.

Leaving MediaCity, he had to check his bearings, unused to this new route home. the Two Sisters were slightly to the left of where they'd normally be. A few minutes' extra walk, at most. A scruffy expanse of grass fringed by a few straggly trees opened up on his right. Langworthy Park, according to the graffiti-covered sign. A small white building on the corner had a black silhouette painted on its side. A man, crouched in a combat stance. Guy slowed down to read the notice beside the padlocked door.

Classes in Krav Maga. All ages, all abilities – beginners, intermediate, advance. Tues / Wed / Thurs evenings 6 – 8 pm. I also have a Krav Maga Academy (7 – 16 years), Sundays 2 – 4 pm. Build your kids confidence and pride.

Guy checked the windows, but the lower ones had been whitewashed over. Probably to offer some privacy for when people were training inside. He noted that the windowsills and walls were spotless, as was the door and the steps leading up to it. The no-nonsense wording of the sign made him think that the person running the place was ex-Forces.

He'd nearly passed the little City Savers on the road adjacent to his when a window poster of hot buttered toast caught his eye. Bread. You need to buy bread. He slipped through the doors and went directly to the section with loaves. Factory-made crap filled the shelves. Stuff that went mouldy within a day or so of being opened. He suspected it was made that way deliberately: how come Martyna's stuff kept for days in its open paper bag?

Settling for something with a smattering of sunflower seeds stuck to the top, he doubled back to the self-service tills. Only two were open and someone was scanning the last of his items at one of them. From off to the side, a staff member silently watched.

As Guy got closer to the other shopper, he did a double take. Bloody hell, it's the Artful Dodger. The lad from the footbridge. Guy took his time getting to the other till. The youngster flipped a bundle of twenties from his pocket and peeled off a couple. Guy sneaked a look at what he was buying. Kraze. Pot Noodles. Pop Tarts. Cans of Fanta. Pringles. The shop's section of fresh fruit and vegetables was practically non-existent, but Guy had the feeling it was no accident the lad had missed it.

He tapped his card, scooped up the loaf and stepped round the youngster. 'Where's your two mates?'

The lad looked over his shoulder. When he saw Guy, there was a fractional widening of his eyes before he assumed his scowl. 'Fuck do you want?'

Guy lifted his loaf. 'My other one ended up in the Manchester Ship Canal.'

'Pussy,' the lad muttered, turning back to the machine.

Jesus, thought Guy. Not sure I'd have had the balls to do that at his age. He weighed up his options. Say something else, continue on my way or stand here like a lemon who's just been slapped down by a teenager. He started towards the exit.

'Why didn't you take the money?'

Guy's step slowed and he looked back. The lad's head was bowed as he scooped up his change. Guy waited.

'So, why didn't you?' the lad asked, reaching for his carrier bags.

'Do something like that,' Guy said, 'and one thing soon leads to another.'

The lad shook his head, now approaching. 'They'll try again, you know?'

Guy shrugged. 'Thought they might.'

Now side by side, they continued towards the doors.

'Did you really mean it?' the lad suddenly asked. 'When you said you had nothing in your life to lose?'

'Yup.'

'But...say Ads had gone to spark you. What would you have done?'

They were now outside the shop. 'Not sure.'

The lad studied the pavement as he processed the information. 'You didn't look scared,' he said in a voice so low, he could have been talking to himself.

Guy took the opportunity to swiftly look him up and down. Flashy trainers that appeared hardly worn. The standard tracksuit-type outfit completed by a gold chain round his slender neck. His face was all angles that didn't quite fit. The features of someone on his way from boy to man. Guy could remember it well. That anxiety of not quite understanding how the world worked. Of wanting to make your mark. Be someone. Such a vulnerable stage.

'And when he slapped your food all over the floor.' He turned his head, eyebrows unbalanced by a frown. 'Weren't you bothered?'

'Not really, no.'

'Made you look like a pussy. Say Ads had gone to spark you then – would you of fought?'

Guy thought for a second. 'Yeah, probably.'

'You know how to?'

He nodded.

The lad assessed him for a long second. 'What if he'd pulled a knife?'

'I'd have jumped.'

'Jumped?'

'Straight into the canal. Faster than a man on fire.'

The lad guffawed so hard, his shopping bags rocked. 'Fucking funny, that.' His grin quickly faded. 'They'll keep trying, you know? They won't give up.'

'You already said.'

'Yeah. Wasn't sure if you believed me.' He crossed the

road with little steps, skinny arms straining to counter the swing of the bags. At the first side street, he took a right, heading straight for the Two Sisters.

CHAPTER 7

The Three Flags had come up in the world. But, then again, a lot of Salford had since Guy had known it. A decking area had been put in at the front, a line of shrubs and planter pots forming a perimeter around timber tables and benches. A basket of flowers hung on either side of the open doors.

He stepped inside and surveyed an interior that was warm and welcoming. Recessed lighting, shelves lined with copper pots, hardback books and other homely items. Pictures on the walls. Carpets. Nothing like the stark interior he remembered. The hard-faced men who used to drink here. The sense of a fragile and uneasy truce that, at any moment, might shatter.

Andy was already sitting in a corner. He lifted his chin in greeting.

'All right?' Guy asked when he reached the table, 'what are you having?'

He nodded at an almost-finished pint. 'Peroni, cheers.'

The strong stuff, Guy thought. At the bar, he ordered himself a session ale. 3.2%. 'This place has changed,' he announced, setting the two drinks down and taking a seat.

'Yeah?' Andy finished his first drink and glanced about. 'When do you know it from?'

'Over twenty years ago. I grew up not that far from here. Brindle Heath?'

The man gave a little shake of his head. 'Don't know it. Only moved to this bit of town a year before last.'

'It's just the other side of the A6.'

'All right, was it?'

'Not so bad, seeing as it was the edge of Salford. Those days, there were still a lot of fields. We'd cross them to the River Irwell, follow that up to Drinkwater Park. Sneak into the rubbish tip and see what we could salvage to make camps in the woods.'

'When kids could be kids, hey? Life before the internet.'

Guy nodded. 'There's a big industrial estate there now. And the prison: Forest Bank.' He realised he was talking a little too much. 'So, where are you from?'

'Warrington. After school, I started work on construction sites. A while down in London. Too expensive, though. And full of wankers. So we came back up here.'

'We?'

'Me and the wife. No kids. How about you?'

'No, just me. I was married, but we went our separate ways.'

'So you live on your own now?'

'I do.'

Meadows sat back. 'Lucky bastard! What is it, a flat?'

'I suppose so.'

He gazed off to the side for a moment. 'That must be a dream. Free to come and go as you like. No menopausal wife waiting to bust your balls about anything she can think of. Seriously, mate – you dodged a bullet there. My wife is turning mental, the mad bitch.'

Guy thought about the evenings when he didn't speak a single word to another human being. The loneliness.

'Can't be that bad, is it? How long have you two been married?'

'Too fucking long, mate. Too fucking long.' He grabbed his phone. 'Got sent this the other day. Made me laugh.' He swiped briefly at his screen. 'Here you go: The missus called me at work the other day to say the dishwasher was leaking. So I brought back some tampons for her.' He let out a short snarl of a laugh. 'Funny, or what?'

Guy was thinking about how much he hated the term 'missus' as he reached for his pint. 'Not bad.'

'Yeah, London was horrible,' Meadows said. 'Glad to get out of there.'

Guy sensed the conversation turning to an exchange of stories about where they'd previously lived. And he didn't want that. 'So, how long have you been working at the terminal?'

'My first job since moving back up here.'

'Most of the lads there seem pretty decent.'

'Yeah, it's not bad. Plenty of overtime, too, at weekends. You like working nights, then?'

Guy took a slow sip of his beer and set it back down. 'Yeah, I do. I like the peace of it.'

Andy wiped condensation off the side of his glass. 'I used to work the cranes down in London.' He raised his eyes toward the ceiling. 'Proper ones. Messes with your head, eventually.'

'How so?'

'It's working on your own that does it. You're way up in your little cabin, swaying about in the wind. Everyone is so far below. You can see all their faces looking up, willing you to get to their bit of the job. It's weird, but after a while, you think they're all talking about you. Chatting shit about how slow you are. Moaning.' He smiled before taking a long pull on his beer. 'That's working on your own for you.'

Guy didn't like where Andy was steering the

conversation. He knew he was the subject of a few conversations at work – that prick Fenton's questions were proof of that. 'But working the crane in the freight yard is different?'

'It's the height. You're not so far removed from everyone. You know, a lot of ex-military types try working cranes. Gets to them too, though. Eventually.'

The comment hung there. When Guy realised the other man wasn't about to break the silence, he sniffed. 'I like to walk. And doing the rounds on that site: it's huge. I must cover seven miles every night.' He glanced across the table. There was a look of expectation in Andy's eyes. That's your lot, thought Guy. 'So, these collectors. Talk me through how they know which containers to target.'

Andy gulped back the rest of his pint. 'Another?'

The speed of the man's drinking is a worry, thought Guy. That and the fact he was obviously keen not to return home. Will I find out everything I want before he's finished another pint? Probably not. 'Yeah, thanks. Just that ale on the right. Torrs.'

Andy soon appeared with fresh drinks. 'Right,' he said, dropping a load of beer mats on the table. 'First thing to understand is that the UK imports a shitload more than it exports, OK?'

'OK.'

'So, let's say each of these beer mats is one hundred shipping containers.' He divided the little squares of card into two piles. 'This side of the table is Britain, this side is rest of the world. Say, for every four hundred containers that come into the country, one hundred go out.'

'Is that the ratio?'

'Don't know. Probably worse, but work with me.' He moved four from the rest of the world pile into Britain's half of the table and slid one beer mat the other way. 'And we do that again. Four this way, one the other. And again.'

Guy nodded. There was now one beer mat for the rest of the world and nineteen for Britain.

'A massive excess of empties soon builds up. Which is why empty storage takes up so much of the site,' Andy stated. 'So, until we do what's called an empty evac – and send those ones with fuck all in them back to an export country – they all just sit at the terminal.'

'Thousands of them.' Guy looked at the pile of mats. 'So how the hell do the collectors know which are the ones with drugs hidden in them?'

Andy cupped his fingers round his pint in a protective stance. 'What do you think?'

'There has to be an inventory somewhere on site. Like a master plan of which container is in which slot. It's probably protected but, somehow, they must have access to that.'

'A protected master plan?' Andy smiled. 'Nothing so complicated, pal. I don't suppose you've seen it, but the cab of my crane has a tablet screen. So does every RST and EL.'

Reach Stackers and Empty Lifters. Guy pictured the chunky yellow vehicles that shifted laden and empty containers round the site. 'Go on.'

'All of them are linked to the depot control system. When a rail service arrives, the screen tells me which transit bay each container should go in. If it's a laden import, a RST might then take it straight to an empty skel doing a pick up. Or it might go into laden storage. But if it's got nothing in it, chances are an EL will just dump it in empty storage. Where it joins the big collection. Every computer in the office is also linked to the control system. There's complete visibility.'

Guy pondered this for a few seconds. 'So, the containers with drugs hidden inside are coming from…anywhere in the world, I suppose. The official contents are delivered to the customer and the empty container goes back to the depot?'

'Correct.'

'But why wait until then to collect the drugs? I don't get it.'

'It's the least risky stage of the process. Where else are you going to get them out that's safer? I mean, an unlit depot with one guy doing security? No offence, mate – but it's perfect.'

'No, you're right. I'm just there for show.' He took a decent gulp of beer. It tasted bloody good. 'But the whole thing depends on someone on the inside feeding them the containers' locations.'

Andy lifted his glass. 'And it could be absolutely bloody anyone.'

'Have you been approached? For your security pass?'

The other man shook his head. 'Not yet. Don't forget, I drive in. There's a chance someone could follow me home, I suppose. I heard one of the yard lads was approached on the forecourt of the petrol station on Europa Way last month. They'd obviously seen him coming out of the staff car park. What did they say to you, the ones who stopped you?'

'That they wanted my security pass for twenty-four hours. In exchange for £400 in cash.'

Andy's eyes widened. '£400?'

'Yup. And they knew my shift pattern, too. Said it would be returned to me before Friday. Oh, and they know where I live.'

'Little bastards!' He reached for his drink and drained most of it. 'Bastards. What did you say?'

'That I wasn't interested.'

'And they were happy with that?'

'Not particularly. Said I'd soon change my mind.'

Guy reached for his own pint. Still over half full. He was starting to feel the alcohol's effects. You said two pints, he said to himself. Promised. Come on, mate. Stick to the plan.

'My guess is it's mainly heroin. The stuff they're collecting.'

Guy immediately put his glass back down. Heroin. What killed my younger brother. 'Why do you say that?'

Andy tipped the last of his pint back and placed the empty glass in the centre of the table. 'Because of where so many laden containers are coming from.' His eyes dropped momentarily to his empty glass.

I get the hint, Guy thought. 'Time for another?'

Andy checked his watch. 'Not even nine. Go on, then. Cheers.'

Guy knocked back the rest of his pint and headed for the bar.

#

It was like he was going the wrong way along a giant conveyor belt: a foot would swing into view and connect with the pavement in front, but he didn't feel like he was actually going anywhere. Only bins, lamp posts and bus shelters passing jerkily by let him be sure he was moving forward. He got to a corner and swung his head about. Buildings seemed to flex and waver. The lights of passing cars left smears in the air.

How many drinks did they end up having? He'd lost count after Andy had returned with a tray that had pints and chasers. What had it been: rum? Something dark and sweet. You idiot.

The final part of the night had shot past in a mad rush. He remembered ranting that whoever rented their pass out was scum – responsible for spreading misery through the city. Guy winced. Did I mention my brother? He didn't think he had. What had Andy been saying? Something about the real scum being those at the top of the chain. The city's crime bosses. O'Sullivan? McGinn? The one bringing most of the heroin into the city had one of those Celtic-sounding names. And there'd been something about a white car. A Jaguar? An expensive model which he drove.

A series of beeps sounded beside him. That'll be the

little green man. He went to cross the road and began lurching sharply to the left. Someone had to skip out of his way. 'Sorry.' He fixed on the opposite crossing point. That's your target, Haslam. Do it! A ten-step stagger.

When he made it to the other side, the kerb almost tripped him. He clung to some metal fencing for a while, the swoosh of cars inches behind him. You're being weak, he told himself. Sort yourself out. He cracked open some memories of being on his last legs. Delirious with heat exhaustion. Shaking in sub-zero winds. It didn't matter how painful things got, you always handled it. Just get your head right, Guy. That's all you've got to do.

He gulped down air and made it to a bus-stop bench. Sat there long enough for three to come and go. What was the other stuff Andy said about the heroin? Supply routes, that was it. The drugs were coming out of the country Guy had done most of his tours in Afghanistan. From there, it went via Turkey into Europe, then right the way across to the huge freight terminal at Rotterdam. After that, a short trip over the Channel and onto a train up to Manchester.

Guy recalled being out in Afghanistan and coming across a massive poppy field. How they'd spent the best part of a day chopping the plants down and had only destroyed about an eighth of the field. Not that it really mattered: the farmer would have just put in a load of new plants as soon as they'd cleared off.

He noticed a little corner shop behind him. Slow steps took him inside. He surveyed the place. Milk shake. He hooked a carton from the fridge. At the counter, he produced some change and looked questioningly at the guy squashed behind the tiny counter.

'One pound eighty.'

He held his hand out and let the man select the coins. 'Cheers.' Back outside, he chugged most of it down and leaned against the wall. Time for some positive thinking: he imagined the sugary solution passing through the lining of his stomach, flooding his system and thinning the alcohol in his blood. Better, he thought. After a couple of minutes, he eased himself away from the wall and tested his balance. Much better. He finished off the drink and glanced back at the shop. Behind the till, there'd been a few little bottles of spirits...no. He shook his head. Forget it. Before the little voice could speak again, he continued on his way. Which road am I even on? Greengate. Next right takes me past a mini arcade of shops. Another right onto Fitzwarren Street and I'm almost home.

By the time the arcade came into view, he was feeling in control. All the shops' shutters were down, except for one with a brightly lit sign that read, Louisiana Fried Chicken. There were four figures close to it and something about the way they were standing raised a red flag in Guy's head. As he drew closer, he could see three of them were wearing black. The usual cropped hair brushed forward. All in their late teens or early twenties. They'd hemmed the fourth person into the doorway of the adjoining shop: a female, about their age. Words were now audible.

'Come on,' the one on the left said in a low voice. 'Do something. What are you? Fucking do something!'

His companions sniggered. Bullies, thought Guy. If there's one thing I cannot stand, it's bullies. Especially if it's a girl they're picking on.

The one doing the speaking stepped in and slapped her across the side of the head. The security shutter made a cymbal-crash as she fell back against it. Guy heard the beginnings of a sob come from her mouth and the noise triggered an intense reaction in him. His vision seemed to clear and sharpen. He felt his nostrils flare as his breathing quickened. A surge of blood caused his fingers to tingle.

'That's it? You're going to fucking cry? You make me want to puke.' The lad lifted his arm again.

Guy stepped up behind him, caught hold of his wrist, bent it over and put him in a thumb-lock. The lad yelped in surprise and pain as Guy dropped him to his knees. The companions looked on, open-mouthed. Keeping the thumb-lock in place with his left hand, Guy gestured to the pair with his right. 'Which of you two is first? Because I only need one hand to knock your fucking teeth out.' He wiggled his fingers and waited for a reply.

They glanced uncertainly at each other, then back at their mate whose head was bowed, face contorted.

'No?' Guy asked. 'Then back off. Further than that. Further. Good. Move from that spot and I will properly fuck you both up. Now,' he turned his attention to the one at his feet. 'Think you're a bad boy, slapping girls about? You cowardly piece of shit. I'm letting you go and you can try and prove me wrong.' He released the lad and took a step back.

Clutching his right hand to his chest, the lad twisted his head to look up at Guy. Humiliation and rage filled his face. 'It's not even a girl.'

Guy blinked. 'You what?'

The lad was now struggling to his feet. 'It's not even a girl!'

Guy glanced at the figure in the doorway. Short hair with a long fringe, swept to the side. But something about the face. It was like Guy's eyesight had gone faulty. The features seemed to flicker between male and female. He wanted to shake his head to clear his vision.

'It's a fucking tranny freak,' the lad spat, circling Guy to join his mates. 'A batty-boy.'

Guy glanced at the person again. Tears were trapped in long, curling eyelashes. Eyeliner, or maybe mascara, had started to smear. Guy wasn't sure which. Now the others spoke.

'You like his sort, do you?'

They were backing away, voices growing louder as the distance widened.

'Will you be taking it up the shitter?'

Suddenly, Guy was glad of the darkness. They wouldn't be able to see he was blushing as he stepped towards them. 'Fuck off.'

They kept retreating, shouts of abuse echoing down the empty street.

'Thank you.'

The person's voice was too low for that of a female. Southern accent. Probably a student, new to the city. Guy's head turned. 'It's...it's no problem. But,' he gestured at the trio as they disappeared round the corner, 'in this part of town,' his eyes dropped briefly to the person's blouse, 'it isn't safe, you know...'

The person brushed away tears. 'I can dress however I like.' The voice was now harder.

Guy took a step back. 'Yeah, I get that.' A flick of the head shifted the fringe to the side. The person straightened one sleeve, then the other, and stepped out of the doorway. Guy saw little red slip-on shoes with bows at the front. Fuck's sake, no one stood a chance wearing things like that. 'Will you be OK?'

'I'll be fine.'

Unsteady little steps took them up the road.

'Listen.' Guy produced a ten-pound note. 'Take this. Get an Uber or something.'

The person looked back, defiance making their eyes shine. 'Cash? For an Uber?' A snort of derision. 'I don't want your money. Just leave me alone.'

The note was left drooping from Guy's outstretched hand. I don't get this stuff, he said to himself. I really don't.

CHAPTER 8

The bird feeder was no longer in the tree. Must be squirrels clambering up and dislodging it. At this rate, he thought, I'll be buying an air rifle. Sit up here and take the little bastards out. He slid his feet into a pair of trainers, head throbbing when he bent down to do up the laces. Your own bloody fault for drinking that booze, he said to himself, setting off down the stairs with his bag of birdseed.

The feeder was in the alley way this time, lying on the ground. The lid was unclasped again and the wire of the main section had been bent in. He crouched. Like someone's trodden on it, he thought. There was a fair amount of seed on the ground, too. What sort of animal would drag it all the way to here and then leave half the food?

He straightened it out as best he could, refilled it, and sneaked back into the overgrown garden. Once he'd hung it back up, he regarded the ground-floor windows. The curtains could have been frozen in place. There's no way, he thought. If anyone was in that place, they never even looked out the window. Let alone opened the back door to fling my birdfeeder over the fence.

Back up in the bedsit, he scrolled through the airline ticket website as he ate breakfast. The headline prices were all bullshit, unless you were booking way in advance and happy to set off in the small hours of the morning. A seat on a plane in a few days' time? He pushed the laptop aside. Lee's funeral had cleared out a sizeable chunk of his meagre savings. A return flight to Australia would see off the rest, and then some.

What, he asked himself, if I make the flight one way? try to make a new start over there? He had nothing tying him to the UK anymore, that was for sure. He'd known of people who'd gone over and picked up work. Stayed on once their visas expired. As long as they kept clear of the authorities, they got by all right.

He thought about his plan to buy an old Land Rover with a rear compartment that had been adapted for sleeping in. All the places he'd intended to visit. Hidden corners of the Lake District. Isolated Scottish lochs. Deserted coves on the Welsh coast. Well, he said to himself, with the cost of that flight – single or return – you can kiss goodbye to that.

At the sink, he reflected on his mum and dad's decision to emigrate. They'd made no secret of it being their dream. One day, when both their sons had left home. Retirement on the Gold Coast. Endless sun and easy living. He watched the tap water as it filled his bowl. When did life ever work out like in the tourist brochures? Maybe it could have – if Denise hadn't been diagnosed with bowel cancer. Sixty-five years old. They'd not been in the country three years. Soon as she was gone, Harry started his downward spiral. She'd done everything for him. Cooking, cleaning, washing. The bloke had no idea how to fend for himself. No friends or family close by. Lee had to fly out and sort his place in a sheltered living complex. That was the first inkling they'd got that the old man wasn't right. More than just absent minded.

Guy was convinced the condition took hold so quickly

because his dad had, basically, given up. Handed the dementia a free pass. Here you go: hijack my body and rot my mind. See if I care.

He flicked the tap off and ran a cleaning pad over his spoon, then the inside of the bowl. Whatever was left of the old man's mind, it wouldn't be able to cope with knowing Lee was dead. Lee, the son he was so proud of. The one who didn't drop out of school. Didn't get into trouble with the police. Didn't fuck off for years without saying a word. Guy placed the cleaning pad on the draining board and watched bubbles of washing-up liquid circling slowly in his bowl. And he certainly wasn't going to enjoy getting that news from me. In fact, he'll probably refuse to believe it. Tell me to take my lies and piss off.

#

As he walked to MediaCity's tram stop, he noticed quite a few people with blue and red scarves. More of them on the platform. Many had olive skin and dark hair. Must be a mid-week match at Old Trafford. Some European competition.

There were crowds of them as he made his way through Piccadilly Station to the platform for the Sheffield train. Barely twenty minutes later, he was deep into the Peak District National Park. Every time he made the journey, he couldn't help marvelling at the contrast. The litter and grime and the press of concrete to... this. He gazed out at the gently sloping fields dotted with sheep. Purple foxgloves spearing up from dry-stone walls. A solitary buzzard floated high in the blue sky as the train pulled into Haverdale.

He walked down the near-empty carriage to the doors. As they parted with a sigh, he breathed in the air. This, he thought, is what it's all about.

The Land Rover garage was halfway down the village high street. Guy looked at the collection of vehicles on the forecourt. The place was owned by Jim Bennet, who was once in the Royal Electrical and Mechanical Engineers. The man was only interested in restoring old military models, which he did to perfection. There was the Defender 200 Tdi on the far side. The one Guy had his eye on. He gazed hungrily across at it. Such a little beauty.

'You perving at my girls again?'

Jim had emerged from the shadows of the garage, clad in the same oil-stained boiler suit he wore whatever the weather. 'Jim! You old spanner monkey, how's it going?'

'Bloody manic, it is. The lad I was training threw in the towel.'

Guy smiled as he grasped Jim's outstretched hand. 'Another? What are you doing to the poor things?'

Jim made a sour face. 'Can't take a bit of hard work, that's their problem. How's things with you?'

'Yeah, not so bad.'

The garage owner's eyes cut to the Land Rover. 'So, are you here to...?'

'Might have to put that on hold, pal. Something's come up.'

'Oh? Everything OK?'

'It's,' Guy tipped his head from side to side, 'complicated. My old man's not doing so well. Need to visit.'

'Where is he?'

'Brisbane, Australia.'

'Australia? Christ. That won't be cheap.'

'You're not wrong.'

'Over a grand?'

When Guy pointed to the sky, the other man whistled. 'Grand and a half?'

'Now you're getting closer.'

'Ouch.'

Jim regarded the vehicle for a second. 'You've put a deposit down. I'm happy to keep her to one side.'

Guy sent a wistful glance in the vehicle's direction. With what I earn at the freight terminal, he thought, it'll be a long wait. 'If you get a decent offer, take it. I don't know how soon I'll have the money.'

'Well, I hope things work out for him.'

'Yeah, me too.'

'You heading to the tops?' Jim asked, nodding toward the moors which reared up on either side.

'Certainly am.'

'Nice weather for it. Enjoy.'

Guy followed the high street to where a stone bridge crossed the River Noe. A narrow trail followed the water upstream, and he was soon clambering over rocks and brushing aside ferns that had encroached on the path. As he climbed higher, he passed a favourite spot for wild camping. It was a grassy ledge beside a little waterfall which cascaded into a shady pool. He kept his eyes on the clear water and quickly spotted the wavering outline of a trout. 'If I was stopping, you might have been breakfast.'

When he cleared the tree line, the breeze became stronger. He heard the occasional burbling of grouse as he picked his way across to a rocky outcrop where he took a seat. The distant tower blocks of Manchester were just visible through a gap in the hills. The air above the city was stained a weak yellow. Pollution, which everyone who lived there was pulling down into their lungs. He watched as an aircraft lifted itself clear of the Cheshire plain; its fuselage winked in the sun as it banked right before settling on a Westerly trajectory. America, maybe. Or the Caribbean.

He let out a sigh. I'll need to book that seat when I get back to the flat. What do I say when I arrive at the care home? How should I play it? In the storage unit he'd rented following Lee's death, there were his brother's suits among the various boxes and crates that – at some point – he would need to sort out. The two of them had almost been the same height. Guy was heavier set, but not so much that a suit wouldn't fit. He could comb his hair to the side. Maybe even dye it a shade blonder, like Lee's had been. Would it fool his dad? Could it work?

The alternative made him cringe: walking in as himself and making up some story for Lee's absence. A work commitment might wash. Their father was certainly in awe of Lee's media career. Constantly flitting over to New York. Meetings with big studios. Parties, occasionally attended by film stars. But the atmosphere would be horrendous. The sad truth was that Guy needed Lee. And his dad did, too. Without Lee as an intermediary, it would be just the pair of them. The same issues – stretching back decades – would start to uncoil and lift their ugly heads. And what could Guy say when his dad asked the inevitable question: what are you doing with your life?

Well, Dad, you know Simone left me. Lee would have told you that. How long have I been back in the UK? Only a few months. At the moment, I live in Salford. Nice little flat. No, not an apartment like Lee's place in Salford Quays. Yes, Dad, it's on an estate. Is it near the Two Sisters? Yup – if the sun comes out of a morning, I'm practically in their shadow. I work nights. Yes, partly to keep myself out of the pubs. What do I do? I maintain security at a large industrial site. No, it's not a management position. Yes, Dad, I work alone. You're right: I'm a night watchman. And I'm living on my own in a bedsit. Fucking happy now?

Claiming Lee couldn't make it because of work. Or pretending to be him. Either option was better than telling his father that he was the only son left. If anything could make the old man drop dead, it would be that.

#

It was getting dark by the time his train eased back into Piccadilly Station. The first thing he noticed were the clusters of uniformed police dotted about the station. Among them were a few firearms officers. Guy glanced over what they were carrying. MCX 5.56 carbines. Lovely bits of kit, them.

Streams of football supporters were quietly flowing

across the concourse. Guy checked the time: twenty past nine. It was mainly couples or parents and kids. The more acceptable side of a football crowd, heading home. Checking their faces, it was pretty obvious United had lost. Again. He knew that, in the city's pubs and bars, the atmosphere wouldn't be one of resigned acceptance.

As the tram to Eccles slowly trundled through the city, he studied the streets beyond the window. Things were bustling at the top of Canal Street, but the dickheads generally kept away from there. They passed through Piccadilly Gardens where, among the piles of litter, a few dozen young men roaring about how much they hated what the Glazers had done to their club. The only audience they had were wearing police uniforms. And half of them probably agreed. Most of Manchester did. Guy knew nothing much would happen here: too many CCTV cameras. Outside the city centre, though, it could be very different. Plenty of spots in the streets around the stadium for a bit of misbehaving.

A commotion at Deansgate Castlefield made his head turn. It was over on the far platform. Five young men striding towards the exit ramp, all up on the balls of their feet, chests out, jaws clenched. Like a pack of hunting dogs. One looked in Guy's direction and started barking, 'United! United! United!'

It was more of a challenge than a chant. Daring Guy to disagree. He could see it in the person's bulging eyes. Drugs of one sort or another. He'd heard how popular coke had become at football matches. Lines of it being openly snorted in the toilets. He broke eye contact before the one shouting at him did anything stupid. Like crossing the tracks to demand what the fuck Guy was looking at.

As his tram finally pulled away, he wondered how much of the drugs being taken in the city had come from the shipping containers where he worked. At Cornbrook, he was glad when the line divided and his tram branched away from the football stadium.

CHAPTER 9

The brightly lit sign of the twenty-four-hour McDonalds near the Eccles stop drew Guy in. Crossing the car park, he wrinkled his nose at the cloying aroma of fat which weighted the air. Maybe, he thought, that's what the yellowness above the city is. Grease billowing up from the extractor fans of fast-food places. Manchester certainly had enough of them.

He was nearly at the doors when a voice called out. 'Hey – Mister Nothing-in-his-life!'

A slight figure detached itself from the crowd of youngsters draped over the chairs and tables of the outside seating area. Well, well, thought Guy. It's the Artful Dodger. 'You alright?'

'Yeah, sound.' He tossed a cup with the straw still sticking out the lid onto the ground. 'You want to watch them burgers, though. Not good for your gut.' He glanced towards Guy's belly. 'Blokes your age have to be careful, don't they?'

Cheeky little git, thought Guy, one hand resting on the door handle as he sucked his stomach in. 'I'm only grabbing a coffee, so don't you worry.'

The kid cocked his head. 'Yeah, right. Thought any

more about that deal? Could afford plenty of coffees if you say yes.'

Blue-tinged faces were looking up from phone screens. Heads were twisting round. His mates taking an interest in the conversation. Christ, thought Guy. You ever heard of subtlety? But once they saw it was someone old enough to be their dad, interest evaporated.

Guy stepped through the doors without replying. When he came back out with a coffee in his hand, the kid looked like he was holding court. He produced three tenners from the pocket of his top and held them out to the nearest girl. 'Go on, then. Fries and shakes for everyone!'

Guy could see every face beginning to grin. Free drinks off the cool kid with the cash. In Guy's mind, the coming years played out. And the most likely ending was prison. Or maybe an early grave. Exactly where he'd been heading at that age. The kid spotted him wandering away and jumped down from the table. 'Yo! Mister Nothing-Man!'

Guy glanced back. The kid was approaching with an absurd swagger. Guy could see his pupils were massive. Christ, you're on something, too. Is anyone in this city not?

'Got a question for you.'

'Yeah?' Guy kept going, keen to move the conversation beyond the group's earshot. 'What's that?'

'When we was on that bridge. When I said about Ads sparking you. Could you have stopped him?'

This again. 'Could I have stopped him?'

'Yeah.' The lad looked him up and down. 'I mean, you seem like you... I don't know... but Ads is a nasty fucker. I seen him.'

'You're asking if I know how to fight?'

'Yeah,' he nodded.

'I know how to fight.'

'Where? Where did you learn?'

Guy shrugged. 'Here and there.'

'Like MMA? Cage fighting? Did you used to do that?'

Did. Guy smiled. Past tense. Too old for it now. 'None of that stuff, no. But I know how to.' He spotted an opportunity. A way to usher the kid from the path he was striding down. 'Why? You're wanting to learn?'

The kid grinned uncertainly. 'Not boxing. Not interested in King's rules shit. Telling you, that stuff doesn't work in real life.'

'I know it doesn't work in real life. You heard of Krav Maga?'

His eyes widened. 'You know that?'

'I know that. But I'm not teaching you. There's a place that does it close to here. I need to get myself fit.' He tapped the modest bulge of his belly. 'I'm going to go along. Come with me, if you want.'

'What, is it like classes or something?'

Classes, thought Guy. A word guaranteed to kill his interest. 'No – it's training sessions. Once you've learned some moves, they'll get you sparring with someone roughly your size.'

'Really?' He flexed his knees and brought a hand up to shoulder height, Karate style. 'How soon would that be?'

'Sparring? Not long,' Guy lied. 'A little bit on the basics. Some fitness and strengthening. Then a few moves and you'll be away.'

The kid gazed off to the side. 'I like that. Krav Maga – that's the one they teach the special forces in Israel, isn't it?'

'Yeah. Street-fighting, basically. Hand-to-hand combat in small spaces.'

'Sick! When is it?'

'Sunday afternoons.'

'It's not that shit-hole on Vale Walk?'

'What's that?'

'The Zone? All fucking ping-pong tables and wanky youth workers trying to get you on college courses and that.'

'No, it's a little place. Sort of gym by the looks of it. Pretty basic.'

'When?'

'There's a session this Sunday afternoon. Two o'clock.'

'Two? And you reckon it'll be good?'

'Definitely.'

'What would I wear? I ain't wearing shorts or anything like that. No way.'

'Just come in stuff like you've got on. Trackie bottoms and a t-shirt.'

Guy could see he was teetering on the edge of agreeing. Just a bit more to tempt him. 'The bloke who runs it looks like he's been carved out of rock. Pretty sure he's ex-special forces himself.'

'Really? Go on, then. Sounds all right, that does.'

Guy could hardly believe he'd got him to bite. 'OK. Where do you live?'

'Two Sisters.'

'Which one?'

'Conmere.'

'You know I'm on Farrant Road, right? How about the corner of Farrant that's closest to Conmere? One forty-five this Sunday.'

'Yeah, I can do that.'

'Nice one.' Guy started on his way then glanced back. Keeping his voice casual, he asked, 'What's your name?'

'Jayden.'

'OK. I'm Guy. See you Sunday, one forty-five.'

'Don't you forget,' Jayden said, turning away and jogging back towards his mates.

CHAPTER 10

As he crossed the footbridge on his way into work, he could see a row of long-haired teenagers on his favourite bench. Their thin legs seemed welded to the ground by massive Frankenstein boots, and their choice of clothes would have worked fine at a funeral. Most of the make-up was black, too. What he thought of as Goths. He wasn't sure what the correct term was now. The pungent smell of weed drifted in his direction.

He quite liked their type: at least they weren't interesting in creating trouble. A couple of them had started glancing uneasily in his direction as he drew closer. The spliff was being kept well out of sight. He nodded at them as he went past. 'Evening.'

A short pause, then a chorus of murmured replies.

'Evening.'

'Alright?'

'Hello.'

Guy smiled to himself as he cut up the side road to Wharfside Way. Such polite young men. More crow-like figures were walking along the road, all heading in the same direction. Must be a Friday evening gig at the nearby Victoria Warehouse, he concluded. He paused in front of a bus shelter, surprising another cluster of them gathered inside. A tiny plastic bag was being passed round. He glimpsed the white powder inside it. Fuck's sake: the stuff's everywhere.

When he reached the freight terminal car park, he couldn't help scanning the rows of parked vehicles. Scrutinising them for anything a bit too flashy. Which of you fuckers are on the take? A group of yard lads were letting themselves out through the gate. They all wore safety boots and work tops. But their coats were their own. He searched for labels. Stone Island. Popular around Manchester, but not too expensive. Canada Goose. He'd heard those things cost close to a thousand quid. What was a yard lad doing with one of those? He glanced up and his gaze locked with the owner's. Mid-twenties, immaculate haircut.

The man started to frown. 'Problem?'

Guy glanced at the jacket again. Don't be so bloody stupid, he said to himself. What are you going to do? Ask how he could afford it? 'No, mate. Just, you know,' he looked at the terminal behind them, 'facing up to spending the next twelve hours in there.'

The other man's face relaxed. 'Night security?'

'Yup, night security.'

'Got it easy, you have! Drinking tea and watching movies.' He grinned.

Guy smiled back. 'Now you put it like that...' He could hear their chuckles as he swiped himself in. Andy was in the locker room, emptying wrappers from his lunch box into the bin. 'Hey.'

The crane driver's head turned. 'Fuck me, good night the other night, or what?'

Guy half-smiled, half-grimaced. 'Things got a bit hazy after those chasers.'

'Lamb's rum! Thought you'd like that.'

Navy drink, Guy immediately thought. What did he mean by that? What exactly did I tell him?

'Right…so…had a few of them, did we?'

'Nah. Two or three.' He checked they had the room to themselves. 'You got onto a right rant, though. Drug-dealers. Remember?'

'Kind of. Them being scum?'

Andy smirked. 'Them being worse than scum. How they all should have their hands chopped off. Hung by their ankles from the lamp posts down Deansgate.'

Guy cringed. 'I said that?'

'You did.' He reached out and placed a hand on Guy's shoulder. 'And sorry about your brother, mate. That happening, I can see why you said what you did.'

'I told you about Lee?'

'Yeah.' His hand dropped. 'Is…is that – didn't you mean to, or something?'

Guy stepped towards his locker and started turning the dials on his padlock. A few drinks and you started blabbing. Prick. 'It's fine. Just didn't realise I had.' He glanced at the other man. 'Sorry if I went on.'

'No, 'course you didn't. Not at all. That last hour, we just put the world to rights.'

Guy shrugged off his fleece. 'What else was I spouting off about?'

'How do you mean?'

Before here, he wanted to say. Did I say anything about what I did before starting work here? 'I don't know…apart from my rant about drug dealers.'

'That was pretty much it. I mean,' he let out a short laugh, 'don't remember it so well myself.'

'Who was that bloke you mentioned? Head of the crime gang bringing in all the heroin?'

Andy checked around him another time. 'McFadden?'

'He's the one who drives an expensive white car?'

'Yeah, a Mercedes. Complete with personalised number plate. What about him?'

'Nothing. Just wasn't sure what his name actually was.'

'Yeah – McFadden. Don't go trying to chop his hands

off. Not with his history. Listen, fancy a few more next time you're off? Pretty decent pub, the Three Flags, isn't it?'

'Yeah, it is. I'll have to see. Money's tight at the moment.'

'Oh, right. Fair enough.' He lifted his coat from the locker and draped it across his arm.

Guy couldn't help but notice the inner label. Burton. Cheap as chips.

'Well, I'd better be off. See you when I see you, yeah?'

'Yeah. Cheers, Andy.'

The locker room door had hardly closed before the hinges creaked as it swung open again. Guy turned to see Nathan Fenton. Great.

'Freight Master's very own man of mystery! How are we this most wonderful Friday night?'

Guy shut his locker. 'Not so bad. You?'

Fenton brushed at the sleeves of his top. Fred Perry. They charged a lot for those things. 'I am tickety-boo. Tick-e-ty-boo! Hitting the pub tonight. Afters at a mate's house. Who knows where the night will take me? And you? Oh,' he winced, 'forgot. You're in here.'

Guy finished securing his padlock and turned. 'Yeah, well. It's a tough job, but someone's got to do it.'

'Too right.' Fenton raised a forefinger. 'Talking of tough jobs, I had another little thought about –'

Guy closed the gap between them. 'Get fucked, Fenton, you little weasel.'

The other man slid back a step. 'Jesus, mate – no need for that! It's only a bit of banter.'

'No, it's not banter. And I'm not your mate. Just keep away from me. Are we clear?'

The last traces of humour evaporated from Fenton's face. Now all that remained was a barely concealed sneer. 'Loud and clear.'

Guy yanked the door open and marched down the corridor to the manager's office. No sign of Hughes, but there never was once five-thirty came around. Guy slid the logbook off the shelf and checked the previous night. One break in: another reefer. Row 29, stack 11, column B, 2 high.

He crossed the office and studied the map of the terminal on the wall. Fifteen rows away from the one he'd found on his last shift. Fifteen rows. That amounted to thousands of containers. And the collectors knew the exact location of the correct one. So how did the depot control system work? He looked at the computer on Hughes' desk. Even if he turned it on, he had no signing-in details or password. No way of studying the system for himself.

Once the last of the yard lads had left, he removed a radio from the charging rack. Not sure why I even bother taking one, he thought as he set off on his first round. The emergency channel didn't even connect to the police. Rather, it went through to a nearby command centre which consisted of, as far as Guy could gather, a bloke sitting in a prefabricated hut near to Manchester United's stadium.

At the bay where all the RSTs and ELs were neatly parked, he stopped. Andy had mentioned each one was equipped with a tablet that allowed access to the control system. Would it require a log in? Maybe not. He returned to the main building and went back into Hughes' office. The keys for all the vehicles were in a little safe box on the wall behind his desk. Guy checked the set of keys he was approved to carry. All were for doors and gates. Nothing small enough for the safe box. Shit.

Once back outside, he resumed his sweep of the site. The light was fading fast. Seagulls bickered from towards Salford Quays. The gate giving access to Europa Way was the farthest from the terminal building. Simple swipe card mechanism. Beyond the fence, a taxi cruised past. He studied the ground on his side of the metal bars. Once through the gate, there was about thirty metres of tarmac to cross before you reached some cover offered by an untidy pile of pallets. Just beyond them was the first aisle of empty containers. From there, you could follow the corridors across to where the reefers were located. Yes, he thought. If I was using a borrowed pass to get on site, it would be through this gate.

CHAPTER 11

'Well, there you go,' Hughes said, stepping behind his desk and taking a seat. 'A clean night of no break-ins.'

Makes a change, Guy thought, placing his radio back on the charging rack. 'There was something, actually.'

Hughes had already unscrewed the lid of his blue flask and was about to pour. 'Mmm?'

'It's not to do with security. But I thought you should know there's a good chance I'll have to go to Australia in the next few weeks.'

Hughes' eyebrows lifted as he set the flask back down. 'Australia?'

'Yes. It's my dad. He lives over there, but he hasn't got much longer left – according to the care home he's in.'

'Ah, sorry to hear that. How long would you be gone for?'

'Maybe a week? Ten days?'

Hughes sat back. 'Right. Well, you've obviously not accrued much holiday yet. If any.' He tapped a finger against his chair's armrest. 'I suppose you could take it as compassionate leave. I'd need to check with HR.'

'Could I take it as part of my holiday entitlement for the rest of this year?'

'Don't think it works like that.' He waved a hand. 'We'll sort something out, don't worry. Just let me know the dates as soon as you can.'

'Will do.'

As he left the staff car park, Guy could see four lorries were queueing in the layby on the far side of the road. The driver of one had climbed down from his cab and was pissing into the bushes beyond the barrier. Aware he was visible to any number of people inside the terminal, Guy turned left rather than right. He followed the pavement which ran beside the perimeter fence to the gate which gave access to Europa Way. He then crossed the road. On this side, there was just the barrier with the screen of bushes directly behind it.

Through the leaves, he could see down a steep grassy bank to the Bridgewater Canal. He knew the narrow stretch of water curved away in a northerly direction before, eventually, crossing the Manchester Ship Canal at the Barton Aquaduct. Before then, there were a multitude of places to access the towpath. The bushes provided a perfect observation point for Europa Gate. He made a mental note of the sapling which stood slightly higher than the surrounding vegetation, then continued along the road until it brought him to Wharfside Way. Five minutes later, he was at Martyna's bakery.

Before opening the door, he checked its base. Looking good. 'Morning!' he called out. The aroma of baking bread filled the air.

'Guy?' she called from the back. 'Is that you?'

'It is,' he replied, surveying what was out. She'd made more of the wheel loaves. Excellent, he thought. I get to try it, after all.

'How was your night shift?'

Martyna has appeared behind the counter, brushing her hands on her apron as she always did.

'All quiet,' he replied. 'Just how I like it. All good with you?'

'Oh, yes,' she replied. 'And also with my super-strong door.'

He smiled. 'I see you've got some wheel loaves.'

'And help yourself to a slice of Carpathian custard cake, too.'

He turned to see a full tray of them. 'You didn't make them just for me?'

'Of course I did. I said I would.' She placed a loaf in the slicing machine and started preparing his coffee.

'How's Gabriela?'

'She's well. At her daddy's this weekend. Keeps going on about the donkeys at Scarborough.'

'Yeah – sorry about that. It would make a good day trip, though. You should think about it.' He slid a tenner beneath the napkins while her back was still turned. 'There's a sea life centre there, too. Penguins and seals. Tanks with all sorts of weird fish.'

'I shall google it,' she said, bagging his things. 'Enjoy!'

'How much do I owe you?'

'Nothing. You paid too much last time.'

He crossed the room and, once half out the door, looked back. 'I knew you wouldn't want to take any money for this.'

She nodded. 'Correct.'

'So, you'll find a ten-pound note under those napkins. Bye!' Her mouth was dropping open as the door swung shut behind him.

Back in his kitchen, he popped some slices of bread in the toaster and then fetched his laptop. The clock in the corner said 7:05. Knowing he'd need to sleep soon, he opened his browser and typed in: 'McFadden, Manchester'.

A host of results came up, mostly dominated by Facebook profiles of various people. He clicked on one. Scott McFadden, a logistics manager in Manchester, USA.

He went back to the search field and tried, 'McFadden, gangster, Manchester, England'.

This generated a much smaller list of results. Many

accompanied by thumbnail images of the same, middle-aged, man. The top result was part of an old Manchester Evening Chronicle article. Guy clicked on it and found himself gazing at the face of someone who could have presented the weather on TV. Greying hair neatly combed in a side parting and a well-proportioned, faintly distinguished, face. No broken nose or scarring around the eyebrows. No defiance or menace in his eyes; just an expression of mild concern. Like there might be strong winds forecast for the weekend. Guy shifted his eyes to the headline.

'I'm no "teflon don",' claims Manchester businessman.

The article was over six years old. In the full picture, McFadden was wearing a white shirt and a purple tie. Slimly built. One eighty centimetres, at most. He was on the steps of the Crown Court, near Bridge Street. Now his expression made sense: an innocent man, caught up in a very unfortunate incident. Guy scanned the text. A case brought against him for living off the proceeds of crime had just collapsed. Guy's eyes stopped moving at a quote McFadden himself had provided: 'Unfortunately, this latest action taken against me by GMP forms part of a concerted campaign. This is the third time they've attempted to discredit my name and reputation with spurious, unfounded allegations. Frankly, I've had enough and will be instructing my lawyers to seek substantial damages on my behalf. This type of comical persecution belongs in an episode of The Keystone Cops, not here – not now – in the police force of what I believe to be Britain's finest city.'

Guy shook his head. First the man got a dig in against the police, then he followed it up with an adoring comment about Manchester. It would have raised smiles in pubs from Brinnington to Blackley. Not only that, but he was also then claiming damages. Cocky. Very cocky.

He scrolled down to where all related articles were

listed. One from two years earlier immediately caught his eyes.

'McFadden "acted reasonably" in street-death attack.'

The story outlined how 'controversial businessman' Dale McFadden had been attacked at the gates of his house by a masked assailant carrying a knife. In the struggle that followed, the attacker had suffered a fatal stab wound to the neck. Recording an open verdict at the inquest, the coroner had concluded that McFadden had 'acted reasonably to defend himself', though he had problems with 'several aspects' of McFadden's version of events. Following the verdict, the Crown Prosecution Service had dropped its charge of murder because it could not prove McFadden was 'not acting in self-defence'.

Guy went back to the man's photo. The bloke looked so harmless. No muscular build or fighter's face. Which meant he'd got to where he was through his brains. And, at the end of the day, that made him far more dangerous. He began to close down the tabs, but paused when another headline caught his eye.

Reverie – MediaCity's chic new cocktail lounge.

Reverie, thought Guy. No way. That's the place they've been doing all the work on. I see it each day on my walk home. He leaned forward. How come McFadden had anything to do with that? The initial lines of text described how the venue was the latest venture of locally born businessman, Dale McFadden. The place belonged to him? Guy could hardly believe it. What would the rental on it be? Prime position in the heart of MediaCity? Had to be astronomical. The bloke was moving into big league stuff.

He continued through the rest of the piece, which seemed little more than a regurgitation of something a PR company would send out. Laid back intimate vibe of this classy after-hours watering hole...perfect place for frazzled media executives to unwind…team of mixologists, led by the legendary Tom Harper who forged his reputation at Number 59, Spinningfields.

Guy got to the closing caption. Reverie was hosting a private function this Saturday before opening its doors to the general public the following weekend. He checked how recent the article was. Three days old. Which meant the private party was…tonight.

He sat back and looked around his bedsit. Anything, he thought, beats spending my night off sitting in here, alone.

CHAPTER 12

The main plaza area of MediaCity was thronging with smartly dressed people. Dozens were pouring out of the Lowry, no doubt having just seen a play or concert. Others were disembarking from a tram that had just eased onto the platform. Guy checked his choice of clothes. A beaten-in black leather jacket and dark jeans by Diesel. He was pretty sure the jacket was timeless. And the jeans? Simone had bought them for him years ago. Hopefully, they weren't too dated. Beneath the jacket was a slate-coloured T-shirt he'd got in H&M. Three for a tenner, but who was going to tell? And a pair of black leather shoes. Ones he kept for anything faintly formal.

He looked across to the front of Reverie. There was a line of pillars topped by those fake flame things. And some kind of admissions system going on: red ropes funnelling people to two, no three, door staff. Two male and one female. The shorter bloke had sheets of paper in his hand. So, a guest list of some kind. Shit. He looked around.

Over to his left was a group of women. Mid-twenties maybe, all in clingy little dresses. Hair done up. Two other women were approaching from the tram platform, hands waving. After a few kisses, they all started talking excitedly.

One pointed in the direction of the bars, and the five of them set off. Guy cut across the plaza, and once in hearing range, matched his pace to theirs.

'No, it isn't me. Tamsin got the invite through work.'

'Who's Tamsin?'

'Tamsin. You know Tamsin. Seeing Rohan Palmer.'

'Oh, yeah – I know who you mean. Rohan, who works at Cube?'

'Yup.'

'So why didn't she want to go?'

'Rohan's taken her to Rome for the weekend.'

'Nice.'

'Lucky bitch.'

'I know! So, it's in her name.'

'What do you mean?'

'The name on the – never mind. I'll go first and do the talking. Just make sure you're all looking gorgeous.'

'Which we are.'

'Is it free drinks? Annette said it was free –'

'I did not! I said I thought it might be free drinks.'

'Is it?'

'Don't know. But it's free entry to an opening night. I just want to see who's in there. Apparently, Naomi Levack has been invited.'

Guy had heard enough. He slowed down. They were now about fifteen metres from the entrance. Fishing his phone from his pocket, he came to a stop and pretended to take a call. The group tottered up to the security staff.

'Evening ladies!' the taller male announced, beaming at the sight of them.

Once they'd been waved through, Guy set off once more. The woman noticed him first and gave a perfunctory nod. 'Evening, sir.'

'Hi there,' Guy said, smiling briefly as he returned his phone to his pocket.

'Which name is it?' asked the shorter male, eyes going to his sheets of paper.

'I'm with the group who just went through? Party name's Tamsin.'

'Token bloke, is it?' the tall one asked good-naturedly.

'Token bloody driver, more like,' Guy replied with a grin as they stepped aside to let him pass.

Music was coming through recessed speakers somewhere above the open outer doors. It reminded him of the stuff they used to play in the beach bars of Arugam Bay. Probably played in beach bars across the world. Rolling, hypnotic stuff. Music that made your blood feel syrupy.

Two female staff in fitted white shirts and dark trousers greeted him with relaxed smiles as they slid the inner doors open. The same track was playing inside, though considerably louder. He could smell incense or something similar. An aroma that made you imagine you were somewhere exotic. Somewhere tropical. Foliage of creeping plants cascaded down from high ledges. Huge gourd-like objects were suspended just below the ceiling, greens and oranges and reds forming swirls of pattern across them. The place was awash with muted light: globes that flickered and sparkled in dozens of recessed wall alcoves, clusters of tea lights scattered across every surface. The soft glow gave everyone's faces an air of enchantment. Wondering what it all had cost, his eyes moved to the far corner: dozens of backlit bottles were perfectly aligned on glass shelves. The bar. He threaded his way between clusters of people, aware of their appraising glances as he passed. It was one of those events. More of a parade than a party. The sort of thing he detested.

There were at least six staff behind the bar, all wearing dark green aprons. Sleeves rolled up. One placed a napkin down with an R logo on it. 'What can I get you?'

Guy surveyed the packed shelves. 'Could you do a cocktail that's alcohol free?'

'Of course. You're looking for something tall, short, bitter, sweet?'

'Nothing with an umbrella in,' Guy said with a smile. 'Or coconut milk. Closest you've got to a rum punch would be perfect.'

He nodded. 'Leave it with me.'

Guy perched on a stool and took a closer look round. Directly opposite was a podium. The DJ's area, if that was the right term. To the left of that, a row of bays which led back to the entrance. It was hard to make out how many people were seated in each. Waiting staff were flitting about, ferrying trays of drinks to the shadowy tables. The group he'd snuck in behind was being shown into the last bay before the windows. He turned his attention to the far end of the room. This had been roped off and two big blokes were positioned by the steps up, hands crossed in front of them. Guy shifted his gaze beyond them. There was a large table with a mixture of men and women sat around it. Ice buckets and bottles of fizz. To the side of them, a group of men were standing. All in suits. Handshakes and shoulder slaps. Someone shifted slightly, and he realised McFadden was in the centre.

Once again, Guy was struck by how small he was. Not just height-wise. A lack of bulk, too. There was, however, nothing meek about his body language. He was smiling, but not too widely. Nothing self-congratulatory. There was a reassured air about him as he wound up the conversation with one person, before smoothly acknowledging the next person waiting for a word.

'Cash or card?'

Guy turned to see the barman setting down a squat glass filled with cloudy amber liquid. A dried slice of star fruit lay across a layer of crushed ice. So, no free bar then. Damn. 'Card, cheers.'

The barman produced a little terminal and Guy glimpsed the price displaying on the screen. Twelve quid? For a glass of glorified fruit juice? Jesus. After paying, he moved closer still to the VIP area, eyes drawn to McFadden once more.

The man had really nailed the look. The suit was nothing flash, but immaculately tailored. Open-necked shirt. A watch that wasn't too chunky or ostentatious, but still looked like it had cost thousands. There was never a moment when he didn't look interested or charmed by those around him.

Guy sipped his drink. Oof. That was bloody good.

He glanced down at it. Impossible to tell it was free of booze. He sipped again, trying to fathom the mix of flavours as conversations bubbled around him. He heard an architectural project mentioned. A chat about a shooting schedule. An anecdote about the heating system in the newly built BBC offices over in Leeds being too noisy.

Soon, his eyes were drawn back to McFadden. This close, Guy could see there was something about McFadden's skin that wasn't quite…normal. It had an unnatural smoothness, as if in permanent soft focus. You've had Botox! Vain bastard. And your teeth have definitely been capped, too. The twat probably fancies himself as a politician one day.

McFadden had leaned in to say something to the woman now next to him. One hand was resting on her upper arm. Partner? Something about it was too formal for that. His eyes went back to McFadden's face. The man was looking directly at him. *Can he actually see me in this light? Clearly enough to know I'm watching?* Guy knew the time had come to look away. But he didn't. McFadden finished what he was saying and, as he straightened up, Guy detected a trace of stiffness in the movement. McFadden's finger tapped against his thigh. Three times, then stopped. *He definitely clocked me,* Guy thought.

He'd almost finished his drink when a man took the stool next to him. About the same age. Dark hair swept back. Black polo top with short sleeves that showed off muscular arms. They glanced at each other for a moment.

'What brings you here, then?' he asked in a thick Salford accent.

Guy smiled inwardly. So McFadden was aware of me. He cocked his head. 'What brings me here?'

The man kept eye contact. Guy could see his nose didn't sit quite right. Busted, maybe a few times.

'Nice new place like this opens, you've got to see it for yourself,' Guy said, smiling as he took an appreciative look about.

'From round here, are you?'

'I am. Manchester born. You?'

'What's your name?'

'Andy.' He held a hand out.

The man ignored it. 'Andy who?'

'White.'

'Don't remember an Andy White on the guest list.'

'I'm part of another group.'

'Which group?'

'The one over there. Why?'

'Which group?'

'They've just got a table. Over on the far side. Something up?'

'Finish your drink and fuck off.' The man stood but didn't move away.

Guy did his best to look nonplussed. 'I'm being thrown out? You're throwing me out? Why?'

The man's eyes were cold as he leaned in close. 'Leave. Now.' He headed off to the VIP area and, when he reached the steps, the two security staff stood aside with respectful nods. Guy searched for McFadden. He was now sitting at the table, filling his neighbour's flute with champagne. That's me told, Guy thought, draining his drink and getting to his feet.

He was nearly at the doors when he saw a softly lit sign on his left. Toilets. Well, the least I can do is take a piss in McFadden's new place. Small victories and all that.

CHAPTER 13

The door was of a heavy dark wood and its seal made a slight sucking sound as he pushed it open. Beyond was a wide area with a line of shallow, trough-like sinks down one side. The music was different in here. Not really music, in fact. More the sound of a forest with running water and bursts of distant birdsong. He could see racks of bottles on the shelf above the sinks. Handwash and maybe moisturiser. Wooden dispensers full of thick paper hand towels. Back-lit mirrors.

Facing the sinks was a long row of doors. No way, he thought, there was ever going to be a piss-pan in a place like this. The first door was closed, so he opted for the third one to leave a gap. He was back at the sink washing his hands and marvelling at the expensive-looking toiletries when a stifled giggle came from the occupied cubicle. Next thing, the lock clicked and a couple emerged. Early twenties, both of them. The man spotted Guy and, looking mildly embarrassed, whispered to the woman that he'd see her back inside. Guy watched from the corner of his eye as she brought her face close enough to the mirror to kiss it. A forefinger came up and she ran it round the rim of each nostril. Spotting Guy watching, she turned her head.

'Something you want to say?'

He could see her pupils were heavily dilated. 'Not me,' he replied.

After adjusting an earring, she headed for the door.

Guy dried his hands, then stepped into the cubicle the couple had been in. A few microscopic dots of white were on the top of the wooden shelf behind the toilet cistern. He blew out a thin stream of air and they vanished.

Exactly the type of place Lee would have come to after work, he realised. Maybe, at first, the odd little line at weekends – like the couple who'd just left. Then weekday evenings. After that, his use had crept into the day as well. Binges at weekends. Other drugs entering the mix. Drugs all supplied by people like McFadden. Who was now moving into the club scene and all the profits it led to. Bastard.

He wandered back into the wash area. The copper piping which ran along the wall above the sinks was very thin. He could easily wrench a section off. Use it to shatter the mirrors as water started flooding the room. Take the end of it and smash out the recessed lights above him. Knock the little speakers off the walls. He stared at himself in the mirror.

What's got into me? There was a glint in his eyes. Feral. He had that same feeling he used to get back in the days when he caused trouble. A memory popped up and he couldn't help smile. Clambering onto the roof of a moving car as it had pulled out onto Deansgate. Trying to surf the fucking thing. Flying off into the path of oncoming traffic when the driver hit the brakes. Jumping up and sprinting in the direction of Castlefield Locks. All the late-night bars down there. Fuck it, he thought. Let's have another drink. What's the worst that can happen?

The music had picked up in volume and speed. A few people were now in the open area before the DJ. Drinks in hands, they swayed and shimmied. A prelude to proper dancing. He wove his way back to the bar and signalled to the same bloke as before. 'That last drink you did me? Sure it didn't have any alcohol in it?'

'Only a bit of Guarana.'

'What's that?'

'A bit like the stuff in Red Bull. Bit of a pick-me-up.'

'Yeah? I'll have another, please.'

He perched on the same stool and leaned back against the bar. Spread his arms out. How long, he asked himself, since I've been somewhere like this? He glanced to his right and saw the man from before standing at the edge of the VIP area, arms crossed, staring in his direction. Guy gave him a little smile before turning back to the main bar. What's your end game here, Guy? He wasn't actually sure. Other than trying to irritate McFadden.

His drink hadn't even arrived when two security staff closed in, one from each side. Pincer movement, thought Guy, looking from one to the other. He recognised the tall one from when he'd blagged his way in. 'Alright there?'

The man wasn't smiling now. 'With us. You're leaving.'

'Just ordered a drink.' He jabbed a thumb over his shoulder. 'He's making it now.'

A meaty hand gripped his upper arm. 'You can walk out or be carried out.'

'Really?' Guy looked directly at him. The bouncer had allowed himself to get too close. Guy visualised the headbutt. It would be so easy. Instead, he turned in the direction of the VIP area and flicked a brief salute in the direction of the watching man. Then he eased himself off the bar stool. 'OK, lads, lead the way. None of us want the night ruined, hey?'

The bar man was returning with his drink.

'Sorry mate,' Guy called out. 'Looks like I'm leaving early.'

The taller one kept hold of the back of his sleeve all the way to the doors. Once they were outside, the pair tried to manoeuvre him up against the wall. Two more, including the woman, also closed in.

'Got some ID there, my friend?' the tall one asked, trying to reach into Guy's jacket.

Guy slapped his hand away. 'Get the fuck off.'

'Come on,' he said, reaching out again. 'Management's request.'

Guy stepped right back into the corner. They could come at him, but it would have to be one at a time. 'You'll get me down. Course you will. But I guarantee you this: at least two of you will be coming to hospital with me.'

Looks of uncertainty flitted between them. None looked keen to come any closer. After another second, the tall one grinned and shifted to the side. 'Come here again, and we'll dance all over your face.'

Guy immediately moved forward, eyes searching for the slightest hint of movement. All their hands stayed down at their sides. Once clear, he kept his pace relaxed, all the while listening for a footstep in case anyone tried to get close enough for a cheap shot to the back of his head. Not a sound. Once out on the plaza, he grinned to himself. That had been fun.

CHAPTER 14

Guy looked in the direction of the Two Sisters before checking his watch yet again. Five past two. The kid wasn't coming. Damn it! Why did I even think he'd stick to the arrangement? The sort of life he leads…what do they call it? Chaotic. That was the word.

He strode away from the towers in the direction of the McDonalds. Lunchtime on a Sunday and the place was rammed. Vehicles queuing for the drive-through stretched right round the building and back across the car park. He stepped through the narrow gap between two bumpers and observed the outside seating area. The smell of exhaust fumes mingled with the oily aroma of fried food. A group of teenagers was there, most of their hoods up. He moved closer to the tables for a better look. 'Any of you found a set of keys sitting here?'

The nearest two glanced in his direction with blank faces.

'Keys? Anyone find any?'

The rest of the group finally started to turn. He checked each of their faces. No Jayden. One made a sucking sound through his teeth. Heads were going back down, eyes returning to phone screens.

'No? OK, thanks for your help, anyway.'

Back on the road, he wondered what to do. Was there a chance Jayden had gone straight to the gym? Guy couldn't imagine it; for all his bravado, the kid wasn't that confident. Wandering, alone, into an unknown place to begin learning a martial art? Not a chance. He'd mentioned the youth centre place – The Zone. Ping-pong tables and crappy biscuits. Which meant he had visited in the past. It was worth a try.

The building was a two-minute walk away, at the top of Vale Walk. With its angular design and brightly coloured wall cladding, Guy guessed it had been purposely built. Probably within the last few years. A sign above the large overhang of the front porch read 'Transforming Young Lives'. To the side was a concrete area with several curved ramps and low railings. A mini skate part, he realised. Except the only people on it were a bunch barely into their teens who had no skateboards and were all arguing. Guy turned his head to hear better. Some ridiculous row about the United result. Now he could see the group was split in two: United supporters on one side, City on the other. The rivalry that would last until the end of time. Voices were getting more emotional. One of the lads tried to shove another.

Guy put on his best Liverpool accent. 'Eh, eh, calm down, calm down! What's with all the handbags?'

The group turned as one and began to scrutinise him.

Guy continued flexing one knee, then the other, hands wafting up and down at chest level. 'No need for it!'

One spoke up. 'You a fucking scouser?'

He stood straight and, when he replied, made sure his Mancunian accent was strong. 'No, 'course not. I just wanted you all to remember something.' He pointed off to the side. 'That's where the real enemy is, lads. At the end of the Mersey.'

He waited for the penny to drop, but they continued to

stare at him. The silence was stretching out too long. Jesus. 'Liverpool,' he stated.

Finally, one began to mutter. 'Fucking hate Liverpool.'

Another nodded. 'Yeah! Fucking whining scouse twats.'

'Jurgen cunting Klopp.'

A few laughed at that.

'Glad he fucked off back to Germany.'

Guy clicked his fingers. 'That's what I'm talking about!'

He continued on through the doors and into a spacious foyer. Ping-pong and crappy biscuits? Jayden, that was harsh. Posters covered the noticeboard on his left. Dance classes. Music club. Games design. Talent academy. Young reporters. There were photos of kids doing assault courses in what looked like the Lake District. A girl smashing the living daylights out of a drum kit. Someone with earphones hunched over a mixing desk. A boy holding a microphone boom next to another who was interviewing someone outside the BBC offices in MediaCity.

Thudding music was coming from a side room. At the far end of the hall, Guy spotted a couple of table-tennis tables sitting alongside a pool table and a load of massive beanbags. A door opened to his side and a woman stepped out. Guy had time to clock high cheekbones and a mass of straggly light-brown hair piled up on her head.

'Can I help you?' Her tone was curt.

'Er, I'm not sure.' He hadn't planned what to say if anyone approached him. To state that he was looking for a teenage boy he'd been chatting to outside McDonald's was an obvious no-goer. Stalling for time, he asked, 'Do you work here?' Even as the question was coming out, he could see the identity card clipped to the belt loop of her dark grey trousers. Nice one, Guy.

'I do.' She placed a hand on her hip, bright-blue eyes fixed on him. She obviously didn't take any shit.

'Right.' He glanced back at the noticeboard. 'I was…I was wondering about volunteering opportunities, that was all. I just recently moved to the area.'

'You have experience in youth work?'

'Youth work?' This was going to shit at a rapid rate. 'Not specifically, no. But I do quite a lot of things.'

She frowned. 'Things?'

'Training, sorry. Should have said training. Stuff I can teach.'

She gave a little wiggle of her head and her lips pursed, though Guy couldn't tell if it was with amusement or impatience. Maybe both. 'This training being…?'

'Self-defence. Strength and conditioning.' He was suddenly conscious of the weight he'd put on. His general lack of fitness. 'I mean, I realise I could do with a bit of it myself. But – you know – I could still…' Now he could see the beginnings of a smirk. Jesus. Could this be going any worse? 'Maybe you have an application form or something I could take with me?'

'I do.' She reached behind her and opened the door. 'Step this way.'

He followed her into a small office. Piles of boxes filled the end of the room. The flaps of one were open. Empty sports bottles with jagged lettering down their sides: The Zone. Next to them were polythene sacks stuffed with tote bags, all bearing the same logo. A netting bag full of deflated footballs hung from the wall. The place needed a damn good tidy.

'Tell me,' she said, 'what did you say to the group of boys out there?'

He turned round, realising her windows looked out on the skate area.

'I could see it was about to kick off,' she continued. 'And was about to come out. But then you appeared. What did you say to them?'

She was searching through the drawers of a desk that was covered in layers of paper. He spotted a photo frame beside her phone. It was the woman herself, aged about ten, or her daughter. The same, almost Slavic, face. He guessed daughter. 'Just made a joke. Best way of defusing things, I always think. A bit of humour.'

She straightened up. 'A joke?'

'Yeah, a scouse joke. Cheap shot, I know. But it's always sure to work. In Manchester, at least.'

She was gazing at him with slightly narrowed eyes. The hint of a smile was back. Oh my, he thought, you are so good looking. If slightly scary.

'It certainly did,' she said. 'Listen, I can't find the forms you need. Just jot down your name, address and email on this, will you?' She placed a pad of paper on the desk and dropped a pen onto it. 'I can send you a link to the form.'

'Right, OK – cheers.' He briefly toyed with giving her a false name. But that would only ensure he could never show his face here again. 'There you go.'

Her phone started to ring, and she pushed a strand of hair behind her ear as she reached for the receiver. 'I'll be in touch.'

'Thanks.' The office door had almost swung shut behind him when she spoke again.

'Hello, Amy Jones speaking.'

Amy Jones, he thought. Nice name.

CHAPTER 15

On his first perimeter check of the freight terminal, he paused at the gate out onto Europa Way. Once sure that no one was lurking in the shadows beyond it, he crouched down and swiftly looped a length of cotton round the edge of the gate and the closest part of the security fence. Now anyone letting themselves in would snap the thread.

Once back in the terminal buildings, he went into the main office and opened the small cupboard where the stationery was kept. There, amongst the Post-it notes, staplers and rolls of Sellotape, he found what he was looking for: a stout pair of scissors.

As he headed in the direction of empty storage, music carried from the direction of MediaCity. Sunday night. The place was never quiet. At first, he'd found it odd how the waves of sound rose and fell. One moment, the drumbeat was clearest. Next, a bass line would take over. Or fragments of the singer's vocals. Sometimes, the whoops of actual people. But the rhythms never seemed to quite fit. It had taken him a few nights to realise he was hearing elements of several songs carrying from different venues, all mixed by the breeze. A kaleidoscope of sound.

When he got to the reefer section, he shone his torch at

the doors of a nearby container. He'd never paid much attention to what was written on them. In the top right-hand corner, above a list of weights in both pounds and kilograms, was a series of numbers and letters.

1767-49-4561

He checked what was on the neighbouring container.

3451-82-7748

He guessed it was an identifier – like a car's registration plate. If each container had its own unique number, locating where the ones with drugs in would be simple – as long as you had access to the depot control system. He could picture what the collectors, including Jayden, would be told: blue container, identification ending in 4561, on row 27, stack 4, column A, ground level.

At the first intersection, he turned left and went two aisles deeper into the maze. No one can see me here, he thought, walking round to the refrigeration unit at the rear of a container. Its upper half consisted of a smooth metal panel. A row of heavy bolts formed a perimeter round it. He guessed that, if all of them were removed, the entire panel would lift off. Beneath that, a large extractor fan sat behind thick wire mesh. Below that appeared to be some sort of compressor. He examined the words printed on the control panel next to the extractor fan: set point / code. Air temp. In range. Alarm. Beside that was a long list of codes. As the unit was turned off, nothing was operational.

At the front of the container, he shone his torch across the doors. A pair of vertical rods ran the length of each one. About two-thirds of the way down them was a handle secured by a wire tag. He checked in each direction before producing the scissors. The blades easily severed the thin wire of the right-hand tab. Grasping the handle, he turned the locking rod through one-eighty degrees and yanked. With a low metallic scrape, the door swung outward.

Stale air enveloped him and he held his breath while

swopping the scissors for the torch. The beam lit up a bare interior: stainless steel walls and ceiling and a raised mesh floor. He directed the light at the end wall. If you're stashing drugs, that's the only place to put them, he thought. His work shoes caused a muted clang as they came into contact with the metal floor. He paused to check the door: no way of opening it from the inside. Feeling vaguely uneasy, he continued further into the container's claustrophobic depths.

The panel sheeting of the end wall was attached by a series of screws which would be easy to remove. He tapped the metal surface: hollow. Probably a void behind it filled with insulation wool or something similar. Towards the top was a gap of about forty centimetres. The air vent, he concluded. When the unit was running, cold air would be blasted across the ceiling, before sinking to beneath the raised floor, where it would circulate back to where he was standing. He reached into the gap and had to raise himself on tiptoes before his fingertips made contact with the end of the container. So, a good thirty centimetres behind this inner wall. Plenty of space to hide a shipment of drugs.

When he stepped back onto the asphalt, it was with a sense of relief. Using his shoulder, he swung the door almost closed and kicked the broken security tag aside. Just another break-in by a collector, he thought, making a note of the container's location before returning to the office building.

When the sky started to lighten beyond United's stadium, he carried out one final check of the perimeter. Arriving at Europa Way gate, he almost shouted with frustration. No cotton thread: the little shits had been back through! Right under my nose, too. He glanced toward the empty storage area, knowing that the last part of his shift would be spent trying to locate the actual container which had been targeted. Setting off for the nearest aisle, he couldn't help wondering if it had been Jayden.

#

Once home, he found his mind turning to McFadden again. The way the bloke was building himself a front as a respectable businessman. And all the while bringing in drugs to sell throughout the city and beyond. He opened his laptop and resumed his search for the man's surname. It seemed that there were very few stories about him since the murder charge had been dropped. Eventually, Guy found an article from the entertainment pages of a magazine called *Cheshire Living*. It was about a fund-raising event for a hospice in Alderley Edge. McFadden had bid the highest for six weekend spa tickets at Mottram Lodge – and had promptly donated them to the hospice staff. Guy homed in on the photos. There he was, wearing a dinner jacket, sitting at a table lit by candles with an ornate bouquet of flowers at its centre. The caption described him as owner of Viscount Security Solutions. Guy nodded. Involving yourself with local good causes. Forging connections with the right people. You scummy bastard.

He opened a new tab and typed in Viscount Security Solutions. Doormen, basically. He could provide doormen for established premises, public events, and private functions. The website was professionally put together, but Guy didn't let that cloud his judgement. Controlling security at pubs and clubs across the city also gave you control of what was sold inside. And, for several years now, McFadden had been quietly building his empire with no trouble from the police.

He went back to the laptop's search history and brought up the report from when the case against McFadden for living off the proceeds of crime had collapsed. This time, he carefully read each line of text. Halfway through, he found what he was looking for: Dale McFadden of Orchard Lane, Worsley. A nice-sounding address.

He typed it into google and studied the resulting map. Worsley lay a short way round the M60, just off junction 13. It took him a few minutes to find Orchard Lane. A little curving road that branched off a larger one. It ran alongside a patch of green labelled Wardley Wood, before re-joining the larger road. Guy zoomed in and switched to satellite view. Wardley Wood was just that: a sizeable copse of trees that stretched for about seven hundred metres. There were just eight houses on Orchard Lane, each surrounded by a large garden. One had a tennis court, three had outside pools. Most had multiple cars parked on the drives.

He zoomed out until the M60 came back into view. Running beneath it at junction 13 was a thin ribbon of blue. Well, well, well, thought Guy. The Bridgewater Canal. If I were to walk briskly from the freight terminal, Mr McFadden, I could be on your road within half an hour.

CHAPTER 16

Guy woke with a sense of unease simmering in his gut. He sat up in bed, removed his eye mask, and rested a hand against his chest. Pulse was running a little too quick. He recalled a restless sleep that had been plagued by thoughts of Jayden's predicament. One dream had something to do with them both sitting on the highest container in a stack of six. It had given a sudden jolt as an RSG locked on and began to lift it. The smooth metal surface tilted sharply and Jayden had slid helplessly towards the edge. Guy had shouted at the driver to stop, but it was Nathan Fenton at the wheel and he was laughing.

Guy removed his earplugs and the sound of the day flooded in. The usual indistinct TV commentary drifting down from above. Someone arguing out on the road. The impatient beep of a car horn. He checked the time: almost half-past two in the afternoon. Shit, he thought, I've overslept. He tracked a series of heavy thuds across the ceiling. What the hell was the person doing up there? Learning to hop?

After flicking the kettle on, Guy turned his head to the side. A noise that sounded like a door being opened. At the back of the house. He went over to the window and looked down into the garden. A hunched little figure in a giant overcoat was slowly making its way across the tangled growth that used to be the lawn. Must be the occupant of the ground-floor flat, Guy thought. A faded baseball cap covered the person's head. Spindly little legs and black shoes. The person was making directly for the tree which the birdfeeder hung from. So, it was you. Thought it might be. He'd got the catches of the window across by the time a claw-like hand had started tugging at the branch to bring the feeder lower.

'Hey!' he called down. 'What are you doing?'

The sound of his voice caused the person's shoulders to flinch, but they carried on anyway. The other hand grabbed the feeder and pulled at it.

'Leave it!' he said, more loudly. 'That's my birdfeeder. Just leave it!'

It finally came off and the branch sprang back up. The person twisted round and glared up at him. He realised it was a woman.

'My garden!' she snapped.

Her voice was a rasp and her wrinkled lips curled inward. But what he could see of her hair was dark and her eyes weren't those of an old woman. Christ, he thought. She could be about my age. Maybe younger. Withered by years of booze. 'It's just a birdfeeder. What's your problem?'

'Cats. Don't want cats in my garden.' She was making her way towards the fence. 'Hate them.'

He almost said that witches were meant to like cats, but stopped himself. 'So you're just going to sling it over the fence again?'

'My garden. You keep out, you're not allowed.'

He stared down at her, his anger rapidly gathering strength. She never opened her curtains. What did she care about the shitty garden? She didn't even set foot in it. Did nothing to it. The kettle clicked off beside him and he imagined pouring boiling water down onto her head. That would be… He closed his eyes. What are you thinking, Guy? It's this place, he thought. This street. This whole bloody area. I need to get out of here. It's wearing me down. Turning me mean.

He ducked back in as she hurled the birdfeeder into the air, her chin defiantly jutting out. The window shut with a thud. He paced back and forth, taking deep breaths. It was no good. If I stay here, he thought, I'll end up like those old men I see. Sallow, grey skin. Ill-fitting clothes. Muttering to myself as I shuffle along the street. An image of Jayden popped into his head. This neighbourhood was his whole bloody life. All he'd ever known. It made him want to yell with despair.

Instead, he searched out his phone and brought up the number for Bennet's Garage. 'Jim, it's Guy Haslam here. Are you good to talk?'

'Of course, mate. Just pottering around.'

'Nice. I was thinking about something you said the other day. About that latest apprentice blowing you out.'

The other man let out a groan. 'Not sure why I bother sometimes.'

'But would you be interested? If someone else put their hand up?'

'Don't know. The ones the apprenticeships place send me; they don't really want to be here. Not when they realise what the actual work involves.'

Guy nodded. 'I've come across this kid where I work. Bit rough at the edges, but there's a spark to him. He's able to use his initiative.'

'Why would he want a job out here if he's working with you?'

'Oh, he's not at the freight terminal. But I've seen him hanging around. We've talked a few times. Round here, you know how it is. He'll just end up getting into trouble. The chance of a proper day's work. Learning from a bloke like you. It's all he needs.'

'Guy, this lad. I take it he's not at school?'

'No, I don't think he is.'

'And he's how old?'

'Sixteen or seventeen. As I said, he's a bit rough at the edges. But he's a smart kid.'

Jim sighed heavily. 'Because it's you. That's the only reason. Bring him over and let's have a chat.'

'Right, cheers, Jim. I've got to speak to him first. See if I can persuade him.'

Jim chuckled. 'You've not even run it past him?'

'No point before you'd agreed.'

'Fair enough. Good luck.'

'Thanks,' Guy said, cutting the call. Now I just need to actually find him.

There was a bounce in his step as he walked over to the broom cupboard and opened the door. He took out his walking boots, then removed the camouflage basha tarp and his black beanie hat from their hooks. From the little chest of drawers beside his bed, he lifted out a neatly folded pair of black cargo trousers and a black top. Sorted, he said to himself. The light would fade in a few hours and, because he'd covered for the other night watchman on Friday, he had tonight off.

#

The tow path which ran beside the Bridgewater Canal wasn't wide enough for two people. Each time he encountered a jogger or dog walker, Guy let them get past by positioning himself on the verge closest to the water. After all, who'd like to encounter some bloke dressed all in black on one side of you and a stretch of dirty brown water on the other? They'd think he was there to mug them and push them in.

By the time the canal was passing through the industrial landscape where the freight terminal was located, it had grown properly dark. The bridge he used to cross over the canal on his way to and from work soon came into view. He paused beneath it and, after checking no one was behind him, made his way up the steep slope to the line of bushes. Two parked lorries came into view. He was about fifty metres too early. You're losing your touch, Guy. He dropped back down onto the towpath, counted out fifty paces and re-climbed the slope. The sapling he'd noted before was a metre to his right. Not bad.

As he crawled into the undergrowth, the loamy scent of soil mixed with the delicate smell of new leaves. Memories came surging back. Jungle operations. Days spent camped out, gathering intelligence. The need for perfect stillness, even when leeches were probing at the eyelets of your boots or looping across your hands, seeking the softer skin of the inner wrist.

Once he was close to the fence, he laid out his tarp, wriggled to one side and folded the canvas material back over himself. By lifting the edge directly before his face, he had a direct view of the Europa gate.

At nine-thirty-six, he spotted the other night watchman ambling across the terminal yard. The man got to the edge of laden storage, briefly played his torch in the direction of the empties, then turned round and headed back to the offices. Lazy bastard.

Twelve minutes past ten and a red Audi coupe cruised slowly along the road, coming from the direction of Europa Way. It pulled over less than five metres to Guy's right and its lights went off. Two males in the front. A cigarette lighter flared. Another person in the back. Next, an orange tip glowed several times before it bobbed to the front of the car, where it glowed again. From there, it moved across to the other person in the front before floating back to the rear of the vehicle. A bit of muffled laughter and the rear window lowered enough for the remains of the joint to be thrown out. The engine revved and the car went on its way. Guy watched the tendril of smoke twisting up from the nearby brambles. That familiar cloying smell.

It wasn't until after three in the morning that he heard

footsteps. These were approaching from the direction of Wharfside Way. Two voices: one deeper, one slightly higher. A few seconds later, two darkly dressed figures came into view. When they passed beneath a streetlight, he recognised Jayden. Walking beside him was the one from the footbridge who'd been holding the cash. The white markings on their trainers rose and fell in the dark as they approached the Europa gate. Once they reached it, both did a cursory check of the road before putting on black baseball caps. The older one handed Jayden a small backpack, then stepped up to the gate. A downward motion of his hand and it swung open. So, you are getting hold of people's passes, thought Guy as Jayden slipped through the gap and into the terminal. Crouching low, he ran silently across the tarmac to empty storage, where he vanished down an aisle.

Guy turned his attention to the companion who had now stepped back from the perimeter fence. He lit a cigarette and started studying his phone. Jesus, thought Guy. It's become this fucking casual? Like you're waiting for pizza to arrive? Once the cigarette was finished, he flicked the butt away and started crossing the road in Guy's direction. When the bloke reached the verge, he turned round and perched on the edge of the fence, less than three feet from where Guy lay.

It was tempting to stare at the back of the man's head to get an early indication of him deciding to look around. But Guy's training had taught him that doing so might cause the person to sense he was being watched. Instead, Guy stared at the midpoint between his shoulder blades. Another time and place, he thought, and I would be reaching out to clamp my left hand over your mouth. Right hand would be holding my fighting knife, which would be plunging in and out of your neck and chest before you knew what was happening. Drag you back here, safely out of sight, where I could slice through your vocal cords and let you bleed out in silence. Instead, he lay perfectly still and watched the shine of the screen as the other man made a call.

'Yo, Ads,' he said in a low voice. 'Yeah, sent him in five minutes ago. What was D saying before? Wants him to go where? Fucking Rochdale? For how long? When's the next batch due here? Oh, OK. Rochdale though? Has he? To that same house? If that's what the orders are. OK. Should be with you in about thirty. Safe.'

He ended the call and pocketed the phone. Guy kept his breathing slow and shallow. Sounded like D was giving the orders. And who was being sent to Rochdale? Jayden? Why would Jayden be needed in a house? He couldn't exactly see the kid putting up wallpaper or grouting tiles.

A few minutes later, the man's chin lifted and he got to his feet. In the container yard, Guy glimpsed a shadow flitting back across the tarmac. The older man ambled over to the gate and swiped again. Jayden stepped back through and they immediately set off the way they'd come.

'All good?' the older one asked.

'Yeah,' Jayden replied, a little breathlessly.

'Got it all?'

'Eight. I got eight.'

'Top work, our kid. Top work.'

Guy eased the tarp from his head and shoulders to get a clearer view. The rucksack Jayden wore now hung low on his back. He noted how the older man did not try to reclaim it. Why would he? If the police stopped them, it would be Jayden in possession, not him. The lad didn't have a clue about how badly he was being used.

Guy waited until they'd disappeared round the curve in the road before stuffing the tarp back into his rucksack. Then he vaulted the fence and jogged to where the road rose as it crossed the Bridgewater Canal. He slowed down and, as the T-junction at the end of the road came into view, saw them turning right. He sped up again and, at the corner, peeped round to see them nearing the intersection with Wharfside Way. Keeping well back, he used the same shadowing technique to follow them along Sir Matt Busby Way onto the A56 and then left into the residential roads of Stretford. They passed three side streets before turning into the fourth. Speeding up once more, Guy checked the time: eleven minutes after four. Every window on the street was dark and, apart from the stilted twitters of a few birds, it was completely silent. The chimneys of the houses on his right were starting to stand out against the slowly lightening sky. Further along the road, he saw them turn into the front yard of a house. Silver Polo parked on the drive. He heard four quiet knocks: two fast, two slow. A finger of yellow light widened like a fan across the front step and they disappeared inside. The door closed with a gentle thud.

Guy looked about. There was nowhere to conceal himself except in someone's front garden. Not possible, now dawn was so near. Could he risk walking past the house? No: assuming they'd met Ads from the footbridge inside, any of them only had to glance out the window to recognise him. All he could do was note down the name of the road. Napier Street, off Morland Road, third house on the left.

He turned round and began the long trudge back towards Salford. What, he asked himself, was Jayden likely to do next? He'd just been up half the night on a job. His pockets would be stuffed with cash. Being a teenager, he'll be starving. Guy nodded. You're right, mate. There's only one place he'll have in mind: McDonalds.

CHAPTER 17

He was on his second coffee, sitting at the outside tables and watching the trickle of morning traffic steadily build, when a familiar figure came into view from the direction of Trafford Park. Jayden, talking on his phone.

Guy bowed his head and waiting until he could hear the lad's footsteps before glancing up. Their eyes immediately met. Feigning surprise, Guy lifted a hand in greeting.

'Mr Nothing-Man!' Jayden announced with a grin.

Guy gave him a nod. 'What happened to you? Stood at the end of my road like a right bell-end waiting for you.'

The lad's expression didn't change. 'You what?'

'The Krav Maga class? Sunday afternoon?'

'Oh, right. Yeah.'

'Oh right? It was you who told me not to bloody forget.'

He shrugged. 'Something else came up.'

No offer of an apology, Guy noted. Not even a flicker of embarrassment. Here was someone used to promises being broken, to plans not being kept. It was totally normal. 'So,' Guy said, sitting back. 'You're up early.'

'So are you.' His eyes shifted to the rucksack next to Guy. 'Off hiking, are you?'

A good trait, Guy thought. Being observant. 'Yeah, I am. Probably around Haverdale. You know it?'

Jayden shook his head. 'Nope. Should I?'

'No, not really. Schools go on trips there sometimes.' He gestured to the seating on the opposite side of the table. 'Sit down, if you want.'

Jayden glanced towards the restaurant building. Searching for someone, or checking no one he knew was already inside. He slid onto the empty bench and draped both arms across the backrest.

'I'm off hiking,' Guy stated. 'How come you're already out and about?'

'Don't mind being up early. Doesn't bother me.'

'That because of the work you do, is it?'

'What work's that, then?'

'You know – the freight terminal. Those two blokes you were with that time. Ads and...?'

Jayden let his head loll to the side, ignoring the question.

'You know they're using you, right? First sign of trouble, don't expect them to help you. Because they won't.' He took a sip of his drink.

'What are you?' Jayden asked. 'A fucking expert?'

Guy studied his cup. 'I grew up around here. Your age? I was doing similar stuff. The lot I was with...I thought they were, like, mates? Even though they were all older than me. But they weren't my mates.'

'And you still don't seem to have any. Mates. Do you?'

Guy raised his cup. 'You got me there,' he smiled. 'I don't. But listen: what are you hoping for? Where do you see things heading?'

'Things heading?' He started to laugh. 'Like I have a plan?'

'Come on. You must have. Things you'd like. I mean,

you're not wanting to live in the Two Sisters your whole life, are you?'

Jayden's eyes drifted to the side. 'No,' he murmured. 'I'm going to get me a nice pad.' He jabbed a thumb over his shoulder. 'One of them flash ones in Salford Quays. With a big bastard of a balcony. Somewhere to sit out of an evening.'

Christ, thought Guy. Just like my brother. He couldn't help glance in that direction. The tops of the tallest apartment blocks just showed against the pale sky. So that's it, he thought. The scope of your dreams involves swopping one flat for another that's barely a mile down the road. 'You never thought about getting away?'

'From where?'

'Here. The city.'

'How do you mean?'

'Live somewhere different. The countryside. Somewhere with a bit of greenery. Not all this dirt and pollution and…crap.'

Jayden was looking at him with a puzzled expression. 'The countryside? You are fucking weird.'

Someone came to a stop beside their table. Guy turned his head. It was a girl. Fourteen, fifteen? Eyes still puffy from sleep, hair loosely constrained by an untidy bun. A North Face puffer jacket over what looked suspiciously like pyjamas. Or maybe fluffy leggings. Without even a glance at Guy, she uncrossed her arms and held out a hand. 'Fucking starving.'

'Yeah, yeah,' Jayden replied, reaching into a pocket and sliding out a twenty. 'Get me the breakfast roll meal, chocolate milkshake and some pancakes.'

She yanked the money from his fingers. 'We eating in?' she asked, eyes finally touching on Guy for the briefest of moments.

'Yup,' Jayden replied.

Guy watched as she headed for the doors. Girlfriend?

The way she'd acted seemed too…arsey. He guessed younger sister.

'The countryside?' Jayden repeated. 'Why?'

'You could get away from all this. Learn a proper skill. You're older than sixteen, right?'

He nodded.

'OK. I know…some people. People who could set you up with a decent enough job.'

Jayden placed a hand on the table. Tapped the fake wood with a forefinger. 'You know how much money I make?'

'If those two you were with are offering hundreds for a security pass, it's probably loads. Probably miles more than I'm earning.'

'Yeah,' Jayden said. 'It fucking is. And not for a shitty twelve-hour shift, either.'

'But what's it going to lead to? The ones who're giving you these jobs – you think they care about you? Actually care?'

Jayden flexed his fingers back and forth, jaw now set tight. 'The fuck are you to talk about people who care? Sitting there like a loner. What do you know about anything?'

'I'm not having a go at you, Jayden. It's just…any organisation needs foot soldiers. People to do the grunt work. Take the risks. Say you were arrested. That Ads and his mate, and whoever they work for, you think they'd visit you in Forest Bank or wherever you end up?' He shook his head. 'They'll be finding someone to take your place. That's what they'll be doing.'

He could see his comments had connected on some level. Jayden's face seemed to shed a few years, and he suddenly looked exactly like what he was: a teenager. A teenager who, more than anything, needed a sense of belonging.

'McFadden, is it?' Guy quietly asked. 'Who Ads and the other one work for?'

Jayden's eyes widened.

Something banged loudly against the window beside them. Guy looked to see the girl on the other side of the glass. Food, she mouthed, pointing to a full tray on a nearby table.

Jayden started getting to his feet.

'Listen,' Guy said. 'I'm just trying to…I don't know…it doesn't have to go the way it's going. That's all. And if you need anything. Even just to talk, I'm here. That's what I'm trying to say.'

Jayden looked down at him. 'You're there, are you? Mr Nothing-Man?' His voice was scathing. 'Yeah, right.'

Guy smiled sadly. The kid had a point.

'And another thing?' Jayden dropped his voice. 'That name you just mentioned? Don't be throwing that about. Unless you want grief. Serious grief.'

Guy watched in silence as Jayden turned round and strode through the doors. Shit, I really messed that up. The kid's furious. He reached for his bag, then changed his mind. Should I go in, try to patch things up? He watched from the corner of his eye as Jayden arrived at the table where the girl was sitting. Her head partly turned in Guy's direction, a questioning look on her face as she said something. Jayden shook his head in reply, then scooped up his burger and took a huge bite.

Guy was still contemplating what to do when he felt a vibration in his coat pocket. Who's calling at this time…? His stomach took a downward lurch. He still had Lee's SIM in the phone. 'Hello, Lee Haslam speaking.'

'Lee, sorry if I woke you. It's Martin, from Brookfield House?'

'No, it's fine. I was awake.' He sat forward and closed his eyes. 'What's up, Martin?'

CHAPTER 18

Guy stared despondently at the flight prices displaying across the screen of his laptop. They'd crept up another two hundred and fifty quid since he'd last looked. Oh well, he thought, credit card bill's going to cripple me. He picked a flight in two days' time purely because it was marginally more affordable than the others. Then he rapidly ticked the last few boxes, fretting his seat would vanish before the damned thing had been confirmed as his.

At the centre of the screen, a ring of dots circled round and round for what felt like ages. Finally, an inner box popped up.

Congratulations, Guy! You're going to Australia. Please check your inbox for our confirmation email.

He took a couple of deep breaths in, not daring to believe anything until he'd seen the actual email. As he waited, Martin's words started replaying in his head. A stroke. Lucky it had happened when it did: just as they were getting him ready for mid-afternoon tea. Tests were still ongoing, but at least it looked like Harry would live. For now.

Above him came the same laborious thud. He glanced at the ceiling with gritted teeth. In his head, he saw a grotesquely overweight bloke. Rolls of blubber restricting his movement. An email coming in caused a two-note chime. He clicked on the mail tab and frowned. It wasn't from *The Flight Place*. Subject line read 'Voluntary Work'. He stared at the sender's name. Amy Jones. Of course, the manager at The Zone. She said she was sending an application form across.

A new message pinged up. This was the one from the flight broker. He opened it: departing from Manchester, at 11.55 am on Thursday. Aeroflot to Bangkok, then Turkish Airlines to Brisbane. He let out a sigh of relief. It was happening.

Closing the message, he went back to the one from Amy. 'Guy, application form attached. We'll also need to get you DBS checked, but just send me the details for the first section in the meantime. Amy.'

Well, that's a no-nonsense way of communicating, he thought. She could be ex-military, sending messages like that. He opened up the form. First section was all standard stuff: address, contact number, date of birth, town or city of birth, National Insurance number. The second section contained information about the DBS check. The types of identification he'd have to provide. Passport. Driving Licence with photo card. Bank statement with address. A full, five-year address history with no gaps. Shit, he thought, picturing the prison cell he'd been trapped in for almost two years. The unbearable African heat and steady supply of mosquitos floating through the bars of the single, miniscule, window. How he'd avoided catching malaria was a miracle; most of the others hadn't been so lucky.

He contemplated the form. Why not fill in the first section, as Amy had asked? She might be able to give him some advice about Jayden before she realised he would never be approved for working with young people. Worth a try. He filled in his details, giving his brother's mobile as his number and sent it back.

Next thing on his list was letting his manager at Freight Master know he'd be needing that time off work. Best do that in person, he decided, checking the time. Just after eight. The bloke was probably at his desk by now, pouring a coffee from the big blue flask.

#

Guy watched the end of Matthew Hughes' pen as it bounced against the pad of paper on his desk. The manager's head was bowed. '11.55 am this Thursday? Christ, it's hardly the advance warning I asked for, Guy.'

'I realise that. If me handing my notice in makes things easier for you, just say. It's not like I've been here that long.'

Hughes looked up. 'Hopefully, there'll be no need for that. You're a good worker, Guy. Punctual. Efficient. Conscientious. I certainly don't want to go through the process of recruiting again.'

'Of course, I'll work tonight and Wednesday, as scheduled.'

'Wednesday? But your flight leaves just before midday on Thursday. That means finishing here and practically going straight to the airport. Are you sure?'

Guy shrugged. 'I can sleep on the plane.'

'And you'll be gone for ten days, you say?'

'Yes, I think that'll be enough. You know, to see him and sort out arrangements.'

'How is he?'

'Too early to say. He's in hospital under observation. They think he's lost the left side of his body. Mentally, he's fairly responsive, apparently. Not sure what that means.'

'Well, however he is, I'm sure he'll feel better seeing his son at this bedside.'

Guy looked away. 'Hopefully.'

'Why don't you get yourself a drink or something? I'll get on to HR at the London office and see what we can work out. I'll come and find you in the canteen.'

'OK.' Guy stood. 'Thanks, I appreciate it.'

He'd hit a morning break, judging by the amount of yard lads lounging about in the canteen. Some were on their phones. One table was playing cards. He searched the room for Andy Meadows. No sign of him, though Nathan Fenton was at a corner table, staring in his direction.

Guy crossed to the drinks machine and punched in the code for a tea. Once the dribble of brown liquid had filled the cup, he slid it from the tray and took a sip. Barely lukewarm. He found an empty table in the corner and had only just opened the newsfeed on his phone when someone cleared their throat. He looked up to see Fenton standing at the other side of the table.

'Hello there.' The man smiled awkwardly. 'Do you…do you mind if I take a seat?'

Guy studied him for a second. *Should I tell him this really isn't a good time for trying to wind me up?* The bloke appeared…chastened. Practically apologetic. Guy could tell the people at the table he had come from were all listening in. 'Doesn't bother me,' he replied, going back to his phone.

'Great, thanks. I thought you might like this. To go with your brew.'

Guy wrenched his eyes from the screen. Fenton had placed a KitKat on the table. He tilted his head. 'What's this about?'

Fenton nervously brushed a hand across the end of his nose. Ducked his head a couple of times before he got his words out. 'I've been acting the dick. This is me, you know, trying to make amends. Peace offering, if you will.'

'Peace offering?'

'Yeah. All that business. Ribbing you about where you'd been before starting here. I was being an idiot.'

Guy locked eyes with the other man. 'You were.'

'Right. Right!' Fenton grinned. 'But, listen, fresh start and all that. How about it?'

Guy placed his phone aside. This, he thought, doesn't add up. 'If I'm honest, I'd be happier if you just kept your distance.'

'And I don't blame you. But all I'm asking for is another chance. Honestly, you'll see I'm not such an arsehole. Well, maybe not such a big one.' He grinned again.

In the periphery of his vision, Guy could see the people at the other table leaning forward slightly, no one speaking. Guy retrieved his phone and went back to the headlines. 'Fair enough.'

Fenton wasn't getting up. After a couple more seconds, he spoke again. 'Got a lot of respect for people like you. A lot.'

Guy lifted his gaze, waiting for an explanation.

Fenton pointed to Guy's forehead. 'When did you get your green lid, then?'

Guy felt a sinking feeling. Shit, did I just hear that right? 'Say again?'

Fenton now tapped a point above his own left eyebrow. The point where the badge on the Royal Marine's distinctive green beret would have been positioned. 'Green lid? The Royal Marines? When did you get in?'

'How do you know about that?'

Fenton's smile stayed in place. 'What, that you were a Royal Marine?'

Guy nodded.

'It was…' He pointed in the general direction of the nearby tables. 'The lads were talking about it earlier.'

Fuck, thought Guy. How the hell did it get out? I'd made it clear to Hughes that no part of my CV was to be shared outside of HR. Not with the embarrassment of how my career ended. Had Hughes let it slip? Maybe someone in HR? Or… His eyes cut to the window. On the far side of the terminal, the crane was trundling its way along. Andy Meadows? That night in the pub. Could, maybe, I have mentioned it myself? But the bloke had said nothing about it next day in the corridor...

'So did you do any tours? Afghanistan and that?' Fenton's eyes had an eager shine.

'Yes, I did.'

'Iraq? Not when things were properly kicking off, obviously. But in the years after that?'

'I've spent some time in Iraq,' Guy said quietly, hating the fact this would all be audible to the nearest tables.

'Yeah? So have you, you know…'

Here it comes, thought Guy. And it's been asked me by a little fucking weasel who has only seen combat via his PlayStation. 'What's that, then?'

Fenton leaned forward. 'Did you ever off anyone?' He made a pistol with his right hand. Flexed his raised thumb. 'Take any fuckers out?'

Guy lowered his gaze and stared at his lap for a couple of seconds. He tried to push the anger back down, but it was no good. Waves of it were flooding his chest. He lifted his eyes to see Fenton's comradely grin. 'Served yourself, did you?'

'No, mate. Kind of fancied it when I was younger. But, you know, never actually got round to it. But I know a bit about the Royal Marines. Read books. All the training you had to get through. Brutal. Hat's off to you.'

'Cheers.'

'So…did you? You must have. How many was it?'

Guy put his phone aside once more. 'You think you can just sit yourself down here and, for the cost of a fucking KitKat, get me to spill my guts?'

Fenton blinked, his smile slipping. 'Eh?'

Guy shoved the snack across the table. 'Stick it up your arse.'

'What's your problem?' Fenton asked. 'Jesus, it's a simple question.'

Simple question? A nice little canteen chat about how many lives I've taken? What it feels like to kill someone? So you can gleefully repeat it all next time you're down the pub? Cunt. He picked up the plastic cup and tipped its contents over Fenton's head. Rivulets of brown liquid made their way down the man's face. The canteen fell silent as a couple of dozen blokes waited to see what would happen next.

Fenton wiped a thumb across one eyebrow then the other. Slowly, he shook his head.

'Guy?'

Glancing to his left, Guy saw Matthew Hughes in the doorway. The man's mouth was hanging open. 'What's going on?'

Guy looked back at Fenton who forced his lips into something that resembled a smile. 'Nothing,' he announced with forced cheer, running a hand through his dripping hair. He got to his feet and shot a quick look at Guy. 'Nothing at all.'

Hughes looked on with a baffled expression as Fenton returned to his table. 'Well, in that case...' His gaze swung back to Guy. 'Good news: I've spoken to HR.'

CHAPTER 19

Guy paused at the turning into Martyna's bakery and looked across to her premises. He checked his watch. Almost eleven. She'd be past her busiest time. It was tempting to pop in for a chat and to grab a coffee. But the adrenaline was still coursing through him after what had happened in the canteen. And he didn't have the time, not with needing to get sorted for Australia.

Instead of heading towards Wharfside Way, he turned left and followed the road to a roundabout where he took the Trafford Park Road exit. More industrial estates and drab depot-type buildings. Eventually, he reached the warehouse of storage units where his brother Lee's possessions were stashed.

Guy took a deep breath. You've definitely been sidestepping this one, he said to himself, removing the set of keys. The outer door gave access to a deserted lobby. A sharp trace of floor cleaner hung in the air. Globular CCTV cameras hung like white fungi from every corner of the ceiling. He approached the door giving access to the blue corridor, and keyed in his personal code: 1981. The year Lee was born. Somehow, it had seemed appropriate when he'd been filling out the forms. Beyond it was a wide, dark corridor which he knew stretched the entire length of the building. Metal door screens lining each side faded into the gloom. He jangled his keys to disturb the mausoleum-like silence and, as he started walking, made sure to bring the heel of each shoe down with a satisfyingly loud thud. Every ten metres or so another ceiling light blinked into life.

The shutter into Lee's unit was secured with a heavy-duty padlock. Once that was off, Guy grasped the twin handles and raised both arms. The metal slats rose smoothly into the roof with a clatter.

Hands on hips, he stared at what remained of his brother's life. Leaning against the backrest of the black leather sofa to his left was a mass of framed pictures. Modern art prints, mostly. That bloke called Rothko, who Lee was always mad about. Next, a stack of four dining chairs, all chrome frames and leather upholstery. Behind them, a few lamp-stands, their bulbs encased in semi-circular shades of copper-coloured material. A mountain bike, barely used. Glass coffee table. A dismantled bed, mattress propped against the end wall, with a full-length mirror leaning against it. A huge, flat screen TV. A load of boxes, the smallest one on the top open. Crammed inside it were several framed photographs. The uppermost one was Lee, up on stage in black tie, collecting some kind of award. The woman handing it over was vaguely familiar. Off some big BBC or Channel 4 production, probably.

Poking out below that frame was another with two pairs of legs, calf-deep in a patch of turquoise sea. Guy knew what the main part of the photo was of: Lee and himself, faces lit pink by the setting sun, an arm draped over each other's shoulder. The family holiday in Turkey when they were in their early teens. Guy smiled sadly to himself. *While things with Dad were still manageable for me. Another couple of years and that spell of relative calm was well and truly over.*

Next to the box was a plastic crate filled with Lee's

booze collection. Grey Goose vodka. Buffalo Trace bourbon. Sipsmith gin. Cinzano. Herradura tequila. Kahlua. Talisker whiskey. Living the dream, weren't you, our kid? Sex, drugs and rock'n'roll. His eyes returned to the coffee table's mirrored surface. How many lines of coke did you inhale off that?

The first of the ceiling lights to come on now clicked off. Guy regarded the door he'd come through, now plunged in shadow. The other lights would soon start going out and the darkness would advance down the corridor to, eventually, engulf him. For some reason, the thought of that happening made him profoundly uncomfortable. He waved his arms hoping to reactivate the timer of the light for his section of corridor, then stepped into the unit and turned to the railing immediately on his right. Lee's clothing hung from it. Gilets, light coats, heavier coats, and casual jackets. Next came the protective suit covers. Six of them. Another light clicked as it went out. The darkness would have moved closer. He lowered the zip of the first one. Russet-coloured tweed. Guy lifted an eyebrow. Maybe acceptable in your line of work, Lee. But I think I'll pass. The next one was slate grey, shot through with threads of dark green. Could work. He unzipped the next: plain black. Can't go wrong with that, Guy thought, fumbling to re-close the zip as another click sounded in the corridor. The last hangar was festooned with Lee's collection of ties. Guy took the whole thing before draping both suits over his forearm. I can decide on the ties back at my place.

He stepped back out of the unit. Just two ceiling lights were still on. Get a grip, he told himself, not letting himself look at the darkness that now filled the far corridor. He dumped the clothing down and lifted a hand for the shutter. At the far end of the storage unit, a faint figure did the same. It's not your brother, he said to himself. It's just your reflection in the mirror. But the thought was now in his head: a forlorn Lee waving a lonely farewell.

'It's not for long, OK?' he mumbled, fingers wrapping round the metal handle. 'I'll be back soon.' He glanced at the mirror again. The motionless figure silently watching. Fuck it. He ducked back into the unit and slid the photo of them both out of the box. 'Come and stay in my flat, our kid. Shit hole that it is.' He retreated and a metallic ripple filled the corridor as he yanked the shutter down.

Back out in the foyer, sunlight was flooding through the glass doors. He pulled them open and, as soon as he stepped outside, his phone gave a beep. Probably no signal in that place, he thought, taking an uneasy look at the screen as he set off back up the road.

Voicemail from an unknown number.

Could it, he thought, be from Australia? He accessed his messaging service while still walking.

'Guy, it's Amy from The Zone.'

Amy. Relief and something warmer tingled in his chest. What's she saying?

'Thanks for sending your details earlier. I realise this response is probably sooner than expected, but can you pop in later today? It would be great to chat things through. Let me know.'

CHAPTER 20

A frustrated-looking bloke in a track suit stood by as groups of kids attempted to play badminton in the main hall of The Zone. Guy watched as they listlessly swiped at a few shuttlecocks. The things were spending more time on the floor. If it was on a PlayStation, he thought, they'd all probably be Olympic level.

Amy's office door opened and she poked her head out. 'Guy. Good of you to swing by.'

'Hey, no problem. I'm not in work for another few hours.'

'Come on in,' she opened the door wider. 'Take a seat.'

'Cheers.' Still looked like she was yet to clear up after a particularly violent earthquake. But there was now a chair facing hers across the desk.

She circled round and sank into her seat with a grateful sigh.

'Tough day?' he asked, perching on the edge of his chair.

'Tough weekend. We took two teams over to a tournament at The Etihad's community facilities. Kids love it: the whole thing about getting to play football at Manchester City.'

'Bet they do. Your work here - it's not just nine-to-five?'

'Far from it. A lot of the stuff needs to take place outside school hours. So it's mainly evenings and weekends.'

Guy could see the photo of the young girl. Wonder how she sorts out her own childcare. Understanding grandparents, maybe?

'Anyway, I'm done until tomorrow afternoon. Lucky me.'

'Sounds like you've earned it.'

She flashed him a smile and reached for a piece of paper. 'So, thanks for sending those details back. Farrant Road?' She looked up. 'You really are close by.'

'I am.' He tried resting his elbows on the armrests of the chair. But it felt unnatural, so he slid them off again.

'Guy, relax. This isn't a job interview. You can sit back in that chair, you know?'

'Right, sorry.' He eased himself properly into it.

'Pretty much the opposite of an interview, to be frank,' Amy said under her breath, eyes on the form.

Guy wondered what she meant by that. She put the piece of paper aside and looked directly at him. 'I saw how you were with that bunch of lads out front the other day. You've obviously got a knack for this kind of thing.'

'I have?'

She nodded. 'Trust me, I've been doing this long enough. You've got the knack.'

Guy wasn't sure what to think. He'd never seen himself working with youngsters. But then again, he'd always hoped to have kids with Simone before their marriage went tits up. Two boys and a girl, that's what he had always imagined. He noticed Amy's gaze had fallen towards the floor.

'Would have got you to sign on the dotted line there and then, to be honest,' she stated. 'Christ knows we need a few people round here who can handle the... more boisterous ones. People who don't resort to shouting when things get challenging. That definitely doesn't work.'

Guy thought back to his time in the Royal Marines. Had to be humour. Certainly for the day-to-day stuff. If you get people smiling, you were halfway there.

'The reason I didn't,' Amy continued, 'was because we need to be careful. This kind of place – it can attract, you know... unsavoury types.'

Guy sat forward, the time he'd spent in prison flashing through his mind. 'I get that. Totally. You mentioned about the DBS check in your email. To be straight with you, Amy, that's not going to be very simple. I... well, my employment history, where I've been living until recently. It's all a bit –'

She lifted a hand. 'It's not a problem.'

'No, really, it is. Or it will be.'

'I have a contact. A sympathetic police officer. She's already checked for you on the system.'

'Sorry?'

'Not a full DBS, obviously. We will need that, but you've got a clean record and that's what I needed to know at this stage.'

Guy's mind flitted back to his first visit. 'So – when you said you couldn't find an application form and got me to just leave my details, was that a ploy? So you could check me out?'

'It was.' Her gaze was unflinching. 'You have no idea the types who try to weasel their way in.'

'But... all you had was a name and address. What if I was using someone else's?'

She turned and pointed to the cabinet behind her. Guy could make out what looked like a webcam wedged between two of the boxes balanced on top of it. 'I sent her your picture, too.'

This lady, he thought, is really something. 'Impressive.'

'I hope you don't mind me cutting corners like that. But I don't have time to waste and we have to be so careful. Having said that, this isn't really an interview. We're desperate for help.'

Guy shifted uneasily in his seat. I'm only here, he thought, to try and find some information on Jayden. 'What did this contact tell you about me?'

Amy reached for a notebook. 'OK – you have some juvenile stuff. That's no big deal. Then you joined the Royal Marines at twenty-one?'

His eyes were on the notebook. The scribbled lines he couldn't quite make out. His throat had gone dry. 'I did, yes.'

'Maybe that's why you had the touch with those lads out there.' She nodded at the window. 'Someone who's been through stuff: the kids sense that. Someone who can connect with them.'

Guy was doing his best to follow her words. But the notebook was a hand grenade with its pin pulled out.

'Does that make sense?' Amy asked.

He looked up. 'Make sense? Yeah, sure.'

She closed the notebook and dropped it in the handbag hanging from the backrest of her chair. 'More funding cuts are due, thanks to bloody austerity. Or the cost-of-living crisis. Or whatever they've decided to call it now. That means less staff, so less stuff we can offer. And those vulture drug-gangs never stop circling, always on the lookout for bored kids who are just hanging about...'

Guy went to speak, then changed his mind. Amy's eyes narrowed. They were, he thought, the most amazing shade of blue.

'Please, feel free,' she said.

'What do the drug-gangs want with the kids?'

'They want to recruit them. Into selling drugs.'

Here's your chance, Guy. Why not? She's certainly not hiding anything from you. 'That first time I popped in here. I was actually looking for a specific kid.'

Her face immediately turned serious.

'It's just when you mentioned drug-gangs. I see him

around. We've talked a bit, and it's what's happening to him. I've been trying to reach out.'

'Why?'

'Why what?'

'Why are you trying to reach out to him?'

'That's a good question.' He glanced to the side, wondering how to phrase it. 'He's got a bit of a spark. Naughty, but he's not... he's not nasty.' He looked back at her. 'In a funny sort of way, I can see myself in him. When I was that age.'

'So this whole volunteering thing. It's not something you're serious about, after all?'

'No, I am. Now you've said that you think I could do it... yeah, I kind of see what you mean.' He lifted his hand and made a circular motion. 'And this place seems really decent. I would like to be involved with it. Assuming I've not just blown things.'

Her eyes were still on him, but she seemed slightly less concerned at his admission. 'When you say it's happening to him, what exactly do you mean?'

'Well, it's the people he's with. They're older than him. A good few years older. A couple of them tried to intimidate me one time. Jayden was there. He didn't do anything other than watch. But it's the fact that he was there. They're showing him the ropes, luring him in. I know how it works. It happened with me.'

'Did you say this kid is called Jayden?'

'That's right. And he lives in Conmere Tower. That's all I've got.'

A knowing look had appeared on her face. 'About seventeen, is he?'

She knows him, he thought. She bloody knows him! 'Yes.'

Amy looked briefly in the direction of the closed door and lowered her voice. 'Sorry to say,' she sighed, 'we had to bar him. He's not allowed through the doors.'

'Why?'

'Why?' She took a set of little keys from her cardigan pocket and unlocked the bottom-most drawer of the cabinet behind her. A white tag on the front of the drawer read, 'S – Z.' She removed a pale blue manila folder. 'This goes no further than us, yes?'

'Of course.'

She opened it, turned to the last sheet and traced a finger down it. 'Yes – I had remembered right. Basically, what that boy can't break into, I don't know. Mostly the store cupboards in the kitchen. Any food he could pilfer. But he also got into the computer suite one time. Tried taking some iPads – which themselves were in a secure cupboard. Let's just say he has a way with locks.'

Guy thought about the freight terminal. No wonder he was being used as a collector. 'That sounds about right.'

She put the folder aside. 'So, what's he doing now?'

'You know I work over at the Freight Master terminal? It's sort of behind Manchester United's ground.'

'The slightly weird industrial area?'

'That's the one. Again, this is confidential, but...' Seeing Amy check her watch, he hesitated.

She waved her fingers in apology. 'Not being rude here, but I didn't bring any lunch in. Do you mind if we continue this in the little cafe over the road? My stomach's doing somersaults.' She turned a full smile on him. 'Surprised you've not heard it.'

Guy hoped the jolt he'd felt run through him hadn't shown in his eyes. He could drink in that smile all day long. 'No... not at all.'

'Oh, that's brilliant. I'll just let Brandon out here know I'm heading off. Two seconds.'

She started round the desk. Once he heard the office door open, he leaned across and peeked at the sticker on the inside page of Jayden's folder.

CHAPTER 21

'Tarik, hi! You OK?'

The dark-haired man behind the cafe counter beamed a welcoming smile. 'Amy, good to see you.'

She made a beeline for a corner table, dropped her bag on the chair nearest the wall and began shrugging off her jacket.

Guy swept the room with interested eyes. A greasy spoon, but it looked like a decent one. Immaculately clean, so food probably spot on. The walls were covered with brightly coloured circles of card which listed the prices of items. Fantastic value. His sort of place. Between the price cards were several framed pictures. He immediately recognised the rugged stone landscapes. Atlas mountains, Morocco. Done a few savage treks across those things, he thought.

Amy folded her jacket over and place it on her bag. 'Grab a seat,' she said, turning to Tarik. 'Cappuccino, please. Guy, anything to drink?'

'Well, a tea, if that's –'

'And a tea!' She sat down and slid a menu in his direction. 'I'm having a cheese and mushroom omelette, which I can promise you are... amazing.'

He liked how she'd said the word. Separating out the three syllables, lowering her voice on the middle one.

'Have you had lunch?'

'Actually, no. But I –'

She jabbed a finger at the menu. 'Order something, for Christ's sake. You won't regret it. Best cafe this side of the Irwell.'

'That so?' He smiled. 'But we're splitting the bill, right?'

'Whatever. So,' she placed her elbows on the table, 'you were saying about Jayden Tucker?'

'Yeah. I work nights at the freight terminal and I've spotted him hanging around beyond the security fence.'

'On his own?'

'No. Usually accompanied by someone older.'

'Up to no good?'

Guy wondered how much to divulge. He decided to tread cautiously. 'I'd say so. The containers that come in... I imagine they must seem like Aladdin's caves if you're into robbing stuff.'

Tarik arrived with their drinks. He placed them down and took a step back. 'Amy, the cheese and mushroom omelette?'

'That predictable? Yes please, Tarik.' She glanced at Guy.

'I'd better follow the recommendation,' Guy said, looking up at the owner.

He showed his approval with a slight incline of his head, then returned behind the counter.

'Is that what you do there?' Amy asked, picking a teaspoon from the pot of cutlery and scraping some foam off the top of her drink. She popped it into her mouth like it was ice cream.

Guy had to make an effort to not stare at her lips. 'Nightwatchman, yeah.'

'And is there a problem with containers being robbed?'

'Yes. Not massive, but it happens.'

'Which would seem to fit Jayden's particular skill set.'

'It's the older blokes that worry me, though. Jayden's seventeen, isn't he?'

'Seventeen and what's classed as a NEET.'

He looked at her questioningly.

'Not in education, employment or training. They're the hard-to-reach kids. And the most susceptible to organised crime.'

Guy checked that the cafe owner wasn't listening in. 'I heard something mentioned about a Dale McFadden one time. In connection to the older guys who Jayden is usually with.'

Amy rolled her eyes. 'Ugh. That man is pure evil. And I don't use that word lightly.'

Guy felt his jaw tighten. 'Why is he evil?'

'The way he exploits people. Those who are younger, weaker or naïve. You know who he is?'

'Just chit-chat. That he is involved with organised crime.'

'It's only ever chit-chat, unfortunately. Yes, it's rumoured – only rumours, of course – that he controls a lot of the drugs coming into Manchester.'

'I hear that, too. All the heroin.'

'There's talk about him running county lines out of the city to nearby towns. Places like Lymm, Buxton, Glossop, Rochdale.'

Rochdale. Guy recalled the conversation he'd overheard Jayden's companion having the previous night. Rochdale had been mentioned. A house there.

'That's not all,' Amy continued. 'Apparently, he's got involved in the sex trade, too. Which is especially bad, in Jayden's case.'

'You don't mean Jayden's going to be –'

Amy cut in. 'Not Jayden. His younger sister. Who he lives with.'

The girl who turned up at McDonalds. He thought about the time he'd seen Jayden getting all the shopping. The junk food that teenagers so relished. He'd been doing the household shop for the two of them. This situation was worse than he thought: it wasn't just Jayden who was in danger. There was a young girl to factor in, too. Seemed McFadden really didn't care whose lives he wrecked in his pursuit of money. 'Any parents?'

'A mum. From what I could gather, she comes and goes. Probably shows her face just to ensure the flat stays in her name.'

'And the dad?'

She shook her head. 'They're basically fending for themselves.'

'Hang on: social services know this and aren't doing anything to help?'

She looked at him for a moment. 'They try not to break up a family unit, if at all possible. The mum is about, though maybe less than the social workers realise. Believe it or not, what they have counts as a viable family unit. In their eyes. You should see some of the situations where they do have to intervene. Besides, Jayden is over sixteen. But the sister – her name's Zara – I think. That's a worry.'

Guy thought about the girl. Fourteen or fifteen, at most. 'Jesus Christ, this is…bloody awful.'

'Yup.'

Tarik appeared with two plates. On each one was a big, glistening omelette, a flatbread of some type and a side salad. Guy checked the wall sticker. Four-quid-fifty for all this? Heaven. Next came a jug of water and two glasses. 'Enjoy.'

'Can see why you come here,' Guy announced.

'Wait until you taste it,' Amy replied, knife and fork already in her hands. She cut off a generous slice and practically shovelled it in her mouth. 'Hope you weren't expecting anything ladylike,' she said through the food. 'Too bloody hungry for that.'

Guy let out a chuckle as he reached for a knife and fork. This woman was ace. There was a little vase beside the cutlery pot and napkin dispenser. In it was a fresh flower. A gerbera or something. Add a lit candle, fast forward to the evening, and this could almost be a dinner date. Except Amy obviously wasn't interested in talking; nothing was said until her plate was scraped clean. He wondered if she'd even had time for breakfast that morning.

'Bloody marvellous,' she stated, slipping a paper napkin out from beneath her plate and dabbing her lips. She peered down at Guy's plate with its last quarter of an omelette. 'You eating that?'

He glanced up, not sure if he'd heard her right.

'Your face!' She burst out laughing. 'I'm joking.'

'Fuck's sake,' he said, smiling. 'Normally it's me asking that.'

Still giggling, she filled their glasses with water. 'Tell me about yourself, then. You were in the Royal Marines for quite a while. Then it's a blank.'

All flavour of what he was chewing leached away. He found himself rolling a ball of egg and bread around in his mouth and had to force it down. But now his throat felt too narrow. He reached for his glass and gulped some water.

Concern was clouding Amy's eyes. 'I'm sorry – I didn't mean to just chuck that at you.'

'No, you're alright. It's a fair question.' He cleared his throat and placed his knife and fork down, all appetite gone. 'I've got quite a bit going on at the moment, that's all. Family stuff which... well, it all connects up.'

'Listen, if I've overstepped the mark... just say. You don't need to tell me anything.'

'No, this is relevant to you. To The Zone.' He met her eyes. 'Actually, I'm going away the day after tomorrow for ten days. Australia. My dad's really ill. He's in a care home over there.'

'I'm sorry to hear that, Guy.'

He glanced at the flower. Christ, now this really does feel like a first date. One of those where you rush into laying everything out for the other person. Still, he somehow felt comfortable doing it. 'He had a stroke – and that's on top of dementia. Probably he – you know – isn't around for much longer.'

'That must be terrible. To have that distance...'

'Yes and no. We fell out years back. It's partly why I joined up, when I think about it. To put some distance between us. I've seen him twice in the last twenty-odd years. And not at all since he retired to Australia.'

'And your mum?'

'They went out there together. But, unfortunately, she passed away within three years of them arriving.' He smiled. 'It's a big mess, to be honest.'

She nodded sadly.

He looked up. 'Still, it is what it is, as they say. And you didn't come here for a run-down of my fucked-up family life.'

'I have absolutely no problem hearing about your fucked-up family life.' She raised her glass of water. 'In fact, here's to fucked-up family lives.'

Guy pictured the photo of the girl on Amy's desk as they clinked drinks. 'The gap you mentioned, after I left the Royal Marines – I need to tell you about that, as well. Then you can decide if you still want me involved in The Zone. Assuming I ever pass that DBS check.' He filled his lungs with air and held it for a moment. 'I was in prison, Amy. For over two years.'

CHAPTER 22

Amy immediately leaned back, widening the distance between them. 'Prison?'

This is it, he thought. This is where she grabs her stuff and makes a quick getaway.

She was staring at him. 'What for? What did you do?'

'That's not an easy one to answer. It wasn't even in this country.'

'Then where?'

'West Africa.'

She frowned and, when she spoke, her voice had a matter-of-fact tone. Just like that first time he'd called in at The Zone. 'Guy, I need to know if this has any bearing on you working with young people. From a safeguarding perspective.'

'Safeguarding?' The word seemed ironic to him, considering the reason he'd been in the country. If anything, he thought, it was me who was meant to be doing the safeguarding.

She ran a hand through her hair. 'You want to talk me through this?'

'How long have you got?'

She checked her watch. 'Half-two. I need to collect my

daughter just after three. School's ten minutes away.'

It was her daughter, he thought. 'It won't take me that long.'

She signalled the cafe owner. 'Can we have another couple of drinks, please, Tarik?' Her eyes moved cautiously back to Guy.

'OK. Where to begin?' He traced a few circles on the table with his forefinger. 'Probably with me leaving the Royal Marines.' He needed to be doing something other than just speaking, so he reached for her plate and started to place her cutlery alongside his. 'I got pretty disillusioned with serving. The stuff we were doing, more and more, it didn't seem right to me. I didn't quite realise this when I first signed up, but the Royal Marines are there to protect the people of this country. And I wanted to do my bit. Even though that might sound corny to you.' He stacked his plate on hers and slid the two of them aside. 'You might go to other countries to do it, but it all feeds back to providing protection.' He glanced at her. 'Am I making sense?'

'You are. I think.'

He nodded. 'Some of the stuff we did was worthwhile. Like trying to disrupt the poppy industry out in Afghanistan. Intercepting shipments, even just chopping plants down once. Anything to reduce the amount of stuff which ends up on the streets over here. It was working, too. Production was dropping. Then America gave up on the country, so we had to get out too.'

'Poppy harvests, I hear, are now the highest they've ever been,' Amy stated quietly.

'Probably. Often, though, it wasn't that. It was business people and their projects we were protecting. Infrastructure stuff. Making sure it was safe for the firms rebuilding the country.'

'Are we still talking Afghanistan here?'

'And Iraq. I've done tours in both.'

'I thought it was all kicking in doors, seizing weapons. Dealing with insurgents.'

'Sometimes, yes. But even that — you'd do a raid, but often the people living in the house were just a dirt-poor family. Babies crying. Grandparents struggling to get themselves out of bed so you could search their room. It hardly made you feel proud.'

Tarik appeared with their drinks and removed the plates as he went.

'But,' Amy said, 'helping to rebuild those countries. That felt good, didn't it?'

He edged the sugar bowl closer and started churning white granules over and over with the spoon. 'A lot of the rebuilding wasn't being done by local firms, Amy. Especially out in Iraq. It was these Western outfits on big contracts. They might subcontract minor projects here and there to the local guys. Toss them a scrap or two. But the money our governments promised the actual people — the Afghans and the Iraqis — it wasn't reaching them. It was all being sucked up in consultancy fees and management costs and executive reports. Bullshit like that.' He shrugged. 'Once I'd seen how it really was, I couldn't unsee it. I just couldn't.'

'So that's why you left?'

'Basically, yeah. I came out in 2015. While I was serving, you're always hearing of opportunities for private work.'

'Private work? You mean being a mercenary?' Amy asked quietly.

The hand holding the spoon stopped moving. 'If you mean being a hired killer, no. What we've been trained to do, it comes in useful for all sorts of situations.'

'Like what?'

Hearing the unease in her voice, he glanced up at her. 'It could be bodyguarding. Or escorting valuable items from A to B. But that was what I wanted to get away from. We also have skills for at sea. So I joined a company doing anti-pirate stuff. Around the Gulf and Horn of Africa, mainly.' He took a sip of tea, then went back to digging at the sugar. 'Did that for a few years. It was decent money and I could do a couple of months on, a couple of months off. While I wasn't working, I was free to do whatever I pleased. That's when I met my ex, Simone. She was a tour rep for an adventure holiday company in Costa Rica. I'd been doing some diving off the coast of Belize. When she came back to Britain, we kept seeing each other, got married and moved to a little place out near Disley.'

'I know it. Close to the Peak District?'

His smile was full of regret. 'Yeah. Suited us for hiking and canoeing. But then I got the offer of the West African job. Different outfit but run by someone I'd served with. He'd been given a very specific project and needed a small team to execute it.' He let go of the spoon and it fell against the rim of the bowl with a small clatter. 'And that's when my life went to shit, basically.'

Amy wrapped her fingers around her cup and stared down into her drink. 'You took the job, whatever it was.'

'I took the job,' he sighed. 'Even though I knew it was shaky. You've heard of those gangs kidnapping entire schools of girls? Taking them out into forest camps and then issuing ransoms?'

'Boko Haram?'

'That's the one which makes the news. But there are others at it, too. Big money to be made. The location of one of these camps had come in and intelligence on it had been gathered. Fifty-three girls, eleven to sixteen, being held by a dozen or so men with Kalashnikovs and a few side arms. Eight of us were 'coptered in. Night mission. Take out the bad guys, free the girls, job done. All quietly green-lit by the regional government.'

'And when you say "take out the bad guys", you mean...?'

He could hear an unmistakable note of disapproval in her voice. 'Amy, these people... they hadn't taken the girls on a school holiday trip. Those offered for ransom are the lucky ones. Plenty never come back out of the forest.'

'The world we live in,' she murmured.

He sought her eyes. 'You get that though, don't you? We're due a big pay day for rescuing the girls. They're due one for ransoming them. We all understood the rules of the game.'

She nodded tentatively. 'I suppose so.'

He looked at her for a moment longer. 'Anyway, the whole thing was bullshit. There were no girls being held captive. It was a rival business concern of this government representative. So we were really just removing a competitor and all his people. The local militia got involved, then the security forces, then – I don't know – government officials, maybe. Three of us died and three of us ended up in prison for over two years.'

'Jesus. How did you get out?'

'There was a lot of negotiating. Very expensive negotiating, apparently.'

'I don't remember hearing about this. Was it in the news?'

He shook his head. 'It didn't make it into the papers. But if you need me to verify what happened, I can do. I have reports and documents.'

'That might be helpful.'

'No problem. When I got back to the UK, I'd lost everything. Including my wife.'

'She left you? While you were stuck in a prison cell?'

'She did. She found someone else who was, as she explained, able to support her.'

'Support her?' Amy grimaced. 'Like a princess needs a knight?'

'One with a very well-paid job.'

'I bet. What does he do?'

He reached for the spoon again, then changed his mind and looked at her instead. 'It's a woman, actually. She left me for another woman.'

Amy's eyes momentarily widened. 'Ah. And were you...how do you feel about that?'

'Hardly left me feeling like a knight in shining armour, that's for sure.'

'Do you want to feel like a knight in shining armour? Is that how you see your role in a relationship?'

He shifted his gaze to beyond her. Through the window, the world was passing by. Neon clothing. Torn clothing. Blue hair. Shaved heads. Green hair. Neck tattoos. Ear buds. Ear studs. Chains stretching from ears to nostrils. Amongst it all was a little old couple. Him in a brown coat, her in beige. Her arm was hooked through his as they shuffled their way along the pavement. 'To be honest, I'm not really sure anymore. I sometimes feel like I'm on the wrong bloody planet.' He smiled. 'What about you? What's the situation with your daughter's dad?'

'Oh.' Amy lifted her shoulders in a shrug. 'I slung him out. Said he could go and live with the woman he'd been screwing. Not sure exactly which one. Turned out, there were several.'

'Like that, was he?'

'Yes. Emotionally immature. Constantly seeking reassurance – in other women's beds. I don't think he'll ever stop. Leopards and their spots.'

'Well shot of him, then.'

'Absolutely. And I didn't want my daughter growing up with him as her example of what a man should be.'

Guy nodded. 'Good for you.' He gulped back the last part of his drink and set the cup down. 'So... I don't know if I'll ever pass that DBS check.'

'But you do still want to volunteer?'

'Yeah, definitely. If you really think I could make a go of it.'

'No doubt about that. Let me talk to someone I know in Child Support Services. See what she thinks about the prison thing.' She checked her watch. 'Shit – I need to be going for Molly.' She started reaching for her coat and bag.

'And I'll ask around about Jayden, too. See what the current score is with social services. I'll share with you whatever I can.'

Guy could see Jayden's folder in his head. Flat 653. 'That would be great, cheers. And Amy? Let me get this.'

But she was already on her feet, purse in her hand. 'Nope. I invited you, remember?'

'Well, let's at least split it.'

'Tell you what,' she said, smiling back at him as she headed for the counter. 'You can get it next time.'

CHAPTER 23

He watched Amy as she deftly wove her way between slower-moving pedestrians. Strong woman, he told himself. Needed to be, running a place like The Zone.

He turned in the opposite direction and set off for his flat. Once into the residential streets behind the main road, he could see the Two Sisters up ahead. He thought of Jayden and his younger sister. The pair of them in that flat in Conmere. McFadden and his crew circling like sharks. Slowly closing in. What if they'd sent Jayden to that house in Rochdale? He wouldn't have been able to refuse. And the sister would now be on her own. Damn it! The Australia trip couldn't have come at a worse time.

He checked the time on his phone. Still a few hours, he thought, before my shift starts. He came to a stop, gaze resting on the twin structures. Should I knock on Jayden's door? Try to warn him about what's going on? How he's being sucked in? No: I can't just turn up at his flat. It'll freak him out.

The turning for Farrant Road soon appeared. As he strode up his street, his eyes kept being dragged to the pair of tower blocks. He couldn't get Jayden's flat number out of his head. 653. It was a matter of minutes to call round.

Maybe, if I can make him see how he's making his sister vulnerable, it will force him into rethinking what he's doing with his life.

He reached into his pocket for his keys. His own front door was just there. But rather than step onto the path leading up to it, he shoved the keys back and kept going. Fuck it. At the very least, Jayden needs to know I'm going away, but only for a while. That I'm not some flake who shows up for a bit, offers his help, and then promptly vanishes without a word.

And Amy? Well, she needn't ever know I got Jayden's flat number from the file on her desk.

A wide expanse of patchy grass formed a border round the base of both towers. Parts of it were charred from where things had been set on fire. A horse – an actual horse – was tethered on the far side. Head down, grazing away among bits of litter. Guy looked at the ranks of windows stretching up towards the sky. Behind some was evidence of who lived inside. The odd football flag. A St George's cross. An NHS rainbow. The insides of some windows had been covered over with what looked like cardboard. Some had a sheet pinned across them. Or flimsy netting. One or two had actual curtains.

He remembered being at school and visiting a classmate who'd lived there. What was his name? Damon something. Kirk? Even back then – when the towers were relatively new – you didn't want to end up living in them. Now within a metre of the doors, he saw they were secured by a fob mechanism. That decides it, then. I can't get in, anyway. As he turned to go, the door opened and a couple of young lads stepped out. Before it could swing shut, he thrust out a hand and caught hold of the handle. I'm in, he said to himself, stepping through into the foyer. On the wall to the side, a stainless-steel noticeboard listed floors and flat numbers. 653. Fourteenth floor. Four from the very top.

To his surprise, the lift that arrived first was pretty

clean. Some attempts at graffiti had been made, but the interior walls had a glossy sheen that marker pens obviously struggled with. Could still be scratched, though, Guy thought, noting the heavily scored surface of the back wall.

The lift doors reopened on a poorly lit corridor. A sign said flats 630 to 679 were on the left. He set off down the corridor. Whatever someone was cooking, it had the same aroma as the stuff he was always smelling in the stairwell of his house. The only thing different about the doors he passed was the numbers stuck to them.

On some, perfunctory black plastic ones had been replaced with more colourful ones. Yellows. Reds. Flower patterns. He got to 645 and slowed. The thud of music was coming from somewhere up ahead. He passed 647, 649, 651 and stopped. The next door had no numbers on at all. The music was coming from inside. He moved to the one after: 655. Turning round, he stared at the blank door. Should I even be doing this? First thing he's going to ask is how I knew which flat he lives in. What do I say? The door to 651 opened and an irritated-looking woman of about fifty stepped out. She was wearing slippers.

'Are you saying anything, or do I?'

He looked at her blankly.

'Fuck's sake,' she said after a pause. 'It'll be me, then.'

Guy moved back as she shuffled up to the door and banged against it with her open palm. 'You've bloody well been told about this! Turn it down! Zara, turn it down!'

The door opened to reveal the girl he'd seen at McDonalds. She was wearing a school uniform, the neck of her white shirt unbuttoned. Something was going on with her skirt, too. Maybe she'd rolled it up at the waist. The hem hardly reached her upper thighs.

'Yeah, yeah,' she said, eyes on her phone as she moved her fingers across the screen. The thudding music immediately dropped in volume. 'Better?'

'Better,' the woman said, her voice softening. 'Even

better if I didn't have to come out here and hammer on your door every other day.' She rolled her eyes at Guy before stepping in the direction of her own flat.

The girl's head twisted as she spotted him for the first time. He nodded. 'I'm looking for Jayden. Is he in?'

The beginning of a frown appeared on her face. 'Who are you?'

From inside the flat, he heard a cough. A male cough. 'Tell him it's Guy.'

'He ain't here.'

'He's not?' Looking beyond her, he could see bare plaster walls and no shade on the light. There were three doors, all of them closed. 'Do you know when he's back?'

'I seen you. You were at Maccy D's earlier.'

'Yeah, that's right.' He heard the flush of a toilet.

'What do you want with Jayden?' she asked suspiciously.

'We were talking about him coming along to a gym session with me. Martial arts.'

'Martial arts?'

'Like kickboxing. Kind of. He was going to try it.'

Her eyes slid down to his feet then slowly back up to his face. 'Go to the gym? With you? Jayden?'

'Yeah,' Guy said, hearing the lack of conviction in his voice. 'So I could do with –'

'You some sort of fucking nonce?'

Guy blinked. 'Say again?'

'Nonce,' she repeated. 'Are you some sort of fucking nonce?'

He shook his head. 'I just need to have a –'

One of the doors opened and the skinnier one from the footbridge stepped into the corridor. The one who'd offered him the cash.

'Zara –' He came to a halt, eyes fixed on Guy.

Fuck. This is bad, thought Guy. Really bad.

'This bloke here,' Zara announced, shifting to the side. 'He's trying to get hold of Jayden.'

'That right?' Still buckling up his belt, the man approached the front door, his eyes never moving from Guy's face. 'And why is he trying to do that?'

'Says it's about taking Jayden to the gym.'

'That so?' His mouth twisted into a smile. 'To the gym?'

'Sounds off, to me,' Zara said. 'Fucking gym.'

Guy ended the stare between him and cash-man by turning back to Zara. Her nostrils were flaring with disgust. Guy cursed himself. What were you fucking thinking of? Just turning up like this. Idiot! 'Doesn't matter.' He turned and started to walk away. It was, he realised with dismay, a long way to the lift. He could feel their stares on the back of his head. Just close the door, he said to himself. Step inside and just close the door.

'Fucking nonce!' Zara spat.

Her words rolled past him, echoing down the corridor. He heard the man laugh and it seemed to encourage Zara.

'Piss off back to your paedo-pad!' she shouted, voice rising to a shriek. 'Kiddy-fiddling perv, fuck off!'

Smarting with embarrassment, he reached the door to the stairs and shoved it open. No way, he thought, am I standing here waiting for a bloody lift to arrive.

CHAPTER 24

He made sure to arrive at the freight terminal just before his shift was due to start. Despite his last-minute arrival, a few yard lads had yet to set off home. He passed a couple in the car park who kept their heads down. Guy decided to test the water. 'Evening.'

No reply.

Another was coming out the main door as he reached it. He stood aside, avoiding eye contact. Looks like I'm the workplace pariah, he thought, walking towards Hughes' office.

Ahead of him, an exterior door opened and Andy Meadows stepped through. Spotting Guy, he came to a halt. 'Well, well...'

Guy closed the gap between them before speaking. 'You heard, then?'

'Tipping a brew over Fenton's head? Oh, yes.' He grinned. 'Fucking weasel's had that coming a long time.'

'Felt like a total leper, just now. Everyone's giving me a wide berth.'

'Really? I wouldn't say that. Plenty of people would have been pissing themselves laughing, even if it wasn't out loud.' His voice grew more serious. 'Fenton, obviously, not included.'

Guy shrugged. 'Too bad. You know why I did it?'

Meadows unzipped his tabard. 'Something about the Royal Marines, wasn't it?'

Guy nodded. 'How did he find that out? Was it you?'

Meadows broke eye contact. 'Me?'

'Did I mention it to you? That night in the Three Flags?'

'Well, yeah, you did...'

Christ, thought Guy. Why did I have those drinks? Never leads to anything but trouble. 'And then you mentioned it to someone here?'

'Didn't realise you were keeping it under wraps. You never said it was, like, supposed to be a secret. Sorry, pal, if I put my foot in it.'

Guy studied the other man's face. He seemed genuine. 'Don't worry. It's my fault. I couldn't have made that clear.'

'Why the secrecy, anyway? Royal Marines? Jesus, you should be proud. I know I would be.'

Not if it led to you doing over two years inside, Guy thought. 'It always attracts the dickheads; Fenton being a prime example of that. Listen, I need to get sorted. My shift starts any minute.'

'OK. Have a good one, yeah? And let's go for another beer or two sometime. Talk a load of shite about stuff.'

'I'm away for ten days, by the way. Day after tomorrow.'

'Oh – how come?'

'Family stuff. But I'll see you after that.' He continued towards the manager's office. To his relief, Hughes had already left. Guy opened the door and plucked a fully charged radio from the rack. A few minutes later, he was in a high-visibility jacket, torch in hand as he set off on his first perimeter check of the night.

When he reached the gate for Europa Way, dusk was

falling. He surveyed the road for anyone loitering nearby. No one in sight. Quickly, he threaded a length of cotton in place then ambled over to the mound of pallets nearby. In case he was being observed from somewhere beyond the fence, he shook his head at the pallets' untidiness. Making no effort to keep quiet, he dismantled the stack and began to arrange them, carefully creating a narrow passage at the rear which led to a small gap right in the centre. Once done, he continued on his way, swinging the torch beam about.

After waiting an hour in the offices, he swopped his coat for a dark fleece, then exited the building via a rear door. Keeping his torch off, he crept the long way back to the pallets and squeezed into the narrow space he'd created earlier.

Peering through the gaps in the pallets' slats, he could clearly see the gate less than thirty metres away. These sorts of jobs, he reminded himself, were all about staying alert. Flexing your toes, rocking on your feet, circling your head, opening and closing your mouth in a series of silent screams. Any little trick to keep the lethargy at bay.

A coolness had crept through the night. He estimated the temperature had dropped by a good four or five degrees, which meant a band of cold air had probably been sucked in from the north and become trapped beneath warmer air from the day. If it was a temperature inversion, Guy knew it could create some interesting phenomena, a couple of which would be useful for him. He tipped his head back and searched for the moon. There it was, in the sky off to his left. But it looked like someone had grasped its upper and lower edges and then stretched it ever so slightly. An inversion was definitely occurring.

Noises, transported effortlessly on the crisp air, were now reaching him from all directions. He remembered an operation where he could hear every word that two sentries whispered from their post almost three-hundred meters away. Now he could make out traffic on the M602, right down to individual cars changing gears. Mixing in with that was the reversing beep of a forklift from one of the industrial parks nearby. Music from the places over at Salford Quays temporarily picked up as people entered or left a bar.

Just after two in the morning, a different sound entered the mix. It was a hard, thin scrape that rapidly repeated itself. Guy closed his eyes to listen better. It was, he suspected, a hacksaw. Some poor bastard's property being broken into. The noise faded and then grew stronger as the air shifted. How far off was it? A hundred metres? Or ten times that distance? Could it be Martyna's place being targeted again? Shit, what if it was? He checked no-one was near the gate then worked his way back out of the pallet tower and jogged silently round to the main entrance.

He let himself out through the pedestrian gate and, when he got to the courtyard of units, waited at the corner. If the sound had been coming from here, it had now stopped. Which meant they'd given up. Or were now inside. He peeped across the car park. Nothing seemed amiss with Martyna's front door. Same for all the others. He padded across the tarmac, careful not to ruin his night vision by looking directly at the exterior lights which clicked on above the entrances to a couple of the properties. When he got to Martyna's, he slipped down the side passage and checked the rear. Nothing amiss. Breathing a sigh of relief, he made his way back to the freight terminal and let himself in through the same gate.

After putting his tabard back on, he set off on another round, torch beam swinging about before him. At Europa gate, he made a show of checking the lock before lowering the torch beam and glancing down. Where was the cotton? No way. Surely not. He crouched and, placing the torch on the ground, pretended to tie a shoelace. The torch threw out enough glow for him to see the remains of the thread hanging from the frame. The little bastards. Another thought hit him: had it been Jayden? And was he still on site? He straightened up and, keeping a casual pace, made his way back to the office buildings. Once inside, he hurried to the same rear door, throwing his tabard off on the way. Within three minutes, he was back in position among the pallets. No one, he thought, leaves via that gate without me seeing them.

The minutes slid slowly by. No music reached him as the bars were long shut. The faintest of breezes brushed at his face and he felt the temperature lift a fraction. That meant the inversion was ending. Visibility remained good until a dim glow showed in the eastern sky. Guy couldn't believe he'd missed them. Had they been watching him all the time? Was the hacksaw a ploy to lure him away? If it was, they were aware of the observation point. No, he shook his head. Surely they weren't that good.

Sliding his way back out of the tower, he contemplated checking the aisles of empty storage for compromised containers. Had it been Jayden? The thought of the lad being so close niggled Guy. He had to know.

A glance at his watch revealed the time: twenty to five. He had about another thirty minutes of ever-decreasing darkness. Just time to make it to the house on Napier Street, if he ran. By the time he reached the end of Sir Matt Busby Way, his lungs felt like giant balls of steel wool were bouncing around inside them. Christ, he thought, slowing to a walk. I am so unfit. That was a five-minute run, at most. Pathetic. The streetlights lining the A56 were still on and he checked the eastern sky once again. A curve of yellow was creeping higher. Maybe fifteen minutes until dawn properly broke. He started to jog.

At the turning to Napier Street, he came to a halt. Both sides of the road were peppered with parked cars – but the one outside number six caught his eye. A white Mercedes SUV. The night with Andy in the Three Flags, he'd mentioned something about the car McFadden drove. Was it a Mercedes with some kind of personalised number plate? He glanced at the nearest houses. Everyone's curtains were still closed, but he could see chinks of light shining in the upstairs windows of two properties. Do I risk making a pass of number six? He knew it was stupid, but the Mercedes was so damn close. Just a glimpse of the registration and I'll know. He thrust his hand into his pockets and set off down the opposite side of the street.

As he drew closer to the vehicle, the view of number six improved. The same silver Polo was parked on the drive. Inside the house, the curtains were drawn and lights were on. That was good: if anyone did look out a window, they would only see their reflection in a black expanse of glass. The curtains of a downstairs room weren't properly drawn. He spotted movement through the narrow gap. Something was going on in there. Almost parallel with the car, he turned his head properly.

MCF 1.

McFadden. Had to be. He kept going, anger making the skin of his scalp itch. The big man himself was paying a visit, then. A lock rattled as a front door began to open. He glanced back. Shit! Someone was emerging from the house. Guy knew he was far too close, and the only person on the street. The nearest parked car to him was a few metres away. He checked the garden immediately to his left. A low scrubby hedge. Grass, not gravel, beyond it. The house itself was dark. No other choice, he thought, vaulting the hedge and dropping to the ground. Voices from the direction of number six as the door closed with a solid thud. Probably reinforced.

'You go get some sleep, kidder.' The deep voice of an older man.

Whoever replied was also male. And though his words were too indistinct to hear, the tone was grateful. And the voice was young.

'Which way you going anyway?' the man asked. 'Yeah? Jump in, I can drop you off.' The locking system pipped. Guy bent a small branch back to create a gap in the foliage.

It was the man from Reverie. The one who'd approached him at the bar, asked a load of questions and then told him to get out. A smile was on his face as he patted someone on the shoulder. 'Could do with more like you.'

The other person nodded his head and turned in Guy's direction. Jayden. Grinning with pride as he walked round the car and opened the passenger door.

CHAPTER 25

Guy waited until the car had driven round the corner before climbing to his feet. As he stepped back over the hedge, he checked the house whose garden he'd been hiding in. Behind an upstairs window, the corner of a curtain had been pulled back. The face of a young boy was staring down at him with a curious expression. He gave a little wave and, what he hoped, was a reassuring smile.

Hurrying back towards the terminal, Guy felt the anger bubbling inside him once more. McFadden – and the other senior people in his set up – how much money were they making by spreading drugs through Manchester and its surroundings? How many lives were they wrecking? How many people were dying because of them? Guy quickened his pace. He had a desire to see more of McFadden. What sort of life he led. The car had been expensive. What about his house? The place he returned to after a day spent sowing misery in all directions. It wouldn't take long getting to the road where the bastard lived.

To his relief, there were no vehicles in the freight terminal's car park. He went straight to Hughes' office, where he filled out a form to say there was nothing to report. No fucker read the things, anyway.

At six on the dot, he was out the door and walking towards Europa Way. When the freight terminal was far enough behind him, he stepped over the fence and dropped onto the towpath of the Bridgewater Canal.

Striding quickly, he saw the raised lanes of the M60 in front of him barely twenty minutes later. The canal veered sharply to the left, at which point a short flight of steps led up to a little car park. A small notice board stood in the corner. Duke's Wharf. Various footpaths led off, including one towards Wardley Wood. He knew the road McFadden lived on bordered that. He looked about. A few cars were already parked up. Morning dog walkers, at a guess.

Next to the notice board were a couple of bins with stickers on to say they accepted dog waste. Hanging from the lowermost branch of the tree behind them was a red dog lead. Bloody perfect, he thought, unhooking it and draping it round his neck. Then he reached into the bin itself and plucked out a used pooh bag. After checking its handles had been properly knotted, he popped it in his pocket. Can never have enough props, he thought. Now, let's see if that stupid dog of mine has run off in the direction of Orchard Lane.

The path was flanked by a mixture of conifers and larger beech trees. Judging by the muted drone of traffic, the M60 wasn't far off to his left. He crossed a cycle way and continued to a fork in the path. As he set off to the right, his phone gave a beep. That familiar dread of it being the care home stopped him dead. Seeing the text was from Amy caused his shoulders to ease a fraction.

> 'Morning, I hope your shift was OK last night. Listen, I'm setting off for the before school club at The Zone. I'll be in most of the day, if you have time to pop by. More on our mutual friend's employment situation. A. X'

He studied her words. She was talking about Jayden. But what did she mean about his employment situation?

Something linking to McFadden, maybe? He typed a reply which said he could be there before three. After adding his name, he scrolled back up to her message. Bollocks. She'd added a kiss. He knew it meant nothing, but still – now he had to add one of his own. And the whole kiss-after-a-message thing made him cringe.

He'd walked another seventy or so metres before a high hedge came into view. The path followed it round to the top of a small road. You've not lost it, Guy thought, noting the nearby sign as he stepped onto the smooth tarmac. Orchard Lane.

The driveways of most of the properties lay behind fences and gates. He took the pooh bag out of his pocket and let it hang from a forefinger as he set off, a suitable look of awe on his face with every glimpse of the impressive properties in the gardens beyond. Eight, he said to himself. That's the number of houses on this road. Which one is yours, McFadden? Noise from the motorway was still reaching him. That was good as it meant all the residences would have excellent soundproofing. Less likely to hear the click of a gate or the crunch of gravel. As he passed each house, he checked for any white vehicle. Third along had a Range Rover Evoque. Another had a Porsche Panamera next to a black Aston Martin. The neighbouring property was undergoing a huge extension. Scaffolding covered the walls and most of the roof. Half the garden was being dug up, too. Maybe a swimming pool going in? The last house had the highest gates of all. Solid wood. Security cameras on each post. Intercom on the right-hand one. This'll be him, Guy thought.

The perimeter fence spanning the front of the property consisted of vertical metal struts not unlike those which encompassed the freight terminal. Through the six-inch gaps, he could see an immaculate lawn. On its far side, a white Mercedes was parked before the house. The driveway was about twenty metres long. A few small bushes dotted the lawns on either side. Another camera was mounted on the corner of the property itself. He noted the name plaque on the left-hand gate as he passed it: The Grange.

So, this is what running your own little criminal empire gets you. A life of loveliness. He glanced back at the plaque. Copper or brass. Was that paid for with the money my brother spent on your drugs before they killed him? Or maybe that money went towards something nice in your big house? An ornament or some jewellery for your wife. Do you have a wife, McFadden? Kids? Places at a private school, while local kids fetch your merchandise from metal containers. The bloke was a parasite. A fucking leech.

At the far end of the road was another sign for a footpath. The narrow track ran down the side of McFadden's property. Halfway along, Guy dropped the pooh bag and, bending to retrieve it, scrutinised the base of the hedge. A fence was immediately behind it. Solid wooden slats set in fifty-centimetre concrete footings. The path curved away to the left, eventually bringing him out on an unkempt patch of field, the trees of Wardley Wood on the opposite side. Guy looked about, pooh bag swinging like a pendulum from his finger. The hedge at the back of McFadden's property was dense and at least four metres high, the house completely hidden behind it. But, about twenty metres away, there was some kind of opening.

Deciding to take the risk, he trudged closer. It was a wrought-iron gate. The top of it was adorned with intricately barbed spikes which rose into the thick arch of hedge above it. Now within touching distance, he could see the gate was secured by a chunky padlock. He slid his phone from his pocket and, keeping his hand by his thigh, snapped a photo.

Only once he was well into the woods and safely out of sight did he stop to check the image. The padlock was an Abus and, judging by the fragments of hedge caught in the hasp, it hadn't been used in a long time. I could easily come back and remove that one night, Guy thought. Then replace it with an identical padlock of my own. And once I've done that, Mr McFadden, I can let myself into your garden whenever I want.

CHAPTER 26

A slow series of thuds dragged Guy from the depths of sleep. He yanked his eye mask off and glared at the ceiling. What the hell was the person doing up there? He tracked the noise as it moved laboriously across to the far side of the room. Jesus Christ. He turned his head and checked the bedside clock. One forty-three. The alarm was set to go off in seventeen minutes. No point trying to get back to sleep now, he thought, swinging his legs from the bed and rubbing the back of his neck. He blinked twice, waiting for the fog in his head to disperse. Shift work, he thought. It's not good for you. Stretching both arms above his head, an involuntary groan prised his jaws apart. 'Come on,' he said under his breath. 'Rise and shine.'

Bending down before his fridge, he studied what was inside. Cheese, ham, bacon and tomatoes. Shredded kale, cucumber, apples, yoghurt. None of it would survive while he was away. He removed the milk and closed the door. Maybe I could offer it all to whoever lives upstairs, he thought. At least it would be a chance to set eyes on my tormentor.

After finishing some toast, he lay clothing out on his bed. Lee's suits were hanging on the back of the door. He glanced at the windowsill and saw the photo of them both propped beside a mirror. 'Better try one on, hey? You always were the skinnier one.'

A faint citrus smell filled his nostrils as he removed the black jacket from its protective cover. There was a drycleaning ticket still attached to the lapel. Mr L Haslam, 3027. 11th March. Guy wondered what his brother had been doing the last time he wore it. A work event? Entertaining clients in town? A date? Had it ended with him back in his apartment, sticking a needle in his arm?

He shrugged it on and flexed his shoulders. Not too bad. Sleeves were a decent length. But when he tried to button it up, he had to breathe in. Letting the jacket hang open, he patted the swell of his stomach. You fat twat. 'Need to sort that out, mate.' His eyes drifted to the photo. Lee's smile. 'Grin all you want,' he said. 'Not all of us can have the build of a bloody racing snake.'

He walked over to the windowsill and checked his reflection in the mirror beside the photo. 'My hair's too short,' he stated. 'You always had yours longer. And more to the side.' He tried to palm his across. 'What do you reckon? Can I pass for you?' His brother's smile wasn't moving. 'I reckon so. Long as I keep the old man's glasses out of his reach.'

#

Amy was at the far end of the hall, surrounded by a group of tables. She saw him coming through the doors and immediately smiled.

'Hello,' he said, a hand raised in greeting. 'What's all this?'

She placed a box in the middle of the nearest table. Monopoly. He checked the other tables. Scrabble. Buckaroo. Connect Four.

'Haven't seen that in years,' he stated, staring at the red and yellow counters. The hours me and Lee used to spend playing that. 'They still go for this stuff, kids these days?'

'They do, believe it or not. Most had never seen a board game before coming here. And it gets them off their phones.'

'So, it's like a games afternoon, then?'

'Exactly that. Wednesdays and Fridays, three-thirty to five-thirty. There's a homework club in the next room, as well. A lot don't have anywhere quiet at home, so we try to offer that.'

Guy nodded. 'No Battleships? You've got to have Battleships.'

'Well,' she gestured towards the doors. 'Feel free to go round the local charity shops. If you find one, grab it.'

'I will. Got to have Battleships.'

'More of a Cluedo girl, myself,' she said, beckoning to him as she set off towards her office. 'After speaking to you yesterday, I called up a contact in Social Services. Told her it was an urgent one.' She opened the door and ushered him through. 'It didn't take her long to get back to me.'

Guy wandered over to the chair. A box of bananas was balanced across the armrests. He lifted it off and looked round.

'Just dump it anywhere,' she said, edging round her desk.

'Here?' he nodded at the boxes of water bottles.

'Yeah, why not?'

'So, what did they say?' he asked, setting them down.

'It's not good, I'm afraid. Have you heard of this thing called cuckooing?'

'Nope,' he replied, taking the seat.

'It's when the place where someone lives gets taken over. Usually as a location for storing drugs. Often for selling them, too.'

'Who do you mean by someone?'

'It's often a person who's classed as vulnerable, for one reason or another. Placed in social housing. Or it's someone who fancies doing a bit of selling and allows them in. Before they know it, their home has been taken over.'

'Was this Rochdale, by any chance?'

Amy's eyebrows lifted. 'How did you know that?'

'Just something I overheard.'

'Overheard?'

He wondered how much to tell her. How he'd lain in wait at the freight terminal. Followed Jayden to the house on Napier Street. Travelled over to check out McFadden's residence. She'd be horrified. And as for calling at Jayden's flat... 'He was outside the McDonald's down the road one time. Gobbing off to these other kids. So, what happened?'

'It's your typical county lines stuff. City-based drug-gang branching out into new markets and the first thing they need is a base to begin operating from. That's where cuckooing comes in. A flat in Rochdale had started attracting complaints about noise and other anti-social activity. Then some kind of altercation occurred – enough to involve the police. They realised it was registered as a place where kids coming out of the care system are temporarily housed. They contacted social services who sent a community out-reach team round. It was clear the girl who had been placed there was no longer in control. One of the out-reach team recognised Jayden among her – what should we call them? – house guests.'

'What happened after that?' Guy asked, sitting forward.

'How do you mean?'

'Did the police get involved?'

'Police?' Amy sounded mildly surprised. 'No. Jayden and the others cleared off. But they'll soon be back. I imagine things will then carry on for a while and, eventually, the out-reach team will move the girl somewhere new and the place will be locked up for a bit.'

'You make it sound like a set process.'

'Pretty much, that's what it is.'

'And Jayden's still out there.'

'He is.'

'What was the altercation which attracted attention in the first place?'

'Not sure. Maybe whoever deals drugs in that area took a dislike to newcomers showing up.'

'God, it makes me angry. Thing is, he's just as much a victim in all this. They're just using him.'

'I realise that, Guy.'

He could see the man outside the property on Napier Street. The fatherly pat he'd given to Jayden. The kid's look of delight. 'Can't we get the police involved? Make some kind of intervention? This is going to end badly for him. I can see it coming a mile off.'

Amy dropped her gaze to the desk. 'The police, if I'm honest, are not equipped for these situations. Their job is to enforce the law. He's dealing drugs, Guy. Or helping distribute them. When the police do eventually act, it'll only be to swoop in and arrest him.'

'Maybe that wouldn't be a bad thing,' Guy muttered, thinking back to his own teenage years. The last magistrate he'd been up before had made it clear: choose a different direction or, the next time, it would be prison. He'd joined the Royal Marines within days. *And I still ended up inside.* The smallest of smiles touched his lips.

'What?' Amy asked.

Guy blinked.

'Something made you smile.'

'Just feels like history repeating itself, that's all.'

'Your history, by any chance?'

He met her gaze. *You are worryingly perceptive.* 'Yes.'

Now she smiled briefly. 'We'll sort this, Guy.'

'How, though?'

'By building a support structure. For him and his sister. I'll invite him back in here, for a start. Try to offer an alternative to what the drug-gang are offering.'

Guy considered his own disastrous attempt at doing just that and couldn't help but shake his head.

'Hey - don't worry.' She was regarding him with a concerned expression. 'Things haven't gone too far. There's still a chance.'

He used a thumb to knead at the palm of his other hand. 'You know what the stupid thing about all this is?'

'What?'

'Here we are, desperately trying to work out ways of keeping Jayden away from McFadden. Maybe we're going about it the wrong way. Maybe it's McFadden who should be stopped from going near everyone else.'

'I'm not sure what you mean.'

'Come on…everyone bloody knows. The yard lads at the freight terminal. You. Me. Jayden. Even the police. Yet he still moves around Manchester doing exactly what he wants. Spreading poison wherever he goes.'

Amy continued looking at him. 'Well…I'm not sure where you're going with that.'

He sighed. 'Me neither.'

'But – back to Jayden – we really need to talk to him.'

'Yeah, good luck with that. The kid is slippier than an eel.' He checked his watch. 'And I fly to Australia tomorrow. It's the worst possible timing.'

'Don't think like that. You can't let this sour the time with your dad. Think how much it will mean to him. His son travelling all that way.'

His son, Lee, thought Guy. Not me. And who knows if the crazy fucking plan will even work?

'Guy?'

He gave another nod and did his best to sound convinced. 'You're right. He'll be… really chuffed.'

'I think he'll be more than that. How long are you going for again?'

'Ten days.'

'It'll be amazing. In the meantime, I can do a bit here. There's an especially good organisation who work with kids who are caught up in this country lines stuff. I'll contact them.'

'Are you sure?' He looked around the room. The amount of stuff piling up. 'You've got enough on as it is.'

'I can always make time for something like this.'

His eyes roved about once again. 'Thirty minutes in here,' he rubbed his hands together. 'That's all I'd need.'

She laughed. 'I can make that wish come true. Shall I book that in for when you're back?'

'Please.'

She picked up an imaginary pen and mimed placing a mark in her diary. 'Done. You know, while I've got this open,' she looked up, 'once you're home again, how about the two of us go for a drink?'

He met her eyes. Suddenly, Simone's face was there, filling his mind. The way she'd deserted him. Not just deserted him. Carefully transferred out their savings, methodically cleared everything she wanted from the house. 'I...I...it still feels like I'm sorting myself out after my marriage, you know – finished. Even though it's been, well, quite a while...'

She lifted her hands. 'It's fine. I completely understand.'

Now I've made you embarrassed. Shit. 'That's not to say I don't find you... well, pretty amazing, if I'm honest.' Now her cheeks reddened. First time, he thought, I've seen you even faintly ruffled.

She turned to the window. 'Uh-o, look what's heading our way. Action stations.'

He glanced to the side. A group of lads were vaulting the low wall into the car park, schoolbags bouncing up above their shoulders as their feet hit the asphalt.

CHAPTER 27

He tried to spoon out some of the white rimy liquid which frothed at the edges of his bacon. Teach me for buying cheap crap, he thought, giving up and dropping two pieces of bread into the toaster. Doing so made him think of Martyna. He hadn't dropped in at the bakery for – what? – four, five days? It felt like he'd been whisked up in a vortex, time zipping by in a stupid rush. And, in about thirty hours, I'll be airborne. Rising through the clouds and into the calm blue above. He decided to give the care home another call, check the latest news on his dad. Maybe he'd have been showing some signs of improvement.

He glanced at his watch to work out the time difference. Three in the morning, out in Australia. He'd wait until nearer midnight on his shift and call when it was their breakfast.

The toast had just popped up when he heard a knocking sound. Was that my door? Surely not. It came again. Followed by another. Who was that? Had to be a resident.

He pulled the door open and looked out. Light shining up from the hallway below added a layer of fuzz to the person's dim outline. The hood of his top was up, and it took Guy a second to realise who it was. Jayden. One hand still on the latch, Guy peered round the lad, wondering how he'd got through the front door. 'Come in,' he said, taking a step back.

Jayden shook his head. Both hands were shoved in his pockets. Furtive. 'Listen, you need to stay out of empty storage. Tonight, between three and four.'

'Why?'

'Why? What do you mean, why? Got a collection. An important one. So you need to sit it out in them office buildings.'

The lad was trying to sound assertive, but there'd been a wobble in his words. Eyes now adjusting to the gloom of the landing, Guy tilted his head. A nasty welt clung like a purple slug below Jayden's left eye. 'You alright, mate? What's happened?'

Jayden's head twisted as he nervously checked the stairs behind him. 'Will you do it? Stay in your office?'

From behind Guy came the hiss and pop of the bacon cooking. He opened the door wider so more light could get out. The kid looked grey. His shoulders were shivering. 'Jayden, come inside. Tell me what's going on.'

'No!' He half-turned, placed a hand on the banister and bent forward for a better look down the stairs. 'Shouldn't even be here,' he whispered, straightening up. 'You'll do it, yeah?'

Guy could see bandages covering his left hand. The tops of his fingers were an angry red. Scolded, Guy thought. Like someone had thrust his hand into boiling water. Was that part of the incident over in Rochdale? A turf war between rival dealers? 'Who did that to you?'

Realising his fingers were on show, Jayden slid his hand behind his back. 'Doesn't matter. All I'm saying is to keep away from empty storage. For your own good.' He stepped toward the top of the stairs. 'Three until about four, got it?'

Now a faint smell of burning announced itself. The bacon, damn it. 'Jayden, whatever's happening here, you don't need to do it.'

There was a desperate look in Jayden's eyes. Guy could remember it from in the Royal Marines. Situations where things started to go south, and it dawned on newer recruits that they were in danger. Life-threatening danger. 'We can get you out of this.'

'We? Who's we?' Jayden croaked.

'Me. I can get you out. Trust me, I can.'

'Yeah? And how will you do that?'

'Get you somewhere away from all this. A place I know that's safe. A new life, Jayden. I can even get you work.'

Jayden's lower lip began to tremble. He's about to cry, Guy thought. The kid's about to start crying. He reached out. Come on, he wanted to say. Let me give you a hug.

But Jayden wiped a hand across his nose and shook his head. 'It's not just me I need to think about, is it?' His voice was ragged with emotion. 'You don't fucking know.'

I do, Guy thought. 'Jayden, the girl who showed up at McDonald's is your sister. I realise that.'

'How –'

'I've been talking to the woman who runs The Zone. She mentioned her. Why do you have to think about your sister in all this?'

Jayden grimaced. 'It's the way they're treating her. I know what they're doing.'

'The way who are treating her? Those two older blokes?'

'Yeah, them. Being all nice. I see them looking at her in that way.'

I don't think you realise cash-man was in your flat, thought Guy. While you were away. 'Listen, Jayden, you're not aware of the people who are out there. People ready to help you and your sister.'

Jayden's eyes lifted. 'How would you –'

A loud beeping noise broke out in the flat. Guy glanced

over his shoulder. Shit! The smoke alarm. The noise shredded whatever had been building between them.

Jayden had a desolate look on his face as he backed away. 'I have to do this. I don't have a choice. But, after – that place you said about? Maybe –'

The alarm out on the landing joined in: two horrible sounds merging into a single ululating wail. Guy glanced towards the cooker. Black smoke was billowing up from the pan. 'Just give me –'

But when he turned back, Jayden was halfway down the stairs.

CHAPTER 28

The group of yard lads swept past without a hint of acknowledgement. Still holding the door open for them, Guy regarded their backs. North Face logos stood out on the backs of two of their coats. Another was wearing Undercover. So much expensive clobber in this place. 'My pleasure, boys.'

They continued toward the car park without breaking step. Guy shrugged. If all they had was a sulky-teenager act, it didn't bother him. He walked down the corridor, wondering who else might still be on site. Canteen was empty. As was the manager's office. No one in the locker room, either. Guy took a big breath in. Just me, then. And whatever's happening in a few hours' time.

Within ten minutes, he was back out of the building and heading straight for the stack of pallets by the Europa gate. About two dozen more had been dumped around its base over the course of the day. That was fine: their haphazard arrangement made his observation point less obvious. Leaving them where they lay, he circled the perimeter fence and attached new loops of cotton to each gate. Back in the manager's office, he opened the stationery cupboard and ferreted through it for an unopened pack of 1.5 volt batteries. He replaced those in the handle of his torch with the new ones. *Don't need that dying on me just as things get interesting.*

The first thing he did after taking a walkie talkie off the rack was to turn it off. That way, any unexpected burst of static wouldn't reveal his position. The hi-vis was staying in his locker, too. Black clothing would be the order of the night.

The last room before the rear doors was used as a store by the mechanics. Guy poked his head in. Shelves of tools. Trays of piping. Spanners of increasing sizes hanging from the far wall. His eyes lingered on the end one. Its handle must have measured fifty centimetres. *Should I?* In any confrontation that would come in very useful. But, he realised, you can't turn up already armed for an incident you weren't meant to know was going to happen.

It seemed to take half of his adult life for midnight to arrive. In that time, he saw and heard nothing except for a lorry driver leaving his cab in order to take a piss. The patter of liquid hitting the undergrowth carried across to where Guy stood in his observation post. Even the noise of the man doing his zip back up.

It was approaching one o'clock when he heard voices. Male, speaking quietly. He turned his head, trying to gauge which direction they were coming from. A minute later, they came into view: three men approaching from the direction of Trafford Park. He immediately knew they were dodgy. They cut straight across the roundabout and onto Europa Way. Within seconds, the first aisle of containers blocked Guy's view of them. He listened to their voices fade. Maybe they were on their way to the industrial units that lined Wharfside Way. Seeing what they could steal from around there.

The closer it got to three in the morning, the more he checked and re-checked in every direction. With about ten minutes to go, a thin scraping noise started to lace its way into the narrow confines of where he stood. Similar in tone as the other night. But the noise wasn't as prolonged. Almost like something being tugged at. A rusty gate or door. He angled his head, trying to get a fix on where it was coming from. Possibly to his right, towards Wharfside Way. Or the industrial units on its far side. It stopped for almost a minute before starting again. Definitely to my right, he decided, edging sideways along the narrow passage.

Once clear of the pallets, he kept low and made directly for the nearest aisle of empty storage. Safely in the shadows, he was able to straighten up. The metal surfaces on either side of him acted as a barrier to all sound, and it was only when he reached the first intersection that noise from the world beyond became audible once more.

The scraping had come to a halt. Have I been spotted? He checked the aisle behind him, uneasy at the lack of cover. Nothing. Lying flat, he inched forward and peered off to his left at the short section of the perimeter fence visible beyond where the aisle of containers ended. Nothing suspicious. He got back to his feet, darted across the intersection and jogged to the next one. The bushes pressing against the fence were slightly higher at this point and he took his time, knowing anyone's outline would be obscured by thick foliage. He was just about to proceed to the next intersection when his eyes narrowed.

Something wasn't right with the fence. It took him a moment to realise that two of the struts were out of alignment. He gauged that the distance from the fence to the end of the aisle was about forty metres. He waited for another minute, eyes trained on the bushes, waiting for any sign of movement. Nothing. Fuck it, he decided. I need to check that properly.

Moving quickly, he got to within a couple of metres of the aisle ending and dropped to his stomach once more. He could now see a much larger stretch of fence – which only emphasised the skewed angles of the struts immediately in front of him.

Crafty bastards. They'd sawn through the bases and then bent the upper sections aside. That's what the noise before had been. In fact, that's what the noise had been the other night, too. A hacksaw working its way through one strut and then the other. But why the switch in tactic? Surely far easier to let yourself in through the gates, like they usually did. Unless they didn't have a pass. In which case, could this be a different group?

A clang of metal came from deep within the grid of stacked containers behind him. They're in already, he realised. Whoever they are. He ran back to the first intersection and checked both left and right. Clear. What next? Keep going straight or go left and head deeper into the maze? Another noise. The way it echoed made it impossible to pinpoint. All he could say was that it had come from further towards the middle. He turned left, trotted to the next intersection and checked round the corner of the lowermost container. No one was visible to the left. Twisting his head, he glimpsed two, maybe three, figures flit across the intersection one row to his right. They were moving in the direction he'd originally come from.

Back on his feet, he ran on tiptoes to the intersection he'd crossed earlier. Quick glance both ways. Clear. He turned left and, as he moved forward, heard a shout. Then another voice crying out in pain. Other voices joined in. Three, or four? This, he thought, is sounding too much for only me. He switched his walkie talkie on. 'Freight Master terminal. I need some help over here.'

He ran properly now, knowing his footsteps couldn't be heard amid the rising melee of voices. As he neared the second to last intersection, a single figure careered round the corner and sprinted away in the direction of Europa gate. Cash-man! The one from the footbridge. Guy was about to give chase, but the commotion away to his left was still going on. He advanced to the next intersection where the voices became clearer.

'Hold him!'

'Fuck, I'm –'

'Yes. Yes!'

They were very close. He looked round the corner container to see a figure in black. He was facing away from Guy, down on one knee, gathering small packages and shoving them into a hold-all.

From somewhere round the side, a voice cried out in pain. Jayden. Guy ran straight past the kneeling man, unlit torch ready in his right hand as he entered the next aisle. Less than fifteen metres away, two figures were trying to pin Jayden to the floor. Both, he could tell, were grown men. Well into their twenties. The lad's legs were scissoring back and forth as he desperately tried to wriggle free.

'Fuck him up! Go on!'

As Guy started forward again, one of them got a knee on Jayden's back, forced his head up, then slammed it down into the asphalt. The base of Guy's torch swung in, connecting heavily with the man's temple. His head jerked to the side and his body went limp, arms and legs splaying out as he flopped across Jayden. The other one was looking up, mouth half-open in surprise. Guy had time to spot a gold incisor tooth before punching the man in the face. His legs went out from under him and he sat heavily on his arse. A footstep right by Guy's side. Knowing he had no time to turn, all Guy could do was raise the torch to protect his head. A heavy impact almost knocked it from his grip. The man with the hold-all, his right arm lifting again. Something in his hand. A cosh? Knees flexing into a combat stance, Guy threw a hopeful jab upwards. His knuckles caught the man full in the throat. Arms windmilling for balance, he stumbled back. To his side, the one with the gold tooth was regaining his feet. Guy looked down. Jayden was trying to kick his way out from beneath the unconscious one, blood streaming from his nose. 'You OK?'

Jayden's head twisted at the sound of Guy's voice. 'Yeah.'

Gold tooth was now back on his feet. His eyes went from Guy to Jayden, then to the one with the cosh. 'Did you get it? Tell me you got it!'

'No.'

'Fuck!'

Jayden had now freed his legs. He stood up a little unsteadily and started trying to run in the direction of the Europa gate. Guy saw he was wearing a little rucksack, the mouth of it hanging open.

'The little shit must have it,' the one with the cosh said, stepping forward.

Guy blocked his path, torch held out before him. 'Go on, try. I will crack your fucking head open.'

Movement to his side: gold tooth darting round him in pursuit of Jayden. There was a groan. The man on the ground lifted a hand as he started coming to. 'Leon...'

Cosh man took another uncertain step towards Guy, weapon raised. 'Out of my way.'

'Fuck off.'

'Leon!' The man on the ground had managed to roll onto his side. 'Help me up, Leon. Help me.'

Guy looked quickly over his shoulder. Jayden still had a bit of distant to cover before the end of the aisle - and gold tooth was quickly catching him. Guy turned back and pointed down at the man. 'Do it, Leon. Police are on their way. This place will soon be swarming.'

Cosh-man glanced at his companion. 'Shit.' Keeping a wary watch on Guy, he moved closer to his companion and reached down.

The moment he did, Guy turned and ran after gold tooth. The other man reached the end of the aisle and disappeared from view. Guy sprinted to the end and emerged into the area before the Europa gate. Streetlight from the road cast a weak yellow wash across the tarmac. The bloke had just caught hold of Jayden's rucksack straps and was swinging him towards the pile of pallets. Both Jayden's feet came off the ground before he crashed into them. The man immediately started trying to tear the rucksack free of Jayden's arms. Whatever was inside, they were desperate to get it.

'Get the fuck off him!' Guy roared, closing in fast.

As the man looked round, Jayden twisted onto his back and kicked out. His foot caught the man full in the groin and he collapsed to one knee. Jayden was clear in an instant and off towards the gate once more. Guy kept going towards the other man as he forced himself back to his feet, doubled over in pain. He turned towards Guy and produced a machete from some kind of holster in his jacket. 'Back! Stay back!'

Guy looked past him. Jayden had reached the gate. After fumbling for a second, he got it open and was off down the road towards Trafford Park. Guy turned to gold tooth. He was still bent forward and, even though he looked like he might throw up, the machete was pointing at Guy.

'You've lost him,' Guy stated, slowing to a halt. 'He's gone. And your mates have set off without you.'

The man looked about.

'My back up's here any minute,' Guy continued. 'So it's your shout: I'm not going to stop you from leaving.'

Gold tooth glanced towards the perimeter fence before dragging a deep breath in. 'Don't come any closer.'

Guy took a large step back. 'No problem.'

The other man started hobbling across the tarmac, machete hanging from his hand. Guy trailed him to the corner of the outermost aisle of containers. From there, it was about fifty or so metres to the gap they'd cut in the fence. The man was about halfway there when Guy's walkie talkie came to life. Fucking typical, he thought, retrieving it from his pocket and turning the volume right down. Best gold tooth still believes the cavalry are on their way. 'Freight Master Terminal to Control.'

'Yeah, did you say something just now? I was making a brew.'

'Yeah, that was me.'

'What's up, then?'

'Incident here. Unauthorised access by three unknown persons. Damage to the perimeter fence.'

'Seriously?'

'Yeah, but they're leaving now.'

'What were they doing? Breaking into containers?'

'Looks that way. It got a bit out of control.'

'Out of control? Are you OK?'

'Yeah, I'm fine.' He lifted a hand to see his fingers shaking. Always the same after any action. Gold tooth was now at the perimeter fence. The other two were out on the road, waiting. 'But you'd better call the police. Make sure we've ticked all the boxes.'

'Of course. What about you? Shall I get an ambulance?'

'No, I'm good. A cup of tea will do me.'

'Right, I'm on it. Speak to you in a bit.'

'In a bit.' Guy began heading back to the Europa gate to make sure it was shut. On the way, he tried to piece together events. Jayden and the older one must have come in through the Europa gate. The other lot had obviously entered via the perimeter fence – but had cut through the struts the previous night. Which meant they had known about the collection Jayden was making in advance.

He got to the gate and gave it a gentle shake. Secure. Something was lying on the ground just beyond it. Guy crouched down and reached through the bars. A security pass. He flipped it over and stared at the name and photo on the other side. No way. No fucking way. Andy Meadows, the crane driver. The one person working here, Guy thought, who I believed was straight. Jesus.

After pocketing it, he continued over to the mess of pallets. Andy fucking Meadows. All the shit he'd come out with in the pub that time. I even told him about my brother. As he piled the pallets back up, he saw a lumpy white package. He felt himself frown. The thing was bigger than the ones the man had been stuffing into his hold-all. Guy looked about. He was alone. Gold tooth's words came back. Did you get it? His companion had said no. Was this what they were after? Had it fallen out of Jayden's rucksack during the tussle? He put the pallet aside and bent down. The object was fairly heavy. And the weight was familiar. Very familiar. The outer layers were cling film. Beneath that, a layer of white cloth. One end was more tapered. Gingerly, he pinched at it with a forefinger and thumb. Oh Christ, Jayden. They sent you to retrieve this? No wonder you were warning me to keep away.

Lights were approaching from the direction of Trafford Park. A single police car. He watched it turn off the roundabout onto Europa Way. Heading to the main entrance, then. He studied the package once more. If the police found out about this, Jayden was in trouble. Serious trouble. Enough for prison. So what should I do? Sling it in the canal? No time for that. He slipped the gun into an inner pocket and made his way towards the offices.

CHAPTER 29

The two police constables sat across the table from Guy. Hughes was behind his desk, looking stressed. Several times during the previous hour, Guy had noticed yard lads trying to get sneaky looks through the window of the closed door.

'Is that OK?' Guy asked, checking his watch. 'Only, I have to be at the airport soon. I'm on a flight to Australia.'

'Australia?' The slightly younger-looking of the two officers sat back. 'Holiday?'

'To see my old man. He lives out there.'

'How long are you going for?'

'Ten days.'

'Nice.'

The older officer's head was still down as he leafed through his notes. 'So, just to confirm, the only name you heard during the incident was that of Leon.'

'Correct.'

'OK. And the container you showed us which they'd been into - can I just double-check I've got the location correct? I have row 19, stack 43, column A, two high.'

Guy glanced at his notebook. 'That's it, yes.'

'Good.' He looked over at Hughes. 'I think that will be enough for now. I'm happy.'

Hughes nodded. 'And when did you say someone will take a look at the damaged section of fence?'

'Forensics? They have a lot on this morning. Perhaps around lunchtime. I can double-check for you.'

'Please do, if that's OK.' Hughes brought his hands together in a soft clap. 'Thank you very much for your help, officers. Guy? Looks like you can be on your way.'

'No problem. I'll see you the weekend after next.'

'Weekend after next it is. Thank you, Guy.'

As soon as he was out of his manager's office, Guy closed his eyes. Was I right to have kept Jayden out of it? Amy's words echoed in his head. The police would only regard the lad as potential arrest material. Fuck it, Guy said to himself, heading down the corridor. If that was the case, they'll get no help from me. He opened up his locker and stared at the bag inside. Buried at the bottom of it was the package he'd found beneath the pallet. It might not be a gun, he told himself. You don't know for sure. Yeah, right. Of course it's a bloody gun. He took his trainers out and started unlacing his safety shoes. Jesus. What am I getting tangled up in?

He was zipping up his fleece when his phone started to ring. The familiar stirring of dread, deep in his gut. The number was Australian, but it wasn't the care home. Here we go, he thought, checking no one was in the room before taking the call. 'Hello?'

'Is that Mr Lee Haslam?'

An unfamiliar voice. The tone was business-like but tempered by a faintly human veneer. Guy's sense of unease quickened. 'Yes, speaking.'

'Mr Haslam, my name is Edward Jackson. Are you free to talk?'

'Yes.'

'I was appointed by your parents as their solicitor?'

Guy immediately looked about. There was a plastic chair in the corner. He started towards it. 'Go on.'

'We spoke on the occasion of your mother sadly passing away, if you remember?'

'I think so, yes. What's happening?'

'Mr Haslam, I'm very sorry to be calling you with this news.'

Guy sat. Fuck. He slipped the bag off his shoulder and placed it on the floor.

'The care home just informed me, Mr Haslam. I'm afraid it's your father. He died earlier this afternoon.'

'He died?'

'Yes, I'm sorry to say.'

It was like a loud wind had started to blow in his head. It's me. Just me. Lee, mum, dad. It's only me now. I was never there at the end for any of them. Not one. He sat forward and pressed the heel of his hand against his forehead. Oh God. 'Did they say... was that all? They only said that?'

'It was just after two o'clock and he was in his bed. It was peaceful, Mr Haslam. They said it was peaceful.'

My dad was alone. Alone in that care home. No family with him. Guy stared down at his trainers. The plastic bit at the end of one lace was splitting. He found himself focusing on it. Did they have a name, those plastic bits?

'As you know,' Jackson continued, 'the arrangements are in place. Your father was very meticulous about that after the shock of his wife – your mother's – passing. So there's no rush, Mr Haslam. No rush at all. But I wanted to let you know as soon as possible since, obviously, he expressed his wish that you deliver the reading at his funeral.'

'His funeral?' Guy wiped the tears from his eyes.

'Indeed.'

'Right, sorry. I'm a bit knocked sideways here. The funeral. So, I'm delivering the reading?'

'Yes.'

'Just me?'

'Yes.'

'There's nothing there about anyone else?'

'Anyone else? Well... details will be passed to other residents at the care home. And I imagine there'll be a presence from the staff.'

'How about family? Is there any mention of any other family?'

'Apart from yourself? No.'

'What about my brother, Guy?'

'No.'

He didn't even want me at his funeral. Not even that.

'So, Lee, a lot of what's involved to put his affairs in order, that's all in place. What I need to do is start...'

The man's words were soon submerged beneath the roil and surge of thoughts in Guy's head. Right to the last. No, beyond the last. For fucking ever. He wanted to push me away for fucking ever. He sucked air in through his nostrils. Why did I ever think it could be different? You were a fool, Guy. He kicked out at his bag and the solid lump at its base made him think of Jayden. The shit that kid had got himself in. He pictured the lad looking up, blood streaming from his nose. The relief in his eyes when he saw me standing there. But the collection had gone wrong. No drugs and not the other thing, either. How would the older ones react to that? What about the man at the top? One thing was for sure: they wouldn't just tell him too bad, maybe you'll have better luck next time. They'd want to know how the other lot knew. Who had been talking.

'Mr Haslam? Lee?'

Guy blinked. 'Sorry, what was that?'

'I was asking about a date. For the crematorium? As I said, we don't need to decide anything now. But if you could call me back when it's convenient.'

Like sunlight breaking through cloud, the solution

appeared in his head. It was simple. Ridiculously simple. He lifted his chin. 'I'm not coming.'

'Sorry?'

'I'm not coming. You've got his plans, right? Everything he wanted to happen?'

'Well, yes.'

'Go ahead without me.'

'Without…? I'm not sure I'm following you.'

'I've got something that needs to be sorted over here.'

'Needs to be…? That's… that's – are you sure? You won't be coming?'

'Correct. Just leave me a message if you need anything. Sorry, Edward, but I've got to go.'

CHAPTER 30

The call handler at the travel agency took a while to come back on the line. 'You have the platinum insurance cover for that booking, sir.'

'I do?' asked Guy, thinking about the series of boxes he'd quickly ticked in his rush to secure the seat. 'What does that mean?'

'Because it's within twelve hours of departure, we can't give you a full refund – but you'll get fifty percent of the outbound ticket's cost back and all of your return.'

Bloody hell, thought Guy, reaching for his bag. 'So how much are we talking about?'

'There's also an admin fee to come off, but I make it to be £1,484.'

He could have smiled. That opened up a whole world of possibilities: the deposit and a month's rent on a property for Jayden and his sister out in Haverdale, for starters. He could take Jayden to Jim's garage and get the kid started on a job that would pay a weekly wage. If needed, he thought, I can add a bit of money to that, too. He nodded to himself as he started down the corridor. It was like he'd had a drink: that same sense of elation. And the younger sister? There were two secondary schools just a bus ride away. And Buxton had that big sixth form college. I can get her any school uniform she needs. This could work. It really could! And the money was far better spent on them than on a flight to Australia to attend a funeral I've not even been invited to. Just need to get the pair of them out of that tower block, and fast.

Voices in the canteen. As Guy passed the door, he spotted Andy Meadows at a table in the middle of the room. Fucking snake. Lying fucking snake.

Seeing Guy come to a stop in the doorway, he raised a hand. 'The man himself! Police finished with you, have they?'

Guy entered the room and all conversation started falling away. Everyone's eyes were on him as he walked over to where Meadows sat.

The crane driver drew himself up in his seat, smile withering as Guy came round the table. 'What the hell happened out there? Are you allowed to say?'

Guy could see people twisting in their seats. The room was now totally silent. He looked down at his colleague, eyes moving to the security pass hanging round his neck. 'They sorted you out with a temporary one, did they?'

Meadows lifted a hand, fingers feeling for the plastic card. 'Yeah.'

'Where's your proper one?'

'If I knew that, mate...' he started to say with a smile. Seeing Guy's stony expression wasn't changing, he dropped it. 'Not sure,' he continued warily. 'Couldn't find it when I set off this morning.'

'Lost it, yeah?'

'Not sure.'

Guy removed it from the pocket of his trousers and slammed it down so hard, liquid jumped from the cups on the table. The bang reverberated round the room. 'So you didn't loan it out to a collector? Because that's who fucking dropped it.'

Meadows tried to clear his throat, eyes cutting one way

then the other. Everyone was watching. 'What the fuck?'

Guy thrust a forefinger into his face. 'A fucking kid was carrying that pass. A fucking kid!'

Meadows tried to bat Guy's hand aside as he started rising to his feet. 'Yeah? And that's nothing to do with –'

Guy grabbed him by the windpipe, cutting off his words. 'Lying piece of shit!'

Meadows hands came up, fingers prising at Guy's iron grip. 'Get your...'

Keeping his elbow locked, Guy began to force the man's head back. 'How much? How much did you take for it?'

Meadows tried to lift a leg, knee aiming for Guy's groin. But he had already angled his hip to protect himself. The move caused Meadows to lose his balance and the two of them fell across the neighbouring table, cups and cans rolling from the surface as it started tipping over. Voices were breaking out and Guy felt hands trying to lift him clear of Meadows, whose face was now turning red, eyes beginning to bulge. He kept his grip on the other man's throat. Just wanted to crush the life out of the lying bastard. Someone grasped Guy's thumb and started bending it back. 'Feel good, does it?' Guy hissed. 'That cash going in your pocket, you fucking scum!'

The only thing that made him stop squeezing was feeling his thumb joint starting to wrench as someone bent it right back. As soon as he let go, people dragged him clear. Meadows slid off the table and crashed to the floor.

'What the hell is this?'

Heads swung in the direction of Hughes, who was standing a couple of tables away. Guy pulled his arms free of the people around him. Meadows was now struggling to his knees, coughing and retching. 'He attacked me!'

Hughes turned to Guy. 'Did you attack that man? Because it looks that way to me.'

'Yeah, I attacked him,' Guy replied. 'Fucking great, it was.'

'You do realise that's it? You...you are no longer employed by this company. And that's with immediate effect!'

Guy glanced about and smiled at his manager. 'Have you any idea about the drugs passing through this place? Or are you just too weak to care?'

'Watch what you say,' a voice beside him whispered.

'Get fucked,' Guy said, eyes still on Hughes. 'Because I really can't work out which one it is.'

'I... I beg your pardon?'

Guy started for the door. 'Know what?' He lifted the pass from his neck and tossed it at Hughes as he went past. 'It's not my problem anymore.'

#

He'd crossed over Wharfside Way and was about halfway along it when he heard a car coming from the direction of the freight yard. The closer it got, the more it slowed. Guy started playing scenarios through in his head. Driver will be far side of the vehicle. To attack me, they'll all have to get out. So, the moment it stops, I target the rear passenger door on my side. Take care of whoever's coming out of that first. Then the front passenger. That would leave the driver and whoever was in the other back seat. They'll both have to exit the vehicle and come round it. And if they circle in different directions, I'll still have the advantage.

The car's speed had now dropped to a crawl. His heart was hammering as a bumper, then the end of a red bonnet entered the corner of his vision. He'd been expecting something bigger. When it had almost come to a stop, he whirled round and lunged for the handle of the rear passenger door. It was half open before he realised Gabriela was looking up at him from her car seat. A smile was still on her face, but her eyes were rapidly filling with fear.

'Guy?'

Martyna's voice. He turned his head. She was twisted round in the driver's seat. Jesus. He relaxed his face, turned to Gabriela and attempted a smile. 'Boo!'

'Boo,' she replied uncertainly.

He closed the rear door and stepped away from the vehicle. Martyna had lowered the front passenger window and he moved across to look in. 'Sorry – I mistook your car for...' He glanced down the road. Deserted. 'Doesn't matter. My mistake.'

'Is everything OK?'

'Yeah, it's fine. How about you two?'

'Your face,' she said. 'It's like the clouds when they're black.'

'Sorry. It's been a long shift. How come you've got Gabriela?'

'The child minder is ill. I have to drop her off at another one, but not until nine.'

'OK.'

'You've not called in. So when I saw you going past, we thought...' she reached to her side. 'Carpathian custard cake.'

He looked at the paper bag she was holding up. My God, he thought. I nearly dragged your little girl from her seat. 'Martyna, you didn't need to.'

'I think I did. What's wrong, Guy?'

It was no use trying to brush her off. He had to give her something. 'Just a bit of bad news. I'm still kind of taking it in. That's all.'

'Can we drive you home?'

'No.' He shook his head. 'You should be in your bakery, not ferrying me about!'

'I will ferry whoever I want. Let us give you a lift.'

'No, honestly, Martyna,' he replied, taking the cake. 'I could do with the walk. Clear my head and all that.' He pressed a finger to Gabriela's window. 'Horse rides with you soon, little lady!'

Now she smiled. A little hand appeared and she

pressed her finger against the same spot as his, just the sheet of glass separating them. For a moment, it was like she was visiting him in prison. Them bringing me food. He dropped his hand, hoping it would dislodge the image from his head.

'Well, call by soon. My coffee machine is feeling lonely.'

'I will. And thanks for this, Martyna.' He raised the paper bag. 'Really, it means a lot right now.'

'And I really mean about you calling in.' She checked her rear-view mirror and started signalling right. 'You men: you need to not be so,' her knuckles whitened, fingers clenching the steering wheel, 'like this.'

CHAPTER 31

He placed the bag with Martyna's cake on the kitchen table, then removed the rucksack from his shoulder and watched in silence as it swung from side to side. He looked at the store cupboard door. I should, he thought, stash it in the strongbox. But getting each key from its hiding place, clearing the stuff off it, undoing both padlocks... too much. Instead, he opened the lid of his kitchen bin. As he removed the package from the bag, he briefly studied its shape. Not possible to tell with all the wrapping. He buried it beneath the upper layers of crumpled packaging. That would have to do. The door of the flat banged shut behind him and he jogged down the stairs, out the front door and started striding in the direction of McDonald's.

Of course Jayden and his sister aren't here, he thought as the fast-food restaurant came into view. He surveyed the outside seating area another time, just to be sure. It's mid-morning on a Thursday. Why did I even bother walking all this way? He turned round and looked back towards the Two Sisters. Nothing else for it, he thought. Going to have to try the flat. Maybe Jayden will still be in bed, sleeping things off. Hopefully, Zara'll be in school. It could actually be the perfect time to call. Give me a chance to talk everything through with Jayden.

When he got to the turnoff which led to The Zone, he almost stopped. Should I let Amy know what's happening? I can't: it will put her in an impossible situation. Sorry. I'll tell you everything once I've got the pair of them somewhere safe.

The horse was no longer tethered on the grass beside Conmere Tower. An old boy in a threadbare cardigan and beaten in shoes was also waiting for a lift. As they both stood there, Guy saw the man's head turn a couple of times. He glanced to the side. 'Take their time, these things, don't they?'

He gave a tentative nod, lips busily working against each other. You're nervous, Guy thought. Not sure about sharing a lift with me. There was a ping and the doors started to open. 'Which floor do you need?' Guy asked as he stepped inside. But the man was already backing away. He shook his head as the doors slid shut. What a place to live, Guy thought, pressing floor number fourteen.

The corridor was quiet. As he walked towards Jayden's flat, he remembered the abuse Zara had flung at him. Nonce. That one had hurt. What if it was only her in again? She would be worse the second time, that was for sure. The door was closed. He listened for a few seconds. A low murmur of music? Someone said something and the song changed. The radio, then. Someone in the flat, listening to the radio. He knocked three times. Not too loud, but firm enough to be heard. Nothing. He waited for the song to finish and tried again. Five quick ones this time. After a minute, he made out the slow shuffle of footsteps. The door opened halfway and a woman with gaunt cheeks and bleary eyes did her best to focus on him.

'Seriously? Don't tell me he hasn't shown up. I told the little twat to get straight round. I bloody did.'

Guy stared at her in confusion. Who the hell was this? And what was she on about? He wondered, for a moment, if he had called at the wrong flat.

'Has he not shown up, then?' she sighed, running a hand through her dishevelled hair.

'No,' Guy replied, stalling for time. 'He hasn't.'

'Fuck's sake, that boy. There's no telling him.' She set off back along the corridor.

Must be the mum, Guy concluded. Which meant she was talking about Jayden. He checked the corridor was still deserted before stepping inside and closing the door. He found her sitting in the kitchen. Or what was once a kitchen. A room with a small table and two chairs. Sink in one corner. Cupboards. Gaps beneath the work surfaces where, he guessed, a fridge, a freezer and, maybe, a dishwasher once lived. On every surface, a mixture of empty food containers, bottles and trays sat amongst crumpled McDonald's packaging. Jesus, thought Guy, it's worse than the verge by the freight terminal. And that's vile.

She nodded at a torn-off scrap of paper on the table before her. 'Should have called your mate, but I thought – for once – he was going to do as he was told.' She sighed. 'Fat fucking chance of that.'

A few other items lay on the table. An ashtray and pack of cigarettes, a lighter, some brown-stained tin foil, a little bag with sand-coloured powder. He guessed she was somewhere in her thirties. 'When was this, when you told him?'

'Jayden?'

Guy nodded.

She let out another long sigh. 'Well... an hour ago. Something like that?'

'And you told him to go to the place on Napier Street?'

'Yeah – that's where your mate said, wasn't it?'

He nodded. Her eyes had drifted to the bag. Heroin, Guy guessed. And she'd obviously just had a hit. Someone had written a phone number on the scrap of paper. Who, he wondered, had called by earlier?

'He had nothing on him,' she mumbled, reaching for a

cigarette. 'You can check his room. Rucksack's in there. If he had anything, I would definitely have called like your mate told me to.'

My mate, Guy thought. He decided to take a risk. 'You mean Ads?'

She looked at him with half-closed eyes. 'Your mate. The curly-haired one.'

Guy raised a hand a few inches higher than his head. 'This tall?'

'Yeah, him. Big lad.'

Definitely Ads, Guy thought. 'Did he give you that, too?' He picked up the bag of powder.

She immediately dropped the cigarette. 'Give us it.' Fingers reaching.

He let it dangle. 'Did he?'

'Yeah.'

'For letting him know if Jayden showed?'

'Yes. Give it!'

Guy handed it back. So, Ads had already come looking for Jayden. Obviously wanting to know what had happened in the freight yard. Along with where the stuff was which Jayden was meant to be collecting. When Jayden had got back, she'd told him to go and sort things out. Which meant they probably now had hold of him. He glanced at the mum. She'd put an elbow on the table and was resting her cheek on the heel of her hand. Unbelievable, he thought. Happy to sell out your own son for a few quid of heroin.

There was a school bag lying on the floor in the corridor. 'And Zara?'

'What about Zara?'

'Where's she?'

'How should I know where they went? He's your fucking mate. Ask him.'

Guy took a long, deep breath in. You've let your teenage daughter go off with... Do not lose your rag, he said to himself. Stay calm. 'I meant, when did they go? What time?'

'Time? I don't know.'

'What do you reckon, roughly?'

'Yeah, about that.'

Christ. Her head had sunk lower, the skin of her cheek rumpling against her hand. His gaze went to the piece of paper beside the lighter. It had been torn from a McDonald's bag. A phone number for Ads. Have I got a pen? He patted his pocket. Thank God for that. He took it out, reached for the bag, tore off another strip and wrote Lee's phone number on it. Then he swopped it for the piece of paper beside the lighter. 'Hey!'

One eye opened up a bit.

'When Zara left - how long ago was it?'

'Don't know. Before Jayden came back.'

He wanted to kick the table aside. Pick her up and shake some life into her. Some realisation of what was going on. Instead, he made for the door and was almost in the corridor when he heard her mumble something.

'You what?' he asked, looking back.

Her eyes were closed again. 'Tell her, will you, when you see her? Pringles. She knows the ones I like. Tell her to bring us some back.'

#

Once clear of the tower, he sat on a low wall to gather his thoughts. Ads had called at the flat and left with Zara, though it didn't sound like it was against her will. So he must have lured her with the promise of something. What? Could have just been attention, he thought. That's how it worked. The promise of being wanted. Of being with people who said nice stuff about you. Who treated you well. That's how these people operated.

And now it looked like they had Jayden, too. The lad was in serious trouble: he had failed to deliver a very important package, not to mention a batch of drugs. But rather than report it straight in, he'd done the worst possible thing and vanished. So now he looked guilty.

He took the bit of paper from his pocket. Ads. Where would he have taken Zara? There was that place in Rochdale. But there was probably other properties closer, including the house on Napier Street. And that's where they'd told Jayden to go. Guy glanced at the phone number again. I get one chance with this, he thought. One chance before they realise they're being tricked. Well, Guy, you'd better make it count.

CHAPTER 32

He stopped at the corner of Napier Street and surveyed the road stretching away before him. With it being during daytime, the volume of cars parked along it had halved. He couldn't see any vans at all. A couple of young women were chatting away on the far side of the street, buggies beside them. Further up, he could see an old man in a front garden adding seed to a birdfeeder which hung from a metal pole. Guy took a quick glance over at number six. The silver Polo was parked on the drive. Curtains still closed in all the windows.

He tilted his baseball cap forward to better shield his face and set off along the far side of the street. A low hedge separated number six from its neighbour. That house had no vehicle parked out in front. Its curtains were all open and the lights were off. He kept walking for another hundred metres, then crossed over and started heading back the way he'd come. One hand went to his coat pocket and checked the plastic ties and gaffer tape he'd got from his toolbox were still there. Before number six came into view, he removed his phone and made sure the text he'd typed out earlier was ready in the outbox. All good.

The two women had set off for the end of the street, wheels of their buggies clattering on the bumpy asphalt. The old man was back in his house. When he reached the neighbouring property, he walked confidently up to the front door and pretended to ring its bell. While standing on the front step, he cocked his head, listening for any nearby sounds. Nothing. Next, he removed his phone and sent the message to Ads.

Keeping close to the front of the house, he moved quickly to the separating hedge and stepped over it into the front garden of number six. Even though he knew the curtains in the front windows were closed, he ducked down and crabbed his way across to beside the front door. The thud of heavy footsteps. A muffled voice, the tone excited. He double-checked the door hinges were on his side. They were, which greatly improved his angle for entry. He resisted the urge to check if anyone was watching from the houses opposite. Things had now gone beyond the point of pulling back. As a lock turned, the person spoke again. This time, the words were audible.

'No, the sister's room. He'd hidden it in there!'

The door opened an inch and Guy pushed himself clear of the wall so his jacket didn't scrape against the bricks when he straightened up. His eyes stayed on the crack in the door. Just a few more inches would do it.

'Thing is, Luke. Why the fuck didn't he just tell them when he had the chance?'

'A rat's a rat. A rat's a fucking rat.'

That was cash-man's voice, further back in the house. So that's your name, Guy thought. Luke. And it has to be Ads on his way out. Keys jangled and the door started swinging inward.

'Tell D I'm getting it, yeah?'

Staying low, Guy exploded upwards into the gap. His shoulder crashed against the woodwork and the door flew inwards, connecting heavily with Ads. Guy's momentum took him through the doorway and into the house. The impact had thrown Ads back against the hallway wall, and now he was sliding towards the floor. Just beyond him, Luke was rooted to the spot, a look of complete bewilderment on his face. Guy kept going forward, knowing he had a precious few seconds before Ads would be able to do anything. His right fist connected with Luke's nose a moment before his left thudded into the side of the man's skull. Seeing how his head snapped to the side, Guy knew that he'd done enough. Already reaching for the cable ties, he turned round. Ads had managed to stop himself from collapsing completely. He was on his knees, right hand placed against the floor, while his left scrabbled for purchase on the wall. Guy kicked the supporting arm out from under him and Ads crashed to the floor. Before the left arm could also drop, Guy grabbed his wrist and looped the first cable tie around it. Then he jammed a knee into the back of Ads' shoulder and reached for his other arm.

#

Guy sat perfectly still, patiently watching them struggle. Eventually, their movements died away until it was just the rapid undulations of their nostrils. Not easy hyperventilating when you've been gagged. He knelt down and yanked the gaffer tape from their eyes.

They both blinked furiously.

Guy retook the kitchen chair. Interrogating captives always left him feeling conflicted. The grotesque imbalance of power made it nothing more than an extreme form of bullying. But, sometimes, it had to be done. And when it was necessary, he knew things were far more successful if it appeared that you were enjoying the process. That inflicting pain on someone who couldn't fight back made you happy. He watched with a smile as they started to look about from their positions on the floor. Blood had crusted round Luke's nose; congealed blobs of it clung to the gaffer tape which covered his mouth. Ads had a big red welt down his forehead from where the edge of the reinforced front door had connected with it.

Luke was staring up with fear-filled eyes. That decides it, Guy thought. You'll be the talker. He shifted his Stanley knife to his other hand, went back down on one knee and peeled some tape away from Luke's mouth. A load of blood poured out. Once it became a trickle, he asked, 'Where's the kid?'

'Fuck you.'

Ads suddenly began bucking his torso back and forth, shoulder muscles straining. Guy let out a sigh. He pressed the tape back across Luke's lips, plonked himself in the chair and sat forward. 'You can't see how you're restrained, so I'll tell you. Your wrists are connected with cable ties. Heavy duty ones. Breaking strain way more than a human can manage, even a gym monkey like you, Ads. So, you want to stop struggling and listen? Both your ankles are the same. Now, your wrists are also connected to the pipes of the radiator behind you. That's why you're head-to-head and up against the base of the wall. You might eventually break free of the pipes. I have seen it done, but it'll take a lot of wrenching about. And a lot of blood loss from your wrists. So, that's the position we're in. Making sense, so far?'

Luke gave a nod. Ads just glared back, head not moving.

'What happens next is easy. Luke: you'll answer all my questions. The quicker you do it, the less trouble you'll both have in later life. With arthritis. And nightmares and that.' He slid off the chair and, this time, knelt beside Ads and reached over him. 'You, big lad, get the shitty end of the stick. But only because your mate there won't keep silent for long. I get the feeling – if it was the other way round – you'd happily let Luke scream his head off before you say a thing.'

Guy put a thumb lock on Ads' right hand before using the Stanley knife to cut the tie round his wrist. As expected, the man immediately tried to wrench his arm free. So Guy increased the pressure until Ads roared with pain behind his gag and the arm went limp. Keeping a tight hold, Guy then swiftly turned himself round so his back was up against Ads' chest. Crossing his legs, he positioned the man's right hand over one of his boots.

'You two seen Blade Runner? Not the sequel with that Ryan Gosling bloke. The original. With Rutger Hauer. Luke? No? Ads? Well, that's a shame. But you've both got a treat in store. Classic film, it is.' While he was speaking, he'd uncurled Ads' little finger. 'There's this scene towards the end where the replicant gets hold of Deckard. Deckard is kind of a cop, sent to track down and take out the replicants. And this particular replicant, he starts breaking Deckard's fingers. Like this.'

He gripped the base of Ads' finger and, with his other hand, yanked it sharply to the side. He felt the knuckle give way as the gristle first popped, then crunched. Behind his masking tape, Ads roared. Guy kept a firm hold of his forearm until the thrashing about stopped. Looking to the side, he saw terror was causing Luke to breathe like a steam train. Thank Christ for that, he thought. I might only have to break the one.

'Luke, I've had a check of the house. Obviously, Jayden's not here. But I overheard what you said earlier, so I know he was. First question is this: where is Jayden now? I'm thinking back at the house in Rochdale, maybe. Did they take him there? Nod for yes, or shake for no.'

Eyes bulging, Luke's stare remained glued to a point across the room.

'Luke? Is it Rochdale? I need a nod or a shake. Still not playing? OK. This, by the way, is for Lee.' He transferred his grip to Ads' ring finger and broke it. Bracing himself against the bloke's convulsing body, Guy stared up at the ceiling. He wanted to retch. 'Telling you, Luke, it gets more painful as we move along. After the forefinger, I go back to the thumb, which is probably the worst. I'll do his hands first, then it's you and Ads' turn to talk.' He got hold of Ads' middle finger. 'Ready? On three. One, two –'

Luke's head shook from side to side.

'What's that?'

Luke shook his head again, a series of rapid grunts coming from behind the gag.

'Not Rochdale?'

Luke nodded.

Guy lifted a hand and wiped at the sweat trickling down his brow. 'OK, Luke, I'm peeling the gaffer tape back again. This time, you speak to me. Shout or anything stupid like that and I'll slice your fucking lips off.' He reached over and tore away the same corner of tape away. 'Where can I find him? Give me a proper address.'

A hysterical little laugh escaped Luke's blood-smeared lips. 'You are as good as dead. You know that?'

Guy slapped him so hard, his head bounced off the kitchen floor. 'I really cannot be arsed, Luke. An address. Now.'

'An address? You want a fucking address? Number ten, bottom of the fucking Manchester Ship Canal.'

Guy blinked. 'What did you say?' In his head, his voice had sounded very small.

'That's where he'll be by now. Good luck finding him.'

Guy felt like the room was zooming away from him. Or he was hurtling backwards. A fairground ride gone wrong. He had to slowly fill his lungs with air. Once the sensation had subsided, he twisted round to check Ads. The bloke's eyes were screwed shut. Guy shifted his gaze to Luke. Oh my fucking God: they're not lying. 'Think you're funny?' He grasped Ads' middle finger in his fist. 'Do you?'

'He's dead,' Luke hissed. 'Just like you will be. When the person we work for finds you, he's going to –'

This time, it was a fist that landed on Luke's face. It wasn't true. It couldn't be. 'Luke, you're playing a really fucking stupid game here. I want the address where –'

The other man's grin was desolate. 'Break all the fingers you want. It's true.'

Shards of ice were raining down on Guy's head. Piling up in his brain, cascading down his vertebrae, needling the nerves in his arms, then his hands, then the very tips of his fingers.

'Who took him?' he whispered.

'We didn't. It wasn't –'

'Who took him?' Guy repeated very quietly.

A sound kept repeating in Luke's mouth, but no words came out.

'McFadden?'

'Not McFadden,' he finally managed. 'His…his men.'

'On McFadden's orders?' He could feel movement behind him. Looking back, he could see Ads desperately shaking his head. 'On his orders?' Guy demanded, turning back to Luke.

He nodded.

'Why…why would he –'

Luke's head twisted, trying to look at Ads. 'Because he was a fucking rat! He's been scuttling around. It was him who told the M13 crew about the collection. That's why they knew to be waiting. He told them. It was him!'

No way, thought Guy. Jayden would never have betrayed you lot. He just wouldn't. He let his head hang forward and, for the next few seconds, just the sound of the other men's breathing filled the room. They'd killed Jayden. Taken a young lad who'd done nothing wrong and…and flung him into…was he conscious when he went in? Had they weighed him down? Tied him to something? Had he watched the glimmer of daylight grow dim as he'd sunk lower and low– 'How many men will be at McFadden's house?'

Luke's eyes widened. 'What?'

Guy uncrossed his legs and got to his knees. His entire body felt numb. Use it, he said to himself. Use this fury. After securing Ads' wrist with a new cable tie, he peeled most of the tape from the man's mouth. Then he sat back on his haunches and gazed at the two men. Both kept their eyes averted. After a few seconds, he spoke. 'No chances anymore. No second questions.' He held the Stanley knife up. 'You don't give me an answer, I slice chunks off your faces. We clear?'

They nodded. Luke had started to cry.

He pointed the tip of the blade at him. 'Where's Zara?'

'McFadden's,' he spluttered, shoulders shaking. 'She went to McFadden's.'

'Why?'

'It's a debt, isn't it? That family owes him. Owe McFadden. So she's the one who has to repay it.'

'What do you mean, repay it?'

'What do you think I mean? By working. She'll have to work. Probably some party he'll take her to. Or just in a house.'

A wave of revulsion caused Guy's throat to tighten. He had to cough before he could speak. 'She's, what? Fourteen?'

Luke looked away. 'Exactly what plenty of men are after.'

'When will this be? This evening? Later on today?'

'Probably.'

He moved the knife to Ads. 'How many people will be at McFadden's house?'

'How many? You're not thinking of –'

'How many?'

'Seven or eight.'

'Including McFadden?'

'Yes.'

'Wife? Kids?'

'McFadden?' His head shook. 'No chance.'

'Will there be any guns at McFadden's house?'

He nodded.

'What sorts of gun?'

'I know of a shotgun he has there. Maybe a Skorpion.

I've heard them say about that once.'

Skorpion, Guy thought. Christ, I hope not. He turned back to Luke. 'Have you ever heard them mention that?'

'Yes.'

Guy took a set of car keys from his pocket. 'You dropped these as I came through the door. They for the Polo on the drive?'

Ads lifted his head slightly. 'Yeah.'

'Where's your phone?'

'Top pocket of my jacket.'

Guy reached over and removed it. 'Code?'

'2306.'

Guy checked it was correct. He took his pen out and wrote it on the back of his left hand. 'And yours?' he asked, turning to Luke.

'Over there. Near the kettle.'

Guy got up and crossed the room. 'Code?'

'1414.'

He checked before writing it on his other hand. 'If there was a raid here, on this house,' he said, recrossing the room, but stopping at the table. 'Like if people were stealing this lot.' He held up one of the bags of pills and powders he'd found stashed in the oven. 'Or this.' He lifted one of the many dark brown blocks that had been neatly stacked beneath the bags. 'By the way, is this heroin?'

Luke gave a nod.

'How would you alert McFadden if someone came to steal it all?'

The two men angled their heads to look at each other.

'Would just send a message,' Ads said.

'Not a special word? Something like that?'

Both their heads shook.

Guy stared down at them. 'If you're lying, I'll come straight back.'

'Not lying,' Luke whispered.

Guy could see that his knees were trembling. 'And if

someone tried to bust in here, who would you send that message to? McFadden himself?'

'T...Tyler,' Luke replied. 'He's in my phone.'

Guy scrolled through the contacts. 'Tyler F?'

'Yes,' Luke replied.

'I've been thinking,' Guy said, sliding both phones into his pocket. 'About the rat who set you up.' He regarded Luke for a long moment. 'I saw you running from the freight terminal. Last night, when it all kicked off. You were out of there, quick as a flash. None of them seemed interested in catching you. Their sole focus was Jayden.'

Luke glanced uneasily at Ads. 'He's full of shit.'

Ads stared back at him, eyes narrowing.

'You want to find the real rat?' Guy asked Ads. He then nodded at Luke. 'No need to look very far.'

'It's total shit!' Luke said, voice too high. 'Seriously, Ads, you going to –'

His words cut off as Guy reattached the tape over his mouth. He then rummaged through one of the bags on the table until he found the tiniest ones, each with a teaspoon of pinkish powder at the bottom. He held one up. 'This amphetamine?'

Ads was still regarding Luke.

'Ads, what is this? Amphetamine?'

'Yeah.'

Guy opened the seal, dabbed the tip of his little finger in and touched it against his tongue. That familiar acrid taste. Memories of going into combat came racing back. Every cell zinging. Sight and sound sharper. Reactions quicker. Wired-up fucking killing machines. That's what we were. He walked from the room without another word.

CHAPTER 33

The hasp of the second padlock popped open and Guy raised the lid of his metal trunk. Inside was all that remained of his previous life. Random items he'd been able to keep from his time in the military. Other things which he'd acquired while working as a private contractor. Various bits of kit that could come in useful, depending on the nature of the job.

The first item he lifted out was an MK4 Osprey tactical vest. Attached to its Molle system of outer hoops was a variety of pouches and pockets – places for safely stashing all the equipment he would need.

Laid out beneath that was an assortment of smaller objects. A plastic box full of stunnies – nasty little devices which let out a rapid series of bangs and flashes. Perfect for lobbing into a room before storming it. He placed the container on the floor beside the vest. Plasma lighter which was windproof, waterproof and, most importantly, silent. He depressed the side button and waited for the purple beam to leap across the two coils at the top. Working fine.

His gaze fell on his blades. The Fairbairn-Sykes Fighting Knife lay in its brown leather sheath. His palm ached with the memory of holding it. Along with the green beret, it was the item which meant the most to him from his time in the Royal Marines. He eased it out. Seven-inch stiletto blade, enough to penetrate several layers of thick clothing before passing on into the ribcage. He pressed his fingertips into the knurled grip then returned it to the sheath. 'You're not coming,' he murmured. 'Not dirtying you on these pieces of shit.' His hand moved to his Mora Kniv, a much shorter bushcraft knife with a carbon steel blade. More uses than simple combat, plus he had an ankle-fastening sheath for it. Better choice.

As he placed it beside the stunnies, a thump sounded on the ceiling. Guy glanced up. Not now. Do not fucking start now. It sounded again.

On the far side of the trunk was what appeared to be an especially fat fountain pen, but with a small round mirror at the top, rather than a nib. He picked it out and extended the telescopic arm to its full thirty centimetres. Satisfied the hinge for the mirror was working, he collapsed it back and placed it alongside the other items.

A fast-draw paddle holster, which could be attached to the belt of his trousers, caught his eye next. He part turned his head, mind on the package which he'd hidden in his bin. They had guns. Well, a shotgun at least. Waving his Mora would be useless against that. But ramming a handgun into someone's face… I'll only need the threat of it, he told himself. If I don't have that, my slight chance of success shrinks to nothing.

He put the holster with the other items and then searched for a lanyard. One end of the short rubber coil would attach to the base of the handgun. The other would connect with a loop on the paddle holster. That way, if he lost hold of the gun, it couldn't go far. Useful thing to have, he thought. Especially as I'll be on my own. He got to his feet.

Claggy remains of porridge had found their way onto the clingfilm encasing the gun. He ripped the layers away and put the cloth-wrapped object on the kitchen table. Are you sure about this? He stared down at it. As if in reply, two thuds came from the ceiling.

Fuck's sake, he thought. It's like a bloody seance.

A flick of his forefinger and the upper layer of material fell back to reveal a pristine Glock. Lips pursed in a silent whistle, he leaned forward for a closer look. It was a seventeen. Fourth generation. NATO's classified sidearm and standard issue for the British Armed Forces. No wonder, he thought, its weight had been so familiar.

He picked it up and rotated his hand around. So, this cost Jayden his life. This. It was all over this. Well, McFadden, seems you'll get to see it, after all. When I shove the barrel in your face and tell you to get on your knees. He could immediately sense there was no magazine in the weapon's handle. The chamber indicator was also sitting flat on the slide, which told him nothing was in the spout either. Habit dictated that he racked it three times, anyway. Once he'd done that, he put the weapon aside.

Next, he opened the cloth out fully. Two fifteen-round magazines were buried in its folds. He examined the line of holes on the rear of each one: both full. He emptied the lot out. Fully jacketed Parabellum rounds. Military grade. Thirty in total. Do I even take them? Or just the gun on its own? The words of his sergeant in Afghanistan came back to him whenever they were preparing to go on a raid. Peace through superior firepower. It generally worked, too. He slid one clip into the base of the Glock and placed the other alongside the weapon.

The roll of tape and packet of plastic ties was still on the table from earlier. He sat down and began looping ties into pairs. Eight men was what they'd said. He created ten sets just to be on the safe side. Sitting back, he looked around. What else?

Another thud sounded above him.

That bloody padlock on the gate into McFadden's rear garden. It would have been the perfect entry point, if only

I'd got the chance to swop it over. He opened his toolbox out and removed a pair of curved jaw locking pliers from the central compartment. They'd have to do.

He was about to start lining the mobile phones up on the table when a series of ceiling bangs caused him to clench his fist and slam it down. You want to play, do you? He tipped his head back as another thump sounded. You do. Fine by me.

Next thing he knew, he was taking the stairs two at a time. The landing above was even dingier. Smells seemed to linger in the noticeably warmer air. The flat he wanted was number seven. Using the heel of his hand, he hit the door three times. Weeks, he said to himself. Weeks you've been making my life a misery. Now it's my turn. The thudding noise started again, each repeat bringing it a little closer to the door. Oh, you're a funny fucker. You are such a funny fucker. He realised he was up on the balls of his feet, fingers curling and uncurling at his sides. We'll see who's laughing in a minute, you prick.

The door had hardly begun to open when it bumped against something.

'One moment,' a tremulous voice said. Same sort of wobble that had eventually crept into his dad's words. That same thump and the door opened a little wider. A wash of fetid air came out. A mixture of damp wallpaper, unwashed clothes and something sweeter. Rotting food?

CHAPTER 34

A heavily overweight man with a fuzz of grey hair peered out. The chunky frames of his glasses belonged to the previous century, their thick lenses giving him a startled look. 'Yes?' he asked uncertainly.

Guy could see that what had obstructed the door was some kind of walking frame. The man was gripping onto its handles, but the thing was slightly lopsided. He was wearing a faded old vest, a pair of baggy tracksuit bottoms, and flip-flops. His arms were sheathed in a layer of pale blubber but, beneath it, Guy could see the bulge of muscles. He had been fit, once. Guy felt his eyes creeping back to the emblem on the vest. Royal Navy. There was a faded tattoo on one thick forearm. Jesus, he'd served at some point.

'I...I live below you,' Guy said. 'Number four.'

The man looked crestfallen. 'It's not leaking again?'

'Sorry?'

'The toilet. Is it leaking again?'

'The toilet?' Guy pictured the tiny bathroom downstairs in his flat. 'Is my toilet leaking?'

'My toilet,' the man replied. 'Is it dripping from the ceiling? It did, back in the winter –'

'Oh. No. You're alright.' Guy's mind felt like it had been lurched sideways. All this time, I've been imagining some malevolent little troll. 'It's just that I hear you sometimes…' He gestured at the walking frame. 'Is that broken or something?'

He grimaced. 'One of the bloody wheels. The home help keeps saying he'll sort it out, but he never does.'

That's why it's tilting, Guy thought, looking down at it as the other man took a shuffling step back. The frame made a thud. The inside of the flat was an utter tip. Piles of newspapers and magazines stacked all over the place. Cups and plates perched on many of them. And beside the sink, dozens and dozens of the same empty plastic bottle. More were sticking out from the top of the bin. Guy could just make out the label; it was one he usually only saw in newsagents or petrol stations. Yazoo milk shake. Christ, it looked like the bloke was surviving on Yazoo fucking milkshake.

'I'd say come in, if you can find a space. Place needs a good tidy, if I'm honest.'

Guy could see that channels cut through the debris covering the floor. One from the bedroom out to a junction towards the centre of the room. From there, another branched off to an armchair and a third to the kitchen area. A shorter one cut back towards the toilet. Home help? Had the person ever so much as stepped inside the flat? 'Have you still got the wheel? The one which came off?'

'Oh, yes. It's over there.' He pointed an elbow towards the armchair. 'Can't bend down, can I? Would have done it myself, if I could.'

'Right. Listen, I've got no time. But when I come back, I'll fix it for you, OK?'

'Thanks.'

Guy could hear the doubt in his voice. 'I'm serious. I will. Nice to meet you, by the way. I'm called Guy.'

The man nodded. 'Ray.'

Guy held a hand across the threshold. 'I've got a toolbox downstairs. We'll get you sorted.'

As the man reached out, Guy glimpsed the length of his nails. Needs a health visitor, too.

'Appreciated, Guy. Thanks.'

'No problem, mate. I've got to go, but see you soon.' He jogged back down to his own flat and was shocked to see that he'd forgotten to close the door. All his stuff – including the Glock – was in plain view. Cool head, Guy, he said to himself as he stepped inside and closed the door. If you don't keep that, you may as well give up now.

Ten minutes later, he opened the door again. Now he was wearing a thigh length jacket over black cargo trousers and boots. A dun-green rucksack was slung over one shoulder. He glanced at the stairs, thinking of the old boy up there. Living in that miserable flat, relying on some harried agency worker to call by once in a while. It was shit.

He re-opened his door, dumped the rucksack on the floor and strode across to his fridge. Anything in it that needed to be used up went into a carrier bag: milk, the last of his bacon, tomatoes, shredded kale, cucumber, apples, yoghurt, cheese and ham. He added the loaf of bread and the bag with the custard cake, then bounded back up the stairs to Ray's flat.

'Take this lot,' he said, hanging it from the handle of the walking frame once the door had opened. 'It's only bread, milk and stuff like that. Some fruit and veg.'

'No, no, no – you don't need to –'

'It's fine. I don't know for sure when I'll be back. Better it gets eaten, hey?'

'Why don't you know when you'll be back?'

'It's just…I need to do something. That's all. I could be away for a bit.'

'Well, are you certain?'

'Absolutely, mate. Fill your boots.'

CHAPTER 35

He parked the Polo on a residential street a couple of minutes' walk away from the turning into Orchard Lane. Rather than immediately switch the engine off, he sat perfectly still, hands on the steering wheel, eyes closed as his mind raced about, trying to check and double-check everything. It was all happening too fast. There hadn't been time to plan. Not properly. And face it, part of him admitted, this isn't a one-man job. It's not even a three-man job. The chances of you pulling this off are absurd. He opened his eyes. This feeling: my blood's actually fizzing. Long time since I've experienced that. And, he had to admit, it didn't feel bad. Not bad at all.

He read through the messages that he'd typed earlier into the phones of Ads and Luke. *Raid need hlp now*. His eyes went to the other screen. *3 of them*. Was it enough to convince Tyler? It would bloody have to be.

As he walked along the road, he made sure his posture was relaxed. A bit slouchy. You're a contractor, he said to himself. Working on the renovations to that house along from McFadden's. Maybe addressing a drainage issue in the pool or whatever it was they're digging. This is your break and you're in no hurry to get back to the job.

A low rumble was coming from the sky and he looked up to see a plane, nose tilted toward the layer of thick grey cloud. Wonder if that's my flight? He checked the time. Christ, there was a chance it was. It could have been me up there.

His mind circled the planet and he contemplated his dad, now lying in an Australian morgue. What would he have thought about this? About what I'm doing? That familiar, despondent head shake, eyes lowered, a puff of air ready in his cheeks? Or maybe a bit of his mind would have perked up, and he would have nodded in approval? I'll never know.

He'd almost drawn level with the scaffolding-clad property when he heard a car engine behind him. Moments later, a Range Rover with tinted windows trundled past. The car's lower sides were spattered with dirty water, and mud caked its tires. It started indicating left. McFadden's property, Guy thought. Was it the crew who had taken Jayden? Driven him off to a secluded point near the ship canal?

The vehicle rolled to a stop before the security gates. Guy guessed that, on the other side, the driver had lowered his window to punch in a code. As a way of keeping his head down, he shrugged the rucksack off and undid the zip. There was only one item inside: the locking pliers.

The gates started to swing inward and, as soon as the Range Rover was through, Guy stopped walking. He was now at the furthest corner of the security fence which ran across the front of McFadden's property. Straggly branches from a neighbour's privet hedge partly hid him. The vehicle parked beside the white Mercedes and all the doors immediately opened. Four men got out, all in their thirties, two of them heavily built. The boot had also started lifting, and the driver reached in to remove a large hold-all. Mud clung to its underside. He handed it to one of the others and gestured to the far corner of the house.

The man carrying it set off in that direction while the rest of them walked in single file across the paving slabs leading up to the front door.

Guy clamped the jaws of the locking pliers at thigh height onto the corner railing. There wouldn't, he knew, be a better moment than this. Anyone inside the property monitoring the security cameras would have been distracted by the four men's arrival. Once the three at the front door were stepping inside the house, he placed a foot on the pliers while reaching up for a decent handgrip. His other foot found a gap between the spikes at the top of the fence and, a moment later, he was landing on McFadden's lawn.

Keeping low, he made straight for the nearest bush and crouched behind it. The front door closed with a muted thud. Now the only windows he could be spotted from were those at the side of the house: two rows of three, the ones on the ground floor perfectly aligned with those on the first floor. He took a moment to study the rest of the property, looking for anything which might give a clue to its interior layout. It was obviously fairly new but designed in a Georgian style: aside from the neatly aligned windows, the exterior was understated. A pair of Dorma windows jutted from the roof. The only characteristic not in keeping with the restrained appearance was the front entrance. Three shallow steps led up to an over-sized portico complete with pillars topped by ornate stone-leaf designs. At the rear of the building, the corner of a glass construction was visible, lights on inside it. A conservatory or orangery or whatever they were called. He realised that, between the plants on the other side of the glass, two heads were visible. Both men were sitting with their backs to him, discussing something.

On the first floor, one window was frosted. Wastewater pipe coming out of the wall below it. So, a bathroom of some sort. Next one was dark, final one lit. Ground floor: furthest two unlit, nearest one lit, but no sign of movement through it. In the centre of the room stood a multi-gym. He could see what appeared to be the top part of a running machine, too. He placed both phones on the grass, took off his coat and stuffed it into the base of the bush. Last check to make sure no one was standing at any of the windows. Next phase.

Grasping the phones in one hand, he sprinted across to the corner of the house and stood with his back pressed against the wall. Now he wasn't visible from any window. His fingers went to the rear pocket of his trousers. He took out the little bag of amphetamine, tipped a pinch of powder into his palm, sniffed it up and waited. Music was coming from somewhere. First floor? He looked about. Seemed to be the first floor. Whatever, it was good news. Nothing worse than going into a silent property. He began another check of his tactical vest. All pouches closed, all kit secure. The first tickles were now building in his head, and he suppressed the urge to nod in time to the music. Plastic ties in a line across the hoops on his left breast. Stunnies in a pouch below them. Ankle knife. His vision was snapping tighter. The twitter of a bird from across the garden sounded hard and sharp. He retrieved the bag of powder from his pocket and tipped the remainder onto the ground. No need for anymore of you, he thought, tossing it. He flexed his fingers and took in a deep breath. Show time, my friend. Fucking show time.

He took out his search mirror, fully extended the arm and laid it on the ground. Next were the two phones: he sent both messages at the same time, turned the phones off, cracked the casings and removed the SIM cards. Then he got into a kneeling position and angled the mirror round the corner of the house for a view of the steps. Within thirty seconds, he heard the front door open. Multiple voices.

'I don't fucking know! Neither are picking up.'
'Same crew who turned up at the freight terminal?'
'Has to be. Fuckers!'

He saw the same four men from earlier jogging towards the Range Rover. Two had baseball bats swinging from their hands. The one with the car keys glanced over his shoulder. 'Mark, keep trying their numbers, yeah?'

He swivelled the mirror back towards the house. A fifth man was on the bottom step. Big bastard, fingers busy at the screen of his phone. 'I am. It's like there's no service.'

Out on the drive, the Range Rover gouged out gravel as it shot backwards. The gears then crunched and it lurched towards the opening gates. The man on the bottom step watched the vehicle race off down the road, then started turning back to the house.

Keeping his feet light, Guy ran towards him. Do not look over your shoulder. Do not look over your shoulder. The front door was half open and he got a glimpse of a large hallway with parquet flooring. Chandelier hanging down. Wide staircase to the right. Then his left arm was going round the man's throat, forearm hard against his larynx. He'd locked it out with his right arm before the man's phone had hit the floor. Both hands lifted as he tried to prise Guy's forearm away. Wrong move, thought Guy, wedging his hip into the base of the man's spine while bending him backwards. The man was forced up onto his tiptoes and his movements became more frantic. Guy kept the forearm-squeeze tight. Not long now. He sensed a shift in the man's weight at the same time he heard a scrape of trainer. Lifting his head, he saw the man had got a foot against the wood of the doorframe. Shit. The man straightened his knee, forcing Guy back. His rear foot came off the edge of the step. Keeping his grip tight, he had to accept the fall. A moment later, he landed on his back with the man on top of him. The impact expelled every last bit of air from his lungs. Glowing blobs filled his vision. All he could do was keep the choke hold and cross his ankles over the man's knees. He clung on, praying the man blacked out before he did. As the neon blobs began to turn red, he felt his arms being jerked from side to side as the bastard bucked and thrashed. Cheek pressed against the back of the man's head, Guy kept opening and closing his mouth, desperately trying to swallow back air. Would the bloke ever stop? Suddenly, his lungs were able to re-inflate. Strength surged back into his arms and he re-tightened his grip.

The man's efforts to break free were now slowing, movements becoming weaker. Guy stayed clamped on until all struggling had stopped. He then counted to five before slowly relaxing his arms. His forefinger found a pulse as he detached a looped pair of cable ties. Once the hands were secure, he removed the battery from the man's phone and checked the hallway. No movement. Tape went across the man's mouth and he dragged him clear of the door, then flipped him into the recovery position. Don't need you dying of positional asphyxia. He checked his watch. Less than two minutes had passed since the Range Rover's departure. Ten-minute drive over to the safe house, if they raced. Call it nine, just to be safe. They discover it was a hoax and phone McFadden. So, a little over seven minutes until the shit hits the fan.

Pain was registering in his right shoulder. Must have been what connected with the ground first, he thought, rotating it as he edged closer to the front door. Search mirror out. Hallway clear. Two doors on the left, both closed. The rooms he'd studied from the outside of the house. A home gym and something else. The lights had been off in it, so probably empty, too. Far end, some kind of archway leading into the rear of the house. A kitchen area, probably. And then it would be that conservatory.

Ads had said seven or eight would be here, including McFadden. Let's call it eight. Four had left in the Range Rover. One is out front, safely cuffed. Two in the conservatory. So that left one other, lurking somewhere in the house.

At the base of the stairs, off to the right, a single door.

Half open. Music definitely coming from the first floor. Similar to the stuff that had been playing in the flat in Conmere Tower. Zara? He returned the mirror to its pouch. First thing, make sure no one's in that room on the right. He glided into the house and over to the doorway, eyes wide, ears straining for any sounds in the room beyond. Something made a light tick. Then another. And again. Clock. He slid through the door and immediately stepped to the side to avoid being outlined. Two sofas, facing each other across a low coffee table. Freestanding lamps. Large clock on dresser in corner.

He came back out of the room and immediately noticed the little telephone console mounted on the wall beside the front door. Green button at the base had a key symbol. So that's how the front gate opens. Carefully, he closed the door of the side room and moved to the base of the stairs. Five wide steps up to a landing. One eighty degree turn and the rest of the flight led to a sort of gallery which overlooked the hallway. A voice, sounding angry, way back in the house. Which probably meant the conservatory area. Another voice replied. Thanks lads, Guy thought. You both stay where you are. He began climbing the first steps, keeping his feet as close to the wall as possible to reduce the likelihood of causing the wood to creak. All the while, his eyes were bouncing from balcony, to hallway, then balcony again. His breath was fast and shallow. Too fast. Too shallow. Breathe, Guy. Breathe. Not a one-person job, this. Four, really. You can't keep every angle covered. Not on your own. You just can't. Shut the fuck up. Keep going. Just keep going.

He crossed the landing and, back pressed against the wall for extra stability, started up the main flight. Each step revealed a little more of the first-floor layout. Door straight ahead at the top of the stairs. Half open, light on. Next door along the balcony, closed. Music coming from behind it. Same room that, when viewed from the outside, was at the rear corner of the house. Further round the balcony, two more doors, both closed. Now three-quarters of the way up, he rechecked the hallway. All good, he said to himself. Nearly there.

He could now see the balcony stretched round three walls, ending at another set of stairs. He recalled the Dorma windows set into the roof. More rooms up there. Maybe bedrooms. Could be a self-contained flat with a kitchen and everything. Somewhere for his security people to stay. God, too many doors and too many fucking stairs. He didn't like the fact the first doorway was partially open. But the light being on inside let him search for the hint of movement through the small gap at the base of the door. Nothing.

He got to the top step and, with two big strides, positioned himself to the side. Silence. Another step took him through the gap. Bedroom, one double bed. Feel of a guestroom. Unused. One inner door, fully open. Tiled floor. Toilet. Ensuite. More fucking rooms to watch out for. He walked softly to the bedroom window and risked a quick look out. As expected, the roof of the conservatory was off to the left. But the ceiling panels were opaque so he couldn't see in. He realised the sky had grown darker. Heavy with rain. It felt very still; not even a whisper of a breeze.

His eyes travelled to the other corner: some kind of extension with a flat roof. Utility room? Where the washing machine and stuff like that would be. Between the two, a patio area with some wooden seating. Carefully, he unlocked the window. Burning. He could smell burning. Barbecue area was across the lawn. At its centre, a firepit. Something smouldering inside it. That hold all, he thought. The one which had been in the boot of the Range Rover.

He gauged the distance down to the flat roof. A simple drop. Escape route, if needed. Time check: four minutes, twenty-six seconds since the Range Rover set off. Still safe for another four-and-a-half minutes. Back on the balcony, he scanned the hallway below. All good.

His head turned to the closed door. There was no key in the lock. If this door opens and it's her inside, he thought, we might just get away with this. I've just got to let her know I'm here to get her out. To safety. Once she understands that, we go down the stairs, hit the green button, then a quick sprint to the gates. He almost smiled. This, Guy, could be up there with your luckiest fucking capers.

Eyes on the hallway below, he moved silently to the closed door and tried the knob. To his relief, it rotated. He opened it a crack and the music became louder. Another check behind him and he eased it open a little further. Corner of a bed, strewn with clothing. Little dresses and crop tops. A pair of cut-off jeans. He pushed the door open another inch.

'That you, Mark? Did you remember the lemonade? I can't drink this fucking stuff without –'

Zara was sitting at a dressing table with her back to him. She was wearing a dark spangly top and purple hot pants. Bare feet. He realised she was looking at him in the reflection of a large mirror. Mouth hanging open, tube of lipstick in her hand. Beside the pots of make-up and brushes was a quarter bottle of vodka. Couple of dark fruits ciders.

'You.'

He lifted a hand, palm towards her. 'It's OK, Zara,' he whispered. 'I've come to get you out of here.' He checked over his shoulder, then looked back at her. 'Can you get some shoes on? We need to leave. Right now.'

She twisted round. 'What the fuck are you doing here?'

He held a finger to his lips. 'There's no time. I'll tell you when we're clear.' He beckoned quickly with his hand. 'Come on, quick.'

Her face was changing. The shocked expression rapidly disappearing. Her eyes shifted to the balcony behind him. 'Mark! Mark!'

No. This was a total nightmare. She doesn't have the

faintest clue about the danger she's in. Guy stepped fully into the room and closed the door. 'Zara, you've got to keep quiet. The men downstairs? They are not –'

She reached over to the portable speaker and killed the music. 'Mark, help! Mark!'

He took a step forward, unsure what to do. Cuff and tape her? I'll never get her down the stairs. Shit!

She grabbed the nearest make-up pots and started flinging them in his direction. One hit the door with a loud crack. 'This fucking weirdo's got in here, Mark!'

They would have heard. They had to have heard. He swivelled round. Key was on the inside of the door. As he removed it, the bottle of vodka shattered against the wall beside him.

'Fuck off, just fuck off! Mark, get here! Mark!'

He stepped back through the door, leaned down to lock it and was just straightening up when it felt like a donkey kicked him in the arse. As he was flung headfirst against the wood, a huge roar took over the world. Splinters and plaster and dust swirled around. His buttocks and thighs felt ridiculously hot as he instinctively dropped to the side. *Did someone just fire on me?*

CHAPTER 36

Keeping his body flat on the floor, he lifted his head. The balustrade where he'd been standing looked like a mini tornado had hit it. Shredded spindles and a gouged-out banister. Small holes pocked the door and wall. Skeet. A shotgun. Jesus fucking Christ. His eyes went back to the balcony's ruined woodwork. That probably just saved my life. Peeping down, he saw a stockily built man with a shaved head climbing the stairs. The side-by-side sawn-off he was holding swung towards Guy. He ducked back down as another blast erupted. A section of wall and ceiling above him disintegrated, raining more plaster down. Guy realised the Glock was already in his right hand. When did I draw that? He took another look. The man had broken his weapon open. Fingers of his right hand were in his pocket. The hand emerged holding two more cartridges, both red. Guy extended his pistol and popped off two shots. Both rounds hit the wall to the man's left. Idiot, Guy. Slow down. The man's eyes had lifted in shock and, fingers shaking, he started trying to slot the cartridges into the breech of his weapon. How long, Guy thought, since I've had any firing practise? He raised himself to a kneeling position and squeezed off two more. This time the man's left arm jerked outward. The other bullet appeared to hit him somewhere in the midriff. He fell back against the wall with a grunt of pain. But the weapon was still in his grip and he began to raise it once more. Guy placed his forearms across the banister and allowed himself an extra fraction of a second to get his aim in properly. Two quick shots, both into the man's chest. Their impact spun him through ninety degrees and he pitched face-first down the stairs, coming to a stop on the landing. The gun lay across the next step up and a light haze of smoke now hung in the air. Beyond the ringing in his head, Guy could hear Zara screaming over and over again. He tried to swallow but couldn't. Mouth totally dry. Fuck. Fuck! Everything, he realised with a sickening feeling, is about to happen very fast.

He sprang to his feet, weapon close to his chest in the compressed-ready position. Moving quickly, he rounded the balcony to the top of the stairs. Hallway area clear. Keeping his back pressed against the wall, he began to rapidly descend the steps, ears straining for any sounds coming from the ground floor. Zara had started pounding on the bedroom door. 'Mark! Tyler! What's happening? He's locked me in!'

Guy kept his gaze on the hallway. At least the ground floor doors were all shut. Check behind! Keep checking behind. You're on your own here. He looked back up the stairs. A waist-high blotch of blood was on the wall at the top of the stairs. The smear followed him down the steps. My blood. The pain in his buttocks and thighs registered for the first time. Fucking shotgun. He wondered how many bits of banister, fragments of trousers and wadding from the cartridges were mixed up in his wounds.

He continued down to the man's crumpled form. Blood was pooling out from beneath his torso. Left hand down to the side of his neck. No sign of life. Pistol retort. A bullet hit the wall inches from his head. Crouching, he directed his weapon towards where the gun had gone off.

Far side of the hall: McFadden. Less than twelve metres away. Weapon still pointing vaguely in Guy's direction as he began turning back to the archway. Wearing a lilac-coloured shirt, grey suit trousers and shooting a fucking gun at me. Chance to take the big man out. Guy fired twice, hoping to get lucky. Both rounds went into the wooden panelling. Bollocks.

Weapon in the compressed-ready position once more, Guy stepped over the dead man, eyes trying to calculate threats as the rest of the hallway swung into view. Zara's shrieks weren't slowing down. Girl had some lungs on her. That archway into the back of the house. Nightmare. This is a four-man job. This is a – shut up, you whining prick. His eyes settled briefly on the panel beside the half-open front door. The button would open the front gates. Your way out of this. Time to bail? Something wasn't right. The door hadn't been that far open before. He peered through the gap. The man he'd subdued earlier was no longer there. Mark. Shit, Mark was gone. Not good. How much time had now passed? Five minutes? Six? He realised there were people out on the road. A couple with a dog looking anxiously towards the house. An elderly man, talking urgently into his phone. Mark was gone. So, a minimum of three, still. McFadden, Mark and maybe another. Possibly Tyler. You could go. Withdraw. Hit that button and get out. Twenty metres to the front gate. You could. It's not too late. He reached out and pressed it. Down the drive, he heard the low whirr of a motor. The gates were swinging inwards. Then Zara started hammering on the door again. 'Let me out! Let me out! Let me out!'

Can't leave her. Can't leave her to these…fucking animals. These fucking animals who've taken her brother. Who took my brother. Who've taken so many people's brothers. Sisters. Sons and daughters. Not leaving her so they can whisk her off to some rank property with a stream of men arriving, day and night. They are not fucking taking her.

He closed the front door and started across the hallway. Each step made a squelching noise. Looking down, he saw blood oozing from the eyelets of his boots. The back of his trousers was hot and sticky. How much am I losing? How much have I lost? Half a pint? More? He used his left hand to untie his laces, gun in his right, trained on the archway. Boots off, then his socks. When he moved forward again, he made no sound.

The archway. He came to a stop while still a few metres away. Don't like it. Really don't like it. Too much open space on the other side. Too much dead ground. Places where someone could hide. And fire from. He looked to his right and saw a small door in the corner. Where did that lead? Same room? Could be. Will they be expecting me to come through the archway? Or will they have a weapon trained on the corner door, too? Ads had mentioned a Skorpion. If that's true, will it already be in someone's hand? Even these muppets couldn't miss with that thing.

Zara took a break from her yelling, and in the brief silence, he heard a couple of quick footsteps. There'd come from beyond the small door. He moved swiftly over to it, then made a quick check behind him. Trail of red footprints. He could feel the blood trickling down his inner thighs and over his calf muscles. Shot in the arse. Embarrassing. He turned back to the door. Unlike the front door, this one wasn't solid wood. Composite material. Hinges on the left, inward opening. The handle turned when he tested it.

Throw a stunnie in first? No point: you do not know the size of the room you're entering. Might not even be a room. Could be a passageway. He blinked twice. This is it. This is it. Follow the door round as it swings open. Get out of the funnel. Back to the wall, work out your arcs and keep moving forward. No stopping. Attack probe. Keep taking ground. His heart felt like it was on a trampoline and a wave of dizziness caused his vison to momentarily distort. Breathe, Guy, breathe.

Gun gripped in both hands, he pressed the upper part of his left arm against the door. It started to swing open. Before taking his first step forward, he leaned back to do a final check on the narrow gap between the doorframe and the edge of the door. Someone was standing directly behind it. They were holding something. Guy pivoted, brought the muzzle of the Glock up to the gap and fired rapidly at leg height. One, two, three, four. Chunks of wood vaporised. A body hit the floor on the other side and a machete skittered across tiles. Gasps of agony. Guy stepped through and immediately moved to his right.

He was in a corner, his back against where two walls converged. Don't want to be here. The room was fucking huge. Stretched across the entire rear of the house. Ignoring the injured person, he scanned for any threats. To his immediate right, a floor-to-ceiling radiator. Then a door, closed. Beyond it, a work surface, sink and cooker arrangement filling the opposite corner.

His eyes moved to the rear wall of the house. Midpoint, sliding doors out to the patio area. Gloomy garden beyond it. At each side of the patio doors was a towering house plant, then – in the far corner – the entrance to the conservatory. Now empty, as far as he could tell. Centre of the room, a large, glass dining table. Four chairs down each side.

His view to the far side of the room was blocked by some kind of partition wall which extended out a metre or so beyond the door he'd just come through. What the fuck was that for? To create some kind of alcove? He could see the rear part of a sofa facing into it. The thud of his heart was going arrhythmic. Amphetamine, adrenaline or blood loss? I can't have bled out that much. Concentrate! Job in hand. Keep moving forward. Keep taking ground. There'll be someone in that alcove bit. Bound to be.

He edged round the radiator, alert for any sound. The man he'd shot through the crack in the door was still on the floor, moaning through clenched teeth. Machete beside him. It was the same person he'd put the choke hold on out front. Mark. Now he was clutching a shattered knee. Not your day, pal. He edged past the radiator, gun sweeping from side to side. Two more people to go. One of them McFadden, with a gun. The closed door was now right beside him. Someone was on the other side. He could hear them quietly trying to fit a key into some kind of lock. The sort of metallic sound the lockers at the freight terminal made. Weapons cabinet? Well Guy, he's not trying to find a fucking mop. No way to check. Not without turning my back on that alcove. Fuck doing that.

Instead, he moved to the far side of the door and, keeping his back to the wall, reached behind with his left hand and rested it lightly on the door handle. Anyone starts opening that, I'll know.

Weapon hand raised, he resumed his check of the main room from his improved position. Over on the opposite side of the room were more chairs, these grouped round a small circular table. In the corner nearest the entrance into the conservatory, a sleek wood-burning stove, silver pipe extending into the roof. Nowhere for anyone to hide over there. Eyes back to the alcove.

About four metres past the first partition wall was a matching one. Corner sofa built into the end of the alcove furthest from him. Then a coffee table. After that, the sofa he'd been able to see when he'd first come through the door. And finally, the bit he couldn't see into. He studied the wall closest to him. Load bearing? He thought not. Cosmetic feature. Just a stud wall and layer of plaster. Anyone's in that corner and they make a sound, I could fire straight through it. Except the big bastard on the floor is making such a fucking racket I can hardly hear a thing. That and Zara kicking the shit out of her bedroom door.

Movement to his right. Out on the patio? His gun swung round and it took a moment for him to work it out. A reflection, caught in the glass of the patio doors. The reflection was the alcove and the movement was McFadden, stealthily moving towards the far partition wall, gun in his hand. A Makarov. Eight rounds, if the magazine was full. Either way, thought Guy, I've got you. As he readied himself to advance, McFadden's head turned and his gaze immediately went to the patio doors where, Guy realised, his own reflection would be visible. McFadden froze and the doorhandle in Guy's left hand began to lower.

CHAPTER 37

Guy withdrew his hand and brought his weapon back into the compressed-ready position. The door began to swing inward inch by inch. Ready to start firing from his sternum while punching the gun towards his target, he tried to keep an eye on McFadden as he willed the other person to emerge.

The gun's stubby little muzzle began to appear. Yup, thought Guy. Looks like a Skorpion. All thirty rounds could come spewing out of it in less than a second. Cannot let that happen.

'By the door!' McFadden suddenly yelled. 'On your right, Tyler, on your right!'

The muzzle immediately began angling towards Guy. Panicking, he lunged forward and grabbed the end with his right hand to force it down and away. Wrong hand, Guy. You've used your wrong hand! The man kept coming through the doorway and their eyes met. Same one from Reverie. The one who told me to get out. This time, his hair was tied back. Lips peeling into a snarl, he head-butted Guy. Hard bone connected with Guy's lips and he was seeing stars again. Keeping hold of the Skorpion's barrel with his right, he swept his left hand up to smash the

Glock into Tyler's face. The bridge of the man's nose tore open and Guy brought his left hand back, ready to fire into his chest.

The Skorpion erupted. A line of impacts raced past Guy's toes and off across the kitchen floor. Guy could feel the muzzle's vibration as he forced it further away from him. The noise was horrific. Now the tiles leading across the floor towards Mark were shattering. Next thing, bullets were tearing into the man's head and shoulders.

Guy lifted his left hand and smashed the butt of his pistol down on the top of Tyler's skull. That caused his head to drop. The gun stopped firing. Guy started trying to wrench it from his grip when a pistol shot rang out. McFadden. Over by the partition wall. The gun went off again and Guy felt like someone had smashed his upper right arm with a sledgehammer. Aware he was horribly exposed, Guy looped the Glock's lanyard round Tyler's neck, yanked him in close and swung him round to create a shield. McFadden kept firing and Guy felt at least two rounds thud into Tyler. Keeping the lanyard tight to stop the other man sinking to the floor, he returned two shots in McFadden's direction before attempting to pull the Skorpion from Tyler's grip. Another shot from McFadden. The Skorpion bucked and Guy registered a sharp pain in his hand as McFadden's bullet ricocheted into the patio door. Guy glanced down. Half his little finger was gone, along with the upper section of his ring finger. Blood was pumping out. Holding the Glock in his left, he loosed off another shot despite the pull of Tyler's weight on the lanyard ruining his aim. A grunt. Did I hit the bastard? Seeing McFadden duck back behind the partition, Guy let Tyler drop. The Skorpion was lying beside him, its housing ruined by the bullet's impact. A bit of Guy's little finger was next to it. He kicked the Skorpion across the floor, slid the Mora from its ankle sheath, severed the lanyard at the base of the Glock and brought the weapon up in two shaking hands. The mechanism was locked back. Empty clip. Fuck! His fingers probed at the pouch where he'd stashed the spare. Nothing. Empty. Out of bullets. The room faded for an instant and he shook his head. Vision's going. Losing too much blood here. Zara had given up shouting. Or can I just not hear anything because of the gunshots? The room was starting to seem very far away. He sucked in air and tried to use the patio window to check on McFadden's position. A spider's web of cracks now covered the glass. No reflections now. Only one thing for it. He laid the Glock down, removed his Mora and started unsteadily towards the partition.

He was halfway there when McFadden burst back into view, roaring at the top of his voice, gun raised. The barrel swung towards Guy and he found himself looking at that little black circle. He's got me. It's over. The skin on the knuckle of McFadden's forefinger whitened as he squeezed the trigger. The gun clicked and Guy blinked again. McFadden kept pulling the trigger, seemingly unable to understand his weapon was empty. They stood looking at each other. Guy could see a decent patch of blood under the other man's right arm pit. So I did get him. Or winged him, at least. McFadden's gaze slid off to the side and Guy saw his eyes widen slightly. He turned his head. The Skorpion was on the floor by the oven. Good luck, thought Guy. It's fucked. McFadden made a dart towards it. Guy saw that, if he moved too, he could get within striking distance of the other man. But, as he transferred his weight onto his right leg, the sole of his foot slipped in his own blood. His leg buckled. Pitching forward, all he could do was stretch out his knife hand and swipe at McFadden's leg. The blade passed across the back of his knee. Yelping, McFadden staggered to the side, colliding with the kitchen table. Guy hit the floor and immediately tried to drag himself back up. But his feet and his hands kept going out from under him. He realised he was flailing around in a layer of his own blood. His lungs didn't seem to be working. McFadden regained his balance and started hopping over to the weapon. With a cry of triumph, he bent down to retrieve it. Guy was on his knees, gasping for breath. His sight was going properly now. Everything was starting to blur. He glanced about, looking for a dry patch of floor. Somewhere not spattered with blood. My fucking blood. The alcove sofa wasn't far away. Fuck it. He slid himself across the stained tiles and tried to grasp the back of the sofa. There was nothing left in his arms. Nothing at all. Giving up, he managed to twist himself round. Now propped against the sofa, he could see McFadden examining the damaged Skorpion with a look of dismay. That's right, you prick. It won't be firing anything. He lifted the knife and mimed sticking it into McFadden. If only I could. Shadows were massing at the periphery of his vision. Struggling here to even keep my eyes open. So damned tired. Had the room been this cold when I first came in?

'Well, well.'

McFadden's voice was like a distant shout across a valley. Guy realised his head had sunk onto his chest. He lifted his chin. McFadden had placed the Skorpion on the work surface and was now holding the Glock.

'This is my gun, isn't it? The one that little rat Jayden was meant to fetch?'

Guy watched as he turned it over in his hands. Above him, inky shapes were spreading across the ceiling. One started to glide down the wall behind McFadden. Sorry, Jayden. I did my best. For you and Zara. I'm sorry.

'You're the one Ads mentioned,' McFadden said, limping closer. 'Security at the freight terminal. And you were in my club on the opening night. Eyeballing me. So, how much did the M13 lot pay you to come here? Into my fucking house?'

Guy stared at him. Keep what strength you have. This isn't over. Not yet.

'Talked round Jayden, too, didn't you – you little fuck? Zara told me about you two at McDonald's.' He lifted the gun. 'Got him to tell you where and when this was coming in, didn't you?'

A moan broke from Guy's lips. No. They killed Jayden because they thought he was working with me. Oh God, it's my fault. This is all my fault. I caused it.

'And now I get to do you with it.' McFadden took another couple of steps closer. His eyes dropped, and he stared for a moment at Mark's body. Then he glanced over at Tyler and shook his head. 'The shit you have caused me.' He turned back to Guy and gave a grim smile.

Guy saw the too-perfect teeth and imagined smashing them in. He wanted to tell the other man he was vermin. Poison. He licked his dry lips. 'You…'

'What?' As McFadden started forward again, he winced. His left hand reached under his right arm pit. 'Fucking hurts, this. Though I doubt as much as yours.'

Guy tucked his knife hand under his thigh so the blade was out of sight. He let his eyes half-close, as if on the verge of fainting. Glock's empty. How close will he come before he tries to shoot? A lot closer if he thinks I'm barely conscious. He let his eyes close completely and sagged his head to the side.

'Hey! Do not pass out. Hey!'

Guy waited another second, then partly opened his eyes. McFadden now loomed above him. Guy's gaze shifted. The shadows had spilled outside the house into the murky garden. He watched as one coalesced behind the cracked glass of the patio door. 'You…' He gave a little cough. 'You are…'

McFadden came to a stop hardly more than a metre away. 'Yes: you are what?'

Just out of reach, Guy thought, tightening his fingers round the knife's handle. Closer. Come closer, my friend.

'You are…an absolute fucking legend?' McFadden asked. 'Is that what you wanted to tell me?'

'You are…' Guy whispered, tipping his head back.

McFadden nodded. 'Ah, I get it. You want me to

shrink the distance a little more? Maybe, in my eagerness to hear you, bend down? So you can ram that nasty-looking blade in my neck?' He laughed. 'You stupid fuck. I couldn't give a shit what you want to say.' Lifting the gun, he flicked the weapon sideways. The empty clip flew out and bounced across the floor. From his trouser pocket, he produced a fresh one. 'Found this out on the front step, next to Mark, over there. Guess you dropped it earlier? I did pay for two, after all.'

Guy watched helplessly as McFadden rammed it into the handle of the gun. The ceiling lights were now fringed by shimmering rainbows. Tiny crimson comets were pinging off in all directions. A few sparkles were catching in the fractured glass of the patio door. It was beautiful. Really beautiful.

'Fifteen rounds, yeah?' McFadden asked. 'And every single one is going in your face.'

Guy couldn't take his eyes off the glittering shards of crimson. The shadow behind the glass was on the move again. Floating closer. Now Guy could make out what looked like a head and hunched shoulders. The red sparkles danced in the cracks of the glass and Guy understood it was a laser. A laser attached to what was probably a MK18 CQBR. He pushed the knife as far away as possible and smiled up at McFadden. 'You are...'

'Yeah, yeah,' he sneered. 'I am what?'

'Fucking dead.'

'I'm fucking dead? Me?' He snorted with irritation. 'Me? No.' He lifted the Glock and took aim at Guy's face. 'Want to know who's fu –'

Muzzle flash on the other side of the patio doors. Two shots. The glass dropped like a sheet of water as McFadden's temple blew outwards. He took a tiny step to the side, a chunk of his head no longer there. Air was seeping from his lips. Eyes rolling upward, he collapsed in on himself: knees, hip, arm and then what remained of his head connecting with the hard kitchen floor.

The first AFO stepped through the window frame. 'Shots fired! Support on black!' Taking little steps to avoid slipping on the shattered glass, he made straight for McFadden, weapon trained on him. 'Cover. Casualties.'

Three others were directly behind, all in black with cameras mounted on their helmets. Two fanned out either side while the third stayed back.

Here we go, thought Guy. First thing they'll do is create a safe working area. He fought to stay conscious as they began to move about.

'Support, trauma.'

'Support, room off room, on me.'

'Room clear!'

'This one's dead.'

'Same here.'

One came back into view and, using a foot, slid the Glock away from McFadden's body. He then trained his weapon on Guy. 'Show us your hands!'

Guy nodded in understanding. Until cuffed, he represented a threat and would be treated as such. Best just grit your teeth and accept what's coming. He managed to lift his left hand a few inches, but his right arm hung down, totally useless.

The officer skirted him and, leaning down, slid the Mora clear. He then grabbed Guy's right arm and yanked it so he keeled over. Guy felt himself being dragged roughly away from the sofa. Hands then flipped him onto his front. A knee came down on his left shoulder and his left hand was wrenched behind him.

'Right arm. Put it in the small of your back. Now!'

'Can't.'

Fingers grabbed his right wrist and bent it across his other arm. Next thing, cuffs clicked. 'Secure!'

The world lurched again as he was rolled onto his side. Now he could see the officer again. He was on one knee, looking down with a curious expression. 'What the fucking hell has happened here?'

'Upst…' Guy murmured.

'You what?'

He cleared his throat and tried again. 'Upstairs. A girl, locked in a room. Make sure she's OK.'

EPILOGUE

Guy wasn't certain what he became conscious of first. Massed beeps which made him think of an endless fleet of reversing lorries. A man's voice, calling over and over. The smell of antiseptic, sharp as the field hospital out in Afghanistan. Is that where I am? On tour? He felt like his mind was immersed in oil. Thick, glutinous oil. All of him, in fact. Even lifting a finger was too much. He gave up and concentrated on the sounds instead.

The beeps, he came to realise, were right beside him. Not beyond the room, or tent, or vehicle, or wherever he was.

'He moved,' the voice repeated from a point somewhere off to his left. 'I swear, he just moved.'

'What did he do?' a female voice asked.

'Moved his face.'

'Moved his face?' Her voice was drifting round to the right.

I'm on my back, Guy realised. Lying on my back.

'Like he was swallowing and starting to blink.'

'You mean his eyes opened?'

'No, but they nearly did.'

'Mr Haslam? Can you hear me?' Her voice was now directly above him. His throat was dry. So horribly dry, he thought that he must be back in the desert. Something was making his right hand feel too heavy. He wanted to sleep again, so didn't try to speak. Didn't try to do anything.

'It's all fine.' Her voice had moved away once more. 'The monitors will pick up any changes. We'll know from them.'

'Right. It was just seeing –'

'You really don't need to keep looking in on him.' Her voice had grown fainter. 'Is it not the corridor you're meant to be keeping watch on?'

'Yeah, it is.'

Keeping watch? I'm under guard? Is that why my hand…I'm handcuffed to the bed? By focusing all his effort on his upper eyelids, he opened them a crack. A bright sea of white flooded in. Colours and shapes began to slowly emerge. An expanse of pale blue. It was a blanket covering the lower half of the bed. He realised he was partly raised up. Pillows? A man in dark clothing was watching him keenly from an open door. Baseball cap with the word 'Police'. An MK18 across his chest.

'Thought you'd come round.'

Guy passed his tongue across his lips. Like licking a lizard.

'I'll get the nurse back, you –'

Guy turned his head slightly from side to side. The action brought his right hand into view. It was down by his waist, partly suspended in some kind of hoist. No handcuffs. Lots of bandages round a kind of plastic tray beneath his palm. A drip line snaking upward. 'Am I under…'

The man checked behind him, then fully entered the room. 'What was that?'

'…under arrest?'

'Arrest?' The man grinned, a hand draped loosely across his weapon. 'You're not a prisoner. You're a hero.'

Hero?

The officer nodded at the far side of the room. 'Check that lot out, mate.'

Guy forced his head to turn. So bloody exhausted. A big window, its sill a mass of cards and bouquets. Pinks and yellows and purples.

'I'm here for you,' the officer stated. 'To keep you safe.'

Me? Guy couldn't keep his eyes open any longer. Sleep, like floodwaters, rising.

#

'So, Mr Haslam, sure you're good?'

This from a man in a dark blue suit, seated in a chair beside the bed. Guy nodded. The drip was gone from his right hand, though the bandages weren't. He could make out the stump of his little finger. Some of the bouquets had gone, too. Fresh ones had taken their places. He didn't know who was sending them. It was hard to believe he'd been here for almost a week.

'Not that you need to do much talking,' the man said, signalling to a younger colleague who was positioned beyond the end of the bed. The man immediately stepped over to the door and closed it.

Guy turned back to the seated one. Early fifties. His head was bowed as he opened a laptop. Neatly cropped hair, receding at each temple. The remains of a fringe. Few more years, thought Guy, and it will be a little island all on its own. Stranded. The man glanced up and caught Guy looking.

'OK, it'll be easiest if I talk you through how we see things as having played out in the residence of Mr Dale McFadden.'

Guy frowned. Seemed an odd approach. But everything had turned bloody weird since he'd woken up. Random hospital staff glancing through the window of the door like he was the new attraction at a zoo. Their coy smiles and little waves.

'This is based on a combination of eyewitness accounts, forensic analysis and ballistic reports at the scene. In essence, you're very lucky to be alive. Having taken it upon yourself to rescue Zara Tucker, who was in imminent danger of sexual trafficking, you –'

'Hang on,' Guy said. 'Is Zara alright?'

The man held up a hand, palm facing Guy. 'You unwittingly walked in on a violent attempt to overthrow McFadden as head of an organised crime gang.'

'An attempt…sorry, say that again.'

The man's nostrils flexed as he breathed in. 'An attempt to overthrow McFadden as head of an organised crime gang. By the senior member or members of the organisation, possibly in conjunction with a rival gang which calls itself M13.'

'How did you work that out?'

'We know McFadden has recently come into conflict with that gang. There have been a few incidents where territories have been disputed. The rights to sell drugs in certain parts of the city. On the day in question, a Range Rover was stopped by an Armed Response Vehicle on Orchard Lane. Known associates of McFadden's were in the vehicle, along with substantial amounts of cash, drugs, and several weapons. Two of the people were carrying injuries, one had some broken fingers. My guess is it was all part of the ongoing tussle, not that any of them are talking.'

Ads and Luke, thought Guy. The little shitheads who sat back and watched as Jayden was taken to the canal and–

'We also had intelligence from sources in Holland that McFadden had purchased a sidearm,' the man stated. 'The weapon was being brought into this country. A Glock. But we had no specifics of the where and when.'

The gun Jayden was sent to retrieve from the freight terminal. The information that Luke had probably leaked to the rival lot. Guy sat back, seeing himself in McFadden's house. Using the gun to drill the one on the stairs with the shotgun. And the one who'd been behind the door of the kitchen. And McFadden himself. 'This gun being the one I...you know. The one...'

'Yes,' the man cut in. 'The one used by McFadden in what followed.'

McFadden? He didn't fire the weapon. Not once. I did.

'To continue, you arrived at McFadden's property. We believe that, by this point, the challenge to McFadden's authority was already underway. You were observed by a neighbour placing one man who appeared to be unconscious into the recovery position before proceeding through the open front door.'

Guy picked at the bandages of his right hand. 'You do know there's a camera by the front steps? I'm guessing you've seen the footage...'

'Frustratingly, the camera wasn't actually recording at the time in question. All we have is the neighbour's testimony.'

Guy was getting the picture. 'You want me to even add anything to this?'

'I think, at this stage, just listen.'

Guy lifted his left shoulder briefly. 'Fine. I'll let you carry on.'

'After ensuring the unconscious man wasn't at risk, we believe you then went to the first-floor bedroom where Zara had been confined.'

'You didn't tell me if she's OK.'

'No, I didn't. And that's not my remit here. I'll leave that to those more qualified.'

What the hell did that mean? Guy glanced over to the man at the door. Got nothing from him, either. Bastards.

'It was at this point, outside the bedroom, that we think you encountered McFadden. We'll let you provide details of what was said in due course. If, indeed, anything was said before you were caught in the crossfire between McFadden and those trying to remove him.'

'The crossfire?'

'Initially, from the stairs. A shotgun.'

'I see.'

'McFadden then used the Glock he'd purchased to kill Scott Collins on the main stairs before descending to the ground floor. He then advanced into the main living area where Mark Dobson and Tyler Farrington were located.'

'What was I doing?'

'You had been badly wounded when Scott Collins discharged the shotgun from his position on the stairs. Though wounded, you followed McFadden down to that main living area. Perhaps you were concerned for the safety of those other men. It's unclear how things unfolded in the main living area. Who was siding with who. But following the altercation, McFadden was the last man standing. And, when you entered the scene, it made you a witness – one McFadden wasn't prepared to let live. When the Authorised Firearms Officers arrived, McFadden was about to execute you with the Glock he'd been using with great effect up to that point. As a result, the lead AFO opened fire and killed McFadden.'

Guy stared down at his left hand. This was going to be the official account. Or the basis of it, at least. He became aware of the mass of cards and flowers. Seemed it already was. 'But what about the paddle holster I was wearing?'

The man gave a frown before consulting his screen. 'Paramedics didn't report any such thing.'

Removed by the AFOs then. Or just deleted from the record. Along with the ankle sheath for my Mora, no doubt. 'Can I ask what I was wearing, then?'

'Cargo trousers. You'd removed your footwear in the hall.'

The man by the door spoke up. 'Maybe you didn't want to ruin McFadden's carpets?'

His sarcastic grin withered under the strength of the look from the seated man, who turned back to his laptop, tapped a few keys, then scrutinised his screen. 'And, judging from this, I'd say a dark-coloured sweatshirt.'

So, Guy thought, no tactical vest. No plastic ties. No stunnies. All of it had ceased to exist. 'And you think this...version of what went on in there is going to wash?' Guy asked in a low voice.

'Tell me this, who's going to challenge it? They're all dead, Mr Haslam.' The man sat back. 'What you did was completely reckless. Bloody stupid, really.' He closed his screen. 'But Dale McFadden has been a pain in our arse for years. And I mean years. The prick has even sued us – and succeeded. What happened in his house was shocking, terrible and,' he met Guy's stare with the faintest of smiles, 'a cause for much celebration. You've been quite the toast of after-works drinks this past week.'

Guy glanced at the other man, who surreptitiously raised a thumb.

'Your statement will be taken soon enough.' The man beside the bed was now getting to his feet. 'This was just an informal appointment. To bring you up to speed, as it were. Is everything clear?'

'Everything's clear,' Guy said. 'Just give me what's needed and I'll sign it.' As the man stepped to the side, Guy noticed a particular card at the end of the windowsill: on the front of it was a silhouette of a Royal Marine with a flag flying from the antennae of the radio mounted on his back. It was based on the famous Yomper photograph from the Falklands War.

'Excuse me: is there anything written in that card? The one with the soldier on the front.'

'This one?' the man asked, picking it up.

Guy nodded, trying to keep the surge of emotions from showing on his face.

'Not much,' he said with a slight frown. 'Just: "Been busy, then? Hope you're healing well. The Boys."'

Guy sat back. His old unit. They'd sent him a card.

'Makes sense to you, does it?' the man asked.

'It does,' Guy said with a smile. 'Now, you've fobbed

me off twice. What the fuck's happened to Zara?'

'You mean the girl who was being held against her will in the upstairs room at McFadden's property?'

'Whatever, is she OK?'

'She's fine. Being cared for.'

He wanted to ask about Jayden. Did they recover his body? Had the ones in the Range Rover revealed where he'd been dumped? Why did no one seem to give a shit?

'As I indicated earlier, there's someone far more qualified to take you through all that. In fact, she's outside. Shall we show her in?'

Guy glanced at the closed door. 'Who is she?'

'Not sure.' He turned to his colleague. 'Justin, you know?'

He shook his head. 'Social services, I guess.'

'Yeah,' Guy said. 'Tell her to come in.'

'Will do.' The man hesitated before stepping back to the side of the bed. 'And Guy? Now we've covered what needed to be covered, I just wanted to say, well played. Well fucking played.' He held his right hand out.

Guy tried to lift his own heavily bandaged hand. 'OK if I use my left?' he asked, reaching across with it.

'Oh, of course. Yes.' Their hands clasped awkwardly above Guy's chest. 'OK, we'll be on our way. We won't be speaking again. Others will take things from here.'

'See you then,' said Guy, watching as they filed from the room. Suits. He let his head fall back against the pillows. Never even told me their names. His eyes were drawn to the ranks of cards. What a crazy situation. Seems I'm the good guy here.

'Hello?'

His head immediately turned at the sound of her voice. Amy. Standing in the open doorway with an uncertain look on her face.

\#

'How are you? Can I come in?'

She was in jeans and a puffer jacket. Day off, then. Guy gestured at the chair. 'Please.'

After giving a cautious nod, she rounded the bed, eyes never leaving his. He tried to read what she was thinking. How much she knew. Was she furious? Appalled? Disgusted? Those bright blue eyes kept probing about his face. Shame suddenly flooded him and he had to lower his gaze. 'I really messed things up. I'm so sorry.'

She settled lightly on the seat and rested a hand on his forearm. 'You don't need to apologise.'

'No, I do.' He had to sniff back the tears. 'Zara. How...how is she?'

'She's fine, Guy. She's fine.'

Glancing up, he could see a smile on her face. Pity? Sympathy? He couldn't tell. 'Really?'

'Really.'

'She's not back in that bloody tower?'

'No. Emergency foster care. A lovely couple who live in Whaley Bridge.'

Near to Haverdale, thought Guy. Edge of the Peak District. 'And she's doing OK?'

'She is.'

'Amy, I don't know what you've heard. But in that house? In McFadden's house? It's not how they're making it out to be.' He nodded at the windowsill. 'Don't believe the cards over there. I went –'

'Stop,' Amy said. 'It doesn't matter. I don't want to know. She's safe, Guy. And she's safe because of you.'

He thought of Jayden and the tears came again. This time he couldn't stop them. 'It was my fault, Amy. Jayden is my fault. They thought – McFadden's lot – that I'd recruited him. They thought he –'

'Guy –'

He shook his head, unable to look at her. 'You need to hear this. They killed him because of me.' A sob rocked him against the pillows. He wanted to slide down and pull the covers over his head.

'Guy, listen.'

He felt her hand on his upper arm. 'The ones who were here just now, they didn't even care. Not even –'

'Guy.' Her voice was firmer. Enough to stop him speaking. 'Did they not say? They didn't tell you?'

'Tell me what? They wouldn't say anything.'

'Can you look at me, Guy?'

He wiped at his eyes and cheeks then, after taking a deep breath, lifted his chin. She was leaning forward and looking into his eyes. And she was…smiling again. Smiling? Nothing, he thought, makes sense anymore.

'Jayden,' she announced quietly. 'Jayden – he isn't dead.'

The periphery of his vision faded out and her face was all he could see. Only her face. 'What?' He watched her lips, needing to see if the words were really coming out.

'He isn't dead, Guy. He got away.'

'I don't understand.'

'After they drove him out to Woods End. A fisherman was walking past. They had to leave the bag…listen, why don't you ask him?'

'Ask him?'

She nodded. 'He's here. If you feel OK to –'

'He's here?' He looked towards the open door. Wanting to laugh. Nearly choking. 'Here? In the hospital?'

Amy called out softly. 'Jayden?'

Out in the corridor, a shadow moved across the floor. And then he appeared. Standing there. Just standing there with that cocky grin.

'You all right, Mr Nothing-Man?'

'Jayden.' The tears got worse. 'Fuck's sake,' he said, wiping furiously with the sleeve of his hospital pyjamas. 'Can't stop crying here. Jayden?'

'Yup, it's me.'

'But they said…I don't…'

'I picked the padlock,' he announced, approaching the bed. 'Of the big hold-all they zipped me up in. While they were talking to the fisherman. So I climbed out and did one.'

That bag, thought Guy. The one they'd set fire to in the garden. Guy found himself laughing. 'You always were good at locks.'

Jayden perched on the end of the bed, looking a little embarrassed.

'I can vouch for that,' Amy said with a smile.

Jayden's eyes roved round the room. 'You've not had the cakes yet!' He was back on his feet.

Guy marvelled at the sight of him as he crossed over to the window and reached for something beside an especially large bouquet. I can't believe this. I cannot believe this.

'Can I have one or what?'

Guy spotted the logo on the side of the bag Jayden was holding up. Martyna's bakery. 'When did that get here?'

'Earlier,' Amy said. 'A lady and her little girl. But you were asleep. A nurse brought them through.'

'So can I?' Jayden asked.

'Of course. What are they?'

Jayden peered into the bag. 'Yellow things. Blobby.'

'Carpathian custard cakes. They're delicious. Apparently. Not actually had one yet.'

He started reaching into the bag. 'Weird.'

'What's weird?'

Jayden withdrew his hand. There was a tenner in his fingers. Guy looked up at the ceiling. 'She got me back.'

'What do you mean?' Amy asked.

'Doesn't matter,' Guy said, shaking his head. 'I'll tell you another time.'

Jayden put the bag on the end of the bed and placed the tenner beside it. There was now a mischievous look in his eyes. 'Them cakes: probably be a lot better with a drink, wouldn't they? From the machines.'

Amy sighed theatrically as she took out her purse. 'Another hot chocolate, is it?'

'Sound. And whatever you two want.'

'Guy?' Amy asked.

He snorted with amusement. 'A tea sounds great, thanks.'

'And two teas, then.' She poured some changed into Jayden's cupped palm.

'Back in no time,' he said, scooting out the door.

Amy watched him go. 'Quite something, isn't he?'

'That he certainly is,' Guy said. 'Is he really handling it so well? The fact they were going to kill him?'

She was quiet for a moment, eyes still on the doorway. 'I think so. I mean, the whole gang thing. He's seen right through that now. He's having counselling, but he's a bit bemused by it. Just chatting shit about stuff, I quote.'

Guy nodded. 'Figures.'

'He's mentioned a place you told him about. And a job?'

'He has?'

'Yes – he's interested. He's even been talking to Zara about the two of them moving. I'm sensing a plan on your part?'

'It's only something I floated past him.'

'Well, he's eighteen next month. Free to make his own decisions. I imagine, if Zara wanted to go with him, social services would do their best to keep them together.'

'I hope so, I really do.'

He felt a light pressure on his bandaged hand and looked down to see her fingertips moving across the material.

'And you? How is everything with you?' she asked gently.

He brought his left hand over and placed it on hers. Her hand immediately flipped over and their fingers sought each other out. The touch of her skin felt so good. He looked up into her eyes and smiled.

THE END

KILLING THE BEASTS – FIRST NOVEL IN THE DI JOHN SPICER SERIES

The Commonwealth Games have come to Manchester and the city is buzzing.

Caught up in the commercial feeding frenzy is Tom Benwell, an advertising executive. But the pressure is getting to Tom - too many deals to make and lies to tell. Meanwhile his friend, DI Jon Spicer, is on the fast track, showing a love for the job that borders on obsession, according to his girlfriend, Alice.

Then, in the aftermath of the Games, a string of brutal murders shatters the city's newfound spirit. Spicer gets the case. Each victim has been murdered in the same bizarre and grotesque manner, yet the lack of motive leaves the police utterly baffled.

With the race on to catch the killer, both men find themselves caught up in a nightmare where the most innocent action can cost the highest price.

KILLING THE BEASTS

PROLOGUE

Leaning forward on the sofa, she gratefully accepted the stick of gum, unwrapped it and then folded it into her mouth. 'Thanks,' she said breathlessly, looking expectantly at her visitor and eagerly chewing.

'My pleasure,' came the reply from the smartly dressed man sitting opposite her. They continued looking at each other for a moment longer. 'Now, if you could just get . . .'

'Oh God, yes, sorry! It's upstairs.' She jumped to her feet. 'I'm all excited. Sorry.'

He smiled. 'No problem.'

She almost skipped across the room, then ran up the stairs. While she was gone the man stood up, walked over to her living room window and checked the street outside. By the time she returned he was sitting down once again.

'Here,' she said, handing him a small booklet.

'Great.' He looked up at her with a slightly embarrassed expression. 'Do you mind if I have a cup of tea before we get started?'

'Oh!' She jumped up again, her dressing gown falling slightly open to reveal a flash of upper thigh. 'I'm so rude. Sorry. Milk? Sugar?'

'Milk and two sugars, thanks.'

Flustered, she paced quickly down the short corridor to the kitchen, bare feet slapping against the lino as she crossed the room. She plucked two mugs from the dirty crockery piled up in the sink and quickly washed them out. As she waited for the kettle to boil she jigged from foot to foot, occasionally taking a deep breath and running her hands through her spiky blonde hair.

A few minutes later she walked back in, a red flush now evident on her throat and cheeks. 'Here you go.' She placed a mug decorated with a cartoon snail on the low table in front of the man's knees. Now furiously chewing on the gum, she went to sit down again but, on impulse, veered towards the hi-fi system in the corner and turned up the music.

'God, I feel like I could dance,' she said urgently, blowing her breath out and running her fingers through her hair once again. 'Is it hot in here? Are you hot?'

The man looked around the room as if heat was a visible thing. 'No,' he replied with a little shake of his head.

'I feel hot,' she said, placing her mug on the table, then waving one hand a little too energetically at her cheek and pulling distractedly at the neck of her dressing gown. The man kept his head lowered, pretending to search for a pen in his jacket pocket.

The girl went to sit down, stumbling against the leg of the coffee table. 'Whoops!' she said with a strange giggle, though panic was beginning to show in her eyes. 'I . . . I'm dizzy.'

The room had begun to shift in and out of focus and her breath wouldn't come properly. She leaned forward and tried to steady herself by putting one hand on the arm of the sofa.

The man watched impassively.

Now visibly distressed, she attempted a half turn to sit down, but her coordination was going and she missed the sofa, crashing onto the carpet. As she lay on her back, her eyes rolled up into her head and then closed completely.

The man calmly got to his feet and put his briefcase on the table. After entering the combination for the lock, he opened it up and removed a long pair of stainless-steel pincers from inside.

CHAPTER 1

30 October 2002

Jon Spicer was driving back to the station when he heard the Community Support Officer's call for help on his police radio. The CSO said he was outside a house in which a corpse had just been discovered. He said the dead girl's mother was still inside, refusing to leave her daughter's body. He went on to explain to the operator that his patrol partner was in the kitchen, trying to comfort her. His voice was high and panicky.

When the address in Berrybridge Road was read out Jon realized he was just a few streets away. Telling the operator he would attend the scene, Jon turned off the main road, cut down a side street and pulled up outside the house.

As he got out of his car and straightened his tie, the sight of a very young and nervous-looking officer confronted him. The officer was trying to reason with an irate woman, who stood with one hand rocking a buggy, stout legs planted firmly apart. As the officer repeated that she wasn't allowed past, the red-faced toddler in the buggy leaned back, shut its eyes and started to bawl.

'You can't stop me getting in my own sodding house,' the woman said, holding another chocolate button in front of the angry infant's face. 'The kid wants his lunch – you can hear, can't you?' In an attempt to keep the cold autumnal breeze off him, she began tucking the tattered blanket around his legs. 'It's all right, Liam.'

Crafty little shit, thought Jon Spicer, noticing how he immediately stopped crying when the button appeared. If his eyes were shut in genuine distress, he wouldn't have known the button was there. Jon had accepted long ago that deviousness was as much a part of human make-up as kindness or joy. What always amazed him was how early people appeared to learn the process of manipulation.

'Sorry madam, we won't be much longer.' Jon intervened, a placatory tone in his voice. Hoping that, if he and Alice had the baby they were trying for, it didn't turn out like that one, he guided the CSO out of earshot. 'Hello. My name's Jon Spicer.'

The young officer glanced at Jon's warrant card, saw his rank, and replied, 'CSO Whyte and I'm glad to see you, sir.'

'You said on the radio that you heard wailing noises from inside the house. Then what?'

He took out his notebook as if in court. 'Yes, that was at 9.55 a.m. We proceeded up the driveway to the front door, which we found to be ajar. On receiving no response from the person in distress within the property, we proceeded inside and found a middle-aged woman sitting on the floor of the living room hugging a deceased woman of around twenty. My patrol partner, CSO Payne, entered the room and crouched down to check for a pulse. At that point she noticed thick white matter at the back of the deceased woman's mouth.' He looked up and breaking from his notes, said, 'It was hanging open you see, though I didn't catch sight of it myself. When we separated the mother from the body, the dead girl's head lay back on the carpet and I couldn't see in.'

Jon nodded. 'So you called for assistance. And no one has been in there except you and your patrol partner?'

'Yes, that's correct, sir.'

'And this woman has confirmed the deceased is her daughter and that her daughter lives in the house?'

'Yes.'

'And no one else lives there?'

'That's correct.'

'OK, good work. Well done.'

A smile broke out momentarily across the young man's face. Then, remembering the gravity of the situation, he reorganized his features into an expression of appropriate seriousness.

The toddler started its bawling once again. His mum gave in and shoved the entire packet of chocolate buttons into his hands. The crying immediately stopped and Jon thought: another victory to the little people. 'So, we've just got to keep Lucifer and his mum, Mrs Beelzebub, at bay for a bit longer,' he murmured, turning back to the woman.

'OK, madam. I'm afraid, because you share a driveway with your neighbour's house – and she's died in what could be suspicious circumstances – I'm having to declare the driveway and front gardens a designated crime scene. Have you a friend you could stay with just while we search this area in front of the house?'

'Pissing hell,' said the woman, pulling a mobile from the pocket of her padded jacket and dialling a number. 'Janine? It's me, Sue. That little blonde ravehead next door won't be keeping me awake with any more loud music. She's turned up dead and the police won't let me up the driveway and into my own frigging house. Can I come round for a cuppa and to give our Liam his lunch? Cheers.'

'Thanks very much, madam,' Jon said, making a mental

note of the ravehead description. 'If I can have your number we'll call as soon as access is possible.'

He jotted it down and she trundled moodily off up the road, the buggy's wheels picking up bits of sodden brown leaves littering the street.

'Right,' said Jon, looking at the house. 'Have you checked the rest of the property?'

'No,' said CSO Whyte, looking alarmed that he'd failed in his duty.

'That's fine,' said Jon. But, having been caught by surprise on a recent murder investigation when the offender had still been hiding in the upstairs of the house, Jon was taking no chances. 'What's your patrol partner's name again?'

'CSO Margaret Payne. She's comforting the girl's mother in the kitchen.'

Jon trod carefully across the patchy lawn, eyes on the driveway for any suspicious objects. When he reached the front doorstep he called over his shoulder, 'CSO Whyte, only people with direct permission from me are allowed past, understood?'

'Yes sir,' he replied, checking down the street as if there was a danger of being charged by a curious crowd.

Pushing from his mind the information he had been given by the officer, Jon turned his attention to the front door. He saw that there were no signs of a forced entry. He stepped into the hallway, keeping his feet as close to the skirting board as possible. Immediately he was struck by an odd smell – sharp and slightly fruity. For some reason he was reminded of DIY superstores. As he made his way along the hall he examined the carpet for anything unusual. Reaching the doorway to the front room, he glanced in. The body of a young white female with bleached spiky hair lay partially on its side by the coffee table. Her pale pink dressing gown was crumpled up around her legs and had partly fallen open at the front, revealing her left breast. He didn't know if it was the lack of obvious injuries, but she didn't look like she was dead. Unconscious, perhaps, but not dead.

He carried on into the kitchen where CSO Payne was sitting, holding the mother's hand across the table. Aware that a six-foot-four stranger with a beaten-up face suddenly stepping into the room could prove unsettling for both women, Jon gently coughed before quietly announcing, 'Hello, my name is Jon Spicer. I'm a detective with Greater Manchester Police.'

The woman lowered a damp handkerchief and looked up at him. Her face had that emptiness which shock and grief instils, but her eyes were alert. He felt them flickering over his face, settling for a second on the lump in the bridge of his nose, which had been broken in a rugby match.

'Could I ask your name, please?' he continued.

'Diane Mather,' she whispered, reaching out and taking a sip of tea from a mug with a snail on it.

'OK, Diane,' said Jon, walking round the table and checking the back door. A bolt was slid across the top and a key was in the lock. 'Has anyone touched this door?' he asked them both.

CSO Payne answered no and he looked at Diane, who also shook her head.

'And have you been in any other parts of the house apart from the hallway, here and the front room?'

'No.' Now she was watching him a little more closely.

Jon walked from the kitchen. Carefully he climbed the stairs, pausing when his head was level with the landing to check where the doors were. The first led into a little bathroom: no one behind the shower curtain. The next was the spare room, only just big enough for a clothes horse that was adorned with vest tops, socks and knickers. The final room was the main bedroom, fairly tidy except for the middle drawer of the chest in the corner. It hung half open, and a few photo albums and booklets lay haphazardly on the corner of the bed, as if dumped there in a hurry. Jon checked under the bed and in the wardrobe. Satisfied no one else was in the house, he walked over to the bedside table and looked in the ashtray. Amongst the Marlboro Light cigarette butts were a few crumpled bits of foil, dried brown crusts on one side. A plastic tube lay next to the small alarm clock.

Jon shook his head. From his earliest days as a uniformed officer, he had watched as more and more drugs crept into Manchester. Now, along with the alcohol riots on Friday and Saturday nights, they were dealing with the devastating effects that crack, heroin, speed and God knew what else were having on people's lives.

At the window he looked down to the road below and saw the CSOs' supervisor had arrived. He went back down the stairs and headed outside.

'Sergeant Evans,' the older man said, shaking Jon's hand over the police tape now cordoning off the driveway and front garden.

'DI Spicer, MISU. I was just passing when I heard the radio call.'

The sergeant nodded. 'So, we have a body inside?'

'Yup,' Jon replied. 'Apparently her throat is blocked with a load of white stuff.' Jon looked at CSO Whyte. 'Could it not have been saliva? An allergic reaction or something?'

The officer looked at him as if he had asked a rhetorical question and was about to supply the answer.

Sergeant Evans then dropped a question into the silence. 'When CSO Payne checked for a pulse, did she say how cold the body felt?'

CSO Whyte thought for a second. 'No. She was trying to get the mother away from the body when she spotted the white stuff . . .' Abruptly, he stopped talking.

'What?' Jon prompted.

The officer stumbled slightly with his words. 'She didn't actually check for a pulse. But the mum – she kept on saying, "She's dead. She's dead." So we just sort of assumed—'

'Jesus Christ,' said Jon. He went to his car, grabbed a pair of latex gloves from inside and hurried back into the house. In the hallway he spotted a pile of women's magazines by the telephone. One by one he laid them across the living room floor, creating a series of stepping stones that enabled him to get to the girl without treading on the carpet.

As he got closer to her, he noticed that the strange smell was getting stronger. As he'd noted before, the dressing gown was crumpled, but he couldn't tell whether she had been assaulted, dragged there, or the disturbance to her clothing was from where her mother had been hugging her.

He crouched down and checked for a pulse. The skin was cold to the touch. He let out a sigh, then examined the rest of her more closely.

No defence wounds to her forearms or hands, no obvious sign of any injury at all. He leaned in for a closer look at her fingers. Apart from being bluish in colour, the nails were fine – no debris under them or damage caused by a struggle.

Next he looked at her face. Her eyes were shut, a few small red dots around them. Mouth slightly open, lips also a faint blue. No blood, saliva or vomit on her lips. No bruising to her throat. Getting up he made his way back across the magazines and into the kitchen. 'CSO Payne,' he said, pointing to her utility belt, 'could I borrow your torch, please?'

In the front room he switched it on and directed the beam into the girl's mouth. Peering in, he saw the back of her throat was completely clogged with something white and viscous. The substance had completely blocked her airways. Death by suffocation? Some sort of lung purge or bizarre vomit?

He bent forward so his head was just above the carpet.

Holding the torch to one side he swept the beam backwards and forwards across the floor, looking to see if the light picked out any tiny fragments lying on the carpet. Nothing apart from fragments of cigarette ash and an old chewing gum wrapper. Standing up, he noted the bin in the corner was full of crushed cans, empty cigarette packets, bits of cigarette paper and other pieces of rubbish. Next to it were a couple of empty three-litre cider bottles.

Back in the kitchen he sat down and quietly asked the mother, 'Do you know what time it was when you discovered your daughter?'

'About quarter to ten,' she replied shakily, stubbing a cigarette out in the full ashtray.

'And you found her in the front room?'

She nodded once.

'On the floor?'

'Yes, lying on her back with her arms out by her sides.'

'How did you get into the house?'

'I have a key. We were going shopping together in town.'

'Was the door locked when you arrived?'

Another nod.

Keeping eye contact, Jon continued. 'OK, Mrs Mather, it's best you go now and let us take over. Margaret here will accompany you down to the station. We'll need to take a statement. Is that OK with you?'

'Yes.' Then she whispered beseechingly, 'What happened to my little girl?'

'We'll find out, Mrs Mather. We'll find out,' Jon said, a note of firmness now in his voice.

As they stood, CSO Payne asked, 'Can we call anyone to meet you at the station?'

She shook her head and Jon wondered if it was an unwillingness to share with anyone else what had happened to her daughter.

He led the way back towards the front door, CSO Payne with her arm round the mother's shoulders. He paused in the doorway to the living room, subtly trying to discourage any further contact. 'We'll be as fast as we can, Mrs Mather. You'll have your daughter back as quickly as possible.' No mention of the coming autopsy, the gutting of her corpse, the sifting-through of her stomach contents.

At the front step he instructed CSO Payne to keep to the grass. Once the two women were back on the street he called out to the young policewoman, 'Oh, your torch. I've left it in the kitchen.'

She walked back across the grass and into the house. Jon was waiting for her. 'Did you touch anything in here?' he asked, handing it back to her.

'I don't think so. We got the mum out of the front room as quickly as we could. I brought her in here and made her a cup of tea . . .' She pointed to the draining board at the side of the sink.

Jon saw that she wasn't pointing at the sink full of dirty cups and glasses. 'Where did you find the mug?'

'Just there, sir, washed up on the draining board. Next to that other one.'

'Washed up? You mean still wet?'

'Yes, I dried it with the tea towel.'

Jon ran his fingers through his cropped brown hair in a gesture of disappointment. 'Go on.'

Aware that she was now being questioned, the officer went on more carefully. 'She smoked three or four cigarettes. Stubbed them out in the ashtray on the table.'

'Yeah, they were Lambert & Butler.' Jon looked into the ashtray and said almost to himself, 'The daughter smoked Marlboro Lights, I think. There's Silk Cut and Benson & Hedges in there, too.' The urge to light up suddenly hit him. He turned away from the ashtray and its stale smell that should have been so unpleasant. 'OK, get her to the station; we'll need her fingerprints, a DNA swab and samples from her clothes. Her fibres will be all over the body.'

'So it's definitely suspicious then, sir?' She sounded

thrilled. 'I thought she might have had a heart attack or something.'

'Don't get too excited – you're in for a bollocking from your sergeant out there. You forgot to check for a pulse. But yeah, I'd say it looks dodgy. The neighbour described her as a ravehead and there are signs of her smoking heroin in the bedroom. And whatever that stuff is blocking her throat, it doesn't look or smell like puke to me.'

As soon as he was alone, Jon went back into the kitchen. Balanced on top of the soiled glasses and cups in the sink was a bowl and spoon, fragments of bran flakes clinging to the surfaces. If the cups and glasses were left over from the night before, and the bowl was from breakfast, why were there just two freshly washed-up cups on the draining board? Had someone else been here that morning? Someone she had offered to make a drink for?

He pulled his phone out and called his base. 'Detective Chief Inspector McCloughlin, please. It's Detective Inspector Spicer.'

After a few moments his senior officer came on the line. 'DI Spicer, I hear you were the first plain clothes officer at the scene of a suspicious death. What have you got?'

'Young female, appears to have choked to death on something. We'll need a post-mortem to ascertain what. My guess is that, if we have a killer, he came in and went out by the front door. It appears the person was let in, so she probably knew them. There's certainly no sign of forced entry or any kind of struggle.'

'So you don't think the case will turn into a runner?'

'I doubt it. My guess is it will be the usual – a friend or family member. I think it should be fairly clear-cut.'

'Right, how do you want to play it?'

'Well, until we've established cause of death, there's no point panicking and calling the whole circus out. We need to photograph her and get a pathologist down to pronounce her, so we can get the body to Tameside

General for an autopsy. The scene is preserved here, so I'll call in a crime scene manager to make sure it stays that way. Then, if cause of death turns out to be suspicious, we can start worrying about calling in a SOCO and the full forensics rigmarole.'

'Sounds like a good way of playing it. Which other cases are you working on?'

'My main one is the gang hooking car keys through people's letter boxes.'

'Operation Fisherman?' asked McCloughlin. 'How many officers are assigned to it?'

'Seven, including me.'

There was a pause as McCloughlin mentally divided up manpower and caseloads.

Jon knew his senior officer was deciding whether to move him to the murder investigation. Before he could decide, Jon said, 'I'd really like to remain on Operation Fisherman, if only in a minor role, while this murder investigation is ongoing.'

'Your partner's still off with his back problem, isn't he?'

'Yeah,' Jon replied.

'Listen. It's time you led a murder investigation yourself. This one seems like it should be quite straightforward. I think it'll be a good one for you to cut your teeth on.'

'You're making me Senior Investigating Officer?'

'You've got it. Just keep me up to speed on everything.'

'And Operation Fisherman?'

'They can do without you while you get this one wrapped up.'

A mixture of excitement and disappointment ran through him. The gang stealing high-performance cars had taken up so much of his time over the last few months, but now he had his own murder case. 'Will do, boss,' Jon replied.

Next he called his base. 'Hello, Detective Inspector Jon Spicer here. We need a pathologist, a photographer and a

CSM at Fifteen Berrybridge Road, Hyde. Who's available for scene management?'

'Nikki Kingston is on duty,' said the duty officer.

Jon immediately smiled — the case had just become a whole lot more attractive. 'Send her down, please,' said Jon, flipping his phone shut and popping a stick of chewing gum in his mouth.

The pathologist and photographer arrived less than fifteen minutes later. While they were still clambering into their white suits, Nikki's car pulled up. She climbed out and went straight round to the boot, opened it up and put on a large red and black jacket that looked like it had been designed for scaling Everest in. As she walked over, the bulky garment only emphasized how petite she was and Jon found himself wanting to scoop her up and hug her.

Looking Jon up and down she said, 'You not freezing your nuts off in that suit?'

Jon grinned. 'Good to see you, Nikki.'

She was already looking at the house. 'So come on then: scores on the doors, please.'

'OK, the two CSOs over there are passing the house on a foot patrol when they hear a commotion inside. They go in to find what turns out to be the victim's mother in the front room hugging the body. One officer retires immediately to call for supervision; the other officer manages to get the mum away from the daughter and into the kitchen. I arrive, check over the rest of the property . . .'

Nikki interrupted. 'So you've been round the rest of the house?'

Jon nodded.

'OK,' said Nikki. 'I'll probably need a scraping from your suit for fibre analysis at some point.'

'No problem,' Jon replied. 'On realizing the body hadn't been checked for a pulse, I re-entered the house and, using a load of magazines for footplates, got to the body. Obviously she was dead.'

Nikki raised her eyebrows. 'Magazines for footplates? Nice bit of improvisation.'

Jon smiled briefly. 'One other thing. There's a cup on the draining board next to the sink and another on the kitchen table with a kiddy-style picture of a snail on it. They're worth bagging up as potential evidence – someone was drinking out of them recently. Problem is the CSO made a brew for the mum in the one with the snail on the side.'

Nikki shook her head. 'We'll be lucky to get anything off that.'

At that moment the ambulance pulled up, so Jon moved his car to allow it to reverse into the mouth of the driveway.

The pathologist and photographer approached the house, pausing on the front doorstep to put on white overshoes, caps and face masks. Laying rubber footplates out before him, the pathologist led the way inside. Almost immediately the front room was filled by white flashes as the photographer went about his work. Ten minutes later the pathologist reappeared in the doorway and beckoned the ambulance men in with the stretcher. Stepping carefully on the footplates, they disappeared into the property.

Nikki and Jon moved round the side of the vehicle, out of sight of the small crowd of onlookers who had now gathered.

'How's giving up going, then?' asked Nikki, still looking towards the house.

He thrust his hands into his pockets as if to stop them scrabbling around for a cigarette. 'Doesn't get much easier. I haven't had one since before the Commonwealth Games, though.'

'That's bloody good. How long is that – three months or so?'

'Yeah, about that. Did you find it a nightmare for this long?'

'Did? Still do. Though on fewer and fewer occasions. Pubs are the place to avoid for me. That and meetings about the divorce with my solicitor.'

'Your ex is still acting the prick, then?'

'Oh yes, he's really honing that skill of his nowadays.'

Jon's lips tightened in sympathy and he said, 'Well, just thank God no kids are involved, I suppose.'

Nikki let out an incredulous laugh. 'There's no way that's ever going to happen. I've seen too many friends go on Prozac immediately after they give birth. Motherhood? No bloody thank you. Anyway.' She clapped her hands together softly to end that part of the conversation. 'You're still using chewing gum. Is that to fight your cigarette cravings or to make sure your breath smells sweet for me?' Impishly, she glanced up at him.

Enjoying the game, Jon caught her eye then looked skywards, only to see Alice's face in the clouds above him. Quickly he looked down and said with a smile, 'In your dreams, Nikki – you know I'm way out of your league.'

'Cheeky bastard.' She laughed, and went to jab him in the ribs.

Jon caught her fist just as the ambulance men reappeared with the body, the pathologist following along behind. Clicking instantly back into professional mode, Nikki pulled her hand free and walked back round the ambulance. Once the body was safely inside, she got the ambulance men to sign their names in the log book for people who had entered the crime scene. Meanwhile Jon had stepped over to the pathologist. 'Any ideas?'

He pulled off his face mask and started removing the white shoe covers. 'Well, I'd say death occurred due to suffocation. All the signs are there: bluish lips, ears and nails, petechiae – burst capillaries around the eyes and on the eyeballs themselves.'

'And the white stuff blocking her airway?'

'It's not any sort of secretion I've seen. I'd say she's had the stuff pumped down her throat somehow, but until

I've seen in her lungs and stomach, I can't say for sure.'

'Can you start the autopsy?'

'Yes, that's fine. Of course, I'll hand over to the home office pathologist as soon as I can confirm it wasn't natural causes.'

'OK – can one of you call me as soon as you know?' said Jon, handing him a card.

He turned to Nikki. 'I need to get away and interview the mum. Can we completely seal the house until the autopsy result is confirmed? If it's suspicious you can arrange for forensics to come over.'

In a voice kept low so none of the onlookers could hear, she said, 'Tighter than a camel's arse in a sandstorm.'

Jon winked in reply and walked over to his car.

#

After a bit of persuasion Mrs Mather had accepted the fact that her fingerprints, a swab from the inside of her cheek for DNA testing and combings from her clothes for fibre analysis were needed. After that, she answered Jon's questions about her daughter, Polly.

Twenty-two years old, single, keen on music and clubbing, worked in the Virgin Megastore on Market Street. As was often the case with people hovering at the edge of an industry, she had ambitions for a more central role. In Polly's case she was lead vocalist of a band, The Soup.

The beer cans and full ashtrays in Polly's front room were the result of the band having been round at her house the night before. Because he had recently been her daughter's boyfriend, Mrs Mather had a phone number for the band's bass player, Phil Wainwright. She asserted that the split had been amicable – the result of Polly wanting to travel round the world while he wanted to concentrate on gigging and trying to find a record deal.

Shortly after Jon had arranged for a patrol car to take her home, his mobile went. It was the home office pathologist. The autopsy had been handed over to him because there were only small amounts of the white substance in the oesophagus and trachea, and none in the lungs or stomach. This meant it had definitely been introduced from the outside, probably while she was still alive. What was confusing the pathologist was how it could have got there. He explained to Jon that for the cough reflex not to function, a person would have to be in a coma or under very heavy sedation. In his opinion this was the case – the substance had formed a neat plug at the back of the girl's throat with almost no evidence of her choking and spluttering. Therefore, with the victim unconscious at the time of the substance being introduced, a third party had to be involved.

'So we'll need a toxicology report then?'

'Yes. If she was subdued with a hospital anaesthetic – propofol or maybe sodium thiopentone – it should be present in her blood in the form of metabolites, but I haven't found any marks so far to suggest she's been injected. Of course, in order to find evidence of narcotics, a full toxicology analysis will be needed. We haven't got the necessary facilities here.'

'Right – can you prepare a blood sample for me? I'll get it sent down to the forensic science lab at Chepstow.'

Next he called DCI McCloughlin. 'Boss? It looks like murder.'

'OK, open an incident room. Ring round and see which stations have any rooms available and I'll start getting a team together for you.'

'Will do.'

After finding a room at the divisional headquarters in Ashton, Jon decided to give Phil Wainwright a ring. As soon as the phone was answered Jon could hear loud talking and music in the background. A second later a gruff voice said, 'Hello?' It was spoken loudly, as if the person was anticipating not being able to hear very well.

'Is that Phil Wainwright?'

'Yeah! Who's this?'

'Detective Inspector Jon Spicer, Greater Manchester Police.'

'Oh, hang on.' The voice disappeared and Jon could hear only background noise until a door shutting caused it to suddenly grow fainter. 'Sorry, you caught me behind the bar. This is about Polly?'

Emotion made the last syllable wobble and Jon thought, he knows already. 'Yes.'

'I thought it would be. Her mum rang me an hour or so ago. You're going to question me, aren't you?'

'Not formally, no. But I need to talk with everyone who was at her house last night. Where are you now, Phil?'

'Peveril of the Peak. I'm a barman here.'

'Nice boozer. Any chance of chatting to you?'

'Well, the evening rush hasn't started yet, if you can get over here.'

'I'll see you in a bit.'

It was dusk as he crossed over the junction for the M60 ring road, a steady stream of cars gliding by beneath him. Following the signs for Aldwinians Rugby Club, he entered Droylsden. The perfectly straight road stretched far off into the distance, regularly interspersed by traffic lights shining red, amber or green. Flanking each side of the road was an endless terrace of the chunky red-brick houses with grey lintels that made up so much of Manchester's Victorian estates.

Abruptly the built-up area came to an end and he emerged into the open space of Sportcity, Manchester City Football Club's new stadium dominating the facilities around it. Then he was past and the road dipped, only to start rising upwards to dark mills that loomed forlorn and empty, brickwork crumbling and broken windows gaping in silent howls. Reaching the crest of the slope he could see beyond them to where the lights of the city centre twinkled, Portland Tower and the CIS building clearly visible. Jon felt an itch of adrenaline as he looked at the city and contemplated all that was happening in its depths.

Dating from the mid-1800s and one of Manchester city centre's proper pubs, Peveril of the Peak was a strangely shaped wedge of a building. Clad in green glazed bricks and tucked away on a little triangular concrete island, it was closed in on all sides by towering office buildings and apartment blocks. Jon parked by some recently completed flats and slipped through the side door of the pub. The bar was in the centre, various rooms leading off to the sides. He looked round the smoke-filled interior, surprised by the lack of people: his mobile phone had made it sound like the place was packed. Instead just a few students and real ale types were dotted about. Jon glanced over the three bar staff, eyes settling on a youngish man with about four days' stubble. He was dragging nervously on a cigarette and wearing a T-shirt from a Radiohead concert.

'Phil Wainwright?'

'Yeah,' he replied, grinding the cigarette out with a bit too much urgency. 'Fancy a drink? The Summer Lightning is a great pint.' His finger pointed to the tap marked 'Guest Beer'.

'Tempting, but no thanks,' said Jon. 'Is there a quiet room we could . . .?'

Phil lifted up a section of the wooden counter and stepped into the customers' side of the pub. 'This room's empty.'

They sat down on some ancient and battered chairs, the upholstery rubbed smooth through years of use. He pulled another cigarette out of a packet of Silk Cut and offered one to Jon.

Another show of hospitality. Another attempt to break down the occasion's formality. Slightly irritated, Jon waved it away and took out his notebook.

'So, how are you feeling?'

Flicking a lighter, Phil dragged hard on the cigarette. 'Pretty numb, actually.' Smoke crept from his lips by the second word.

Jon's eyes strayed to the tip of the lit cigarette and he reached into his pocket for a fresh stick of gum. 'Giving up,' he explained, unwrapping it and regretting the fact he had allowed Phil an angle into him as a person, not a police officer. Before the insight could be seized upon, Jon continued. 'Now, you were round at Polly's last night? What time did everyone leave?'

'Just before midnight.'

Noting this down, Jon continued, 'And was anyone else there apart from the members of your band?'

'No, just us.'

'Did anyone stay the night?'

'No, we all left together. Ade walked back with Deggs – they share a flat. I went about halfway and turned off to go to my own place.'

'How did Polly seem to you last night?'

'Fine.' He paused and frowned. 'Although she's been up to something lately. She's had the odd call on her mobile that she's been really shifty about.'

Jon kept quiet to tease another comment out of him.

'Walking off to have conversations – it was really annoying. I assumed she had started seeing someone else.'

The silence began to stretch out as Phil examined the tip of his cigarette, so Jon said, 'She was due to be going out today with her mum to do a bit of shopping.'

'Yeah, she was looking forward to it. In fact, she hoofed us all out before midnight so she wouldn't be too rough this morning.'

'Did she mention that she was expecting any visitors before her mum?'

'No.'

'OK, what are Ade's and Deggs' full names?'

'Adrian Reeves and Simon Deggerton.'

'Telephone numbers and address?'

Phil pulled out a mobile and started pressing buttons. As he did so Jon suddenly dropped in, 'Why did you and

Polly split up?' watching closely for the reaction.

Phil's finger hovered for a moment over a button as he lost his train of thought. 'Erm, we'd just drifted apart. God, that sounds a cliché, but we had. She was saving up to go backpacking round the world. I wasn't into it.'

'That's bad news I presume – to lose your lead vocalist?'

He looked up, a slightly wounded expression on his face. 'Yeah, but what could we do? It was her decision. You want those numbers?'

Jon noted them down and then drove back to Ashton police station. He removed his box from the car boot and headed up to the incident room on the top floor of the building – the usual soulless set-up of empty desks, blank monitors and silent phones. Putting the box on a corner desk, he got out his paper management system, desk tidy, stapler, hole punch and calculator, then sat back in his chair and blew out a long breath.

The place would be a hive of activity first thing the next morning: office manager, receiver, allocator, indexer, typist, all arranging their stuff on the desks; plants and other personal effects appearing, the outside enquiry team milling around, waiting to be briefed. And him, in charge of it all.

He booted up the computer, entered his name and password, then went on to HOLMES – the Home Office Large Major Enquiry System. The computer package was based on strictly designated roles and procedures in order that every large enquiry progressed in an ordered manner. It was established directly in the wake of the chaotic hunt for the Yorkshire Ripper, when it was discovered that he had been questioned on various occasions, but the paper reports had never been crossmatched.

Jon studied the search indexes, deciding whether to concentrate on any to steer the investigation in a particular direction. With the information he had at this stage, he decided the usual ones would suffice – family, friends, house by house enquiries and victim profile. He then created an additional one marked 'Narcotics/ sedatives'.

On impulse he went on to the Police National Computer's database and typed in all three band members' names.

Nothing showed up for Adrian Reeves or Simon Deggerton, but after he typed in Phil Wainwright the computer pinged up a result: two cautions for possession of cannabis, the second one accompanied by an order to attend a drugs rehabilitation course.

#

It was almost nine thirty by the time he got home. The front door clicked shut behind him, provoking the usual Pavlovian reaction from the kitchen. Paws scrabbled excitedly on the lino floor and an instant later the crumpled face of his boxer dog appeared round the corner, eyebrows hopefully raised.

Jon slapped his hands against his thighs and crouched down. 'Come here, you stupid boy!'

The dog let out a snort of delight through its squashed nose and bounded towards the front door. Jon caught it by its front legs and twisted it onto the faded carpet. Grabbing it by its jowls, he planted a big kiss on its grinning mouth, then released the animal and stood up. Instantly it regained its feet, stumpy tail wagging so violently its entire back half shook.

By now Alice was standing in the doorway to the telly room, arms folded and a smile on her face. 'Nice to see you getting your priorities right,' she said, nodding down at the dog. 'You're late back – you've missed rugby training again.'

Jon let his shoulders drop. 'New case,' he said, walking towards his partner and bending forward to kiss her.

'Not after you've just snogged that ugly hound,' she said, raising her arms and shying away from his puckered lips. 'Go and wash your mouth out first.'

'Did you hear that, Punch?' he asked the dog, feigning outrage. 'You're ugly and Daddy gets no kiss!'

From the corner of his eye he saw that she had lowered her arms. Suddenly he dipped to the side, then straightened his legs so his face burrowed upward to her throat.

Instinctively she pressed her chin down to her sternum to protect her windpipe. Giggling through clenched teeth, she said in a contracted voice, 'Get off!' A foot snaked round the back of his right ankle.

Not fully aware whether it was a play-fight or not, Punch had started up a half-anxious, half-delighted barking. Jon felt Alice's forearm forcing its way across his chest, and realized she was manoeuvring towards one of her tae kwon do throws. He broke the embrace, stepping away from her and laughing breathlessly. 'I'll have none of your martial arts high jinks in my house.'

Her feet now planted firmly apart, Alice flexed her knees and held up the back of one hand to Jon. The tips of her fingers flexed inwards once and she whispered with Hollywood menace, 'Come and try it, motherfucker.'

His eyes flicked over her combat stance and he took another step back, realizing that he'd think twice about taking on someone like that in a real life situation. 'Later,' he smiled, then looked towards the kitchen door and sniffed, signalling that the fooling around was over. 'Something smells good.'

'Shepherd's pie,' Alice answered, relaxing her posture. 'With salad in the fridge.'

'Ah, nice one, Ali,' Jon answered with genuine appreciation. 'Do you mind if I go for a quick r—u—n first?' Having missed rugby training, he was twitching for some exercise.

'Course not; I ate mine hours ago.'

Jon looked down at the dog. 'Fancy a run?'

At the word 'run' the dog let out a moan of delight and padded towards the front door, eyes fixed on his lead hanging from the coat peg.

'How was your day?' he asked as he began climbing the stairs. 'Tell me as I'm getting changed.'

'I was late for work again. The stupid train into Piccadilly was cancelled.' She followed him up to the spare room, stepping over the weights stacked on the floor and sitting down on the gym bench in the corner. Jon was standing at an open wicker unit, pulling his running gear from the assorted items of sports kit piled up on its shelves. Quickly he removed his shoes and socks, hung up his suit and returned his tie to a coat hanger that had another half-dozen threaded through it.

As he began unbuttoning his shirt, Alice said, while innocently examining the nails on one hand, 'Actually Melvyn introduced a new beauty regime to the salon today.'

Clocking her tone, Jon replied guardedly, 'Go on, what's he up to now?'

He dropped his boxer shorts to the floor and bent forward to pick up the neoprene cycling shorts he wore under his cut-off tracksuit bottoms when running. He glanced up and caught her looking meaningfully at his arse.

'It's waxing for men. "Backs, cracks and sacks", Melvyn's calling it.'

Jon digested the information for a second, then looked at her. 'You're not ripping the hair off other men's bollocks?'

She gave him a provocative little grin.

'Oh, sweet mother of God, tell me it isn't true,' he groaned, holding his head in his hands and pretending to cry. 'If this gets out I'm a dead man.' He looked at her again for confirmation that she was having him on.

Alice held his glance for a second longer, then suddenly smiled. 'Why, got a problem with that?'

'Backs I can understand. Cracks maybe at a push – but sacks? Oh, Jesus.'

'Don't worry. It's going to be Melvyn's special

treatment; he's already drooling at the prospect.' She grimaced. 'Can you imagine it? First booking on a Monday morning, pulling some bloke's knackers to the side and . . .' She yanked sharply at the air while making a ripping noise at the back of her throat.

'Don't.' Jon winced. 'It's making me feel ill. What is the world coming to? Backs, cracks and bloody sacks.' He shook his head in disbelief.

'You'd be surprised at the demand for it. And not just gay guys, as you're probably imagining. Besides, you've never objected to me doing other women's bikini lines.'

'Well, that's different, isn't it?' answered Jon, voice suddenly brighter. 'Why, any recent ones to tell me about?'

'Sad,' she replied, as Jon pulled on a running top with reflective panels at the front and back. Downstairs, he clicked the lead on his dog's collar.

'Punch, if you ever catch her creeping up behind you with a waxy strip in her hands, run for the bloody hills.'

He could still hear her laughing as he slammed the door shut.

The cold night air hit him as he ran along Shawbrook Road to Heaton Moor Golf Course. After cutting on to the grass, he kept to the perimeter, making his way round to the playing fields of Heaton School where he could do some sprints up and down the dark and empty football pitches. Rounding the corner of the school buildings, he saw a group of young lads sitting on a low brick wall, the scent of spliff hanging in the air. Having chosen to ignore them, Jon was jogging past when one of them let out a low wolf whistle. A burst of raucous laughter broke out. Jon carried on and another cocky voice said, 'I hate fucking boxer dogs.'

Jon slowed up, turned round and jogged back, Punch's claws tick-tacking on the concrete as they approached. Jon surveyed them for a second, then narrowed his eyes and lowered his voice to a whisper. 'My dog don't like people laughing. He gets the crazy idea you're laughing at him.

Now, if you apologise like I know you're going to, I might convince him that you really didn't mean it.'

From the blank silence he knew they didn't have a clue what he was on about – and certainly no idea which film he was quoting from. 'I thought you lot looked too thick to be anywhere near a school.'

Now aware he was having a go at them, they looked uncertainly at each other, wondering who would be first to speak. Jon switched to bullshit mode. 'I'm doing two circuits of these fields. Next time I pass this point I'll have my warrant card on me. If you're still here, I'll lift you.'

'You a policeman?' one asked, eyes now wide.

'That's right. And I've got better things to be doing with my free time than nicking little twats like you. But I will, if you make me.'

They started getting to their feet, joint now hidden up a coat sleeve. Without another word, Jon turned away and resumed his run.

Back home, he showered and pulled on an old rugby shirt and tracksuit bottoms. After retrieving his supper from the oven, he sat down on the sofa. Punch was already stretched out in front of the gas fire, one brown eye tracking Jon's every move.

'What's this?' he asked, looking at the telly.

'I don't know,' Alice answered sleepily, moving across the sofa to rest her head on his leg. Holding the plate below his chin to stop any bits falling into her hair, he began shovelling great forkfuls of food into his mouth.

After a few seconds he felt her jaw moving as she began to chew. He glanced at the table. Next to a jar of folic acid pills was an open packet of nicotine gum. 'You fighting an urge?' he asked quietly.

'Mmmmm,' she replied without moving. 'It came on just after you went out. First one since lunch, though.'

'That's great; well done babe,' he answered, thinking how close he'd come to sneaking a cigarette earlier that day. 'By the way, this new case I'm on . . . it's a murder investigation and McCloughlin's made me SIO.'

Alice sat up. 'That's brilliant! Why didn't you tell me before?'

Jon scratched his head. 'I was mulling it over, I suppose.'

'Why? Surely you think it's good news?'

He gave a half smile. 'It is and it isn't. It means I'm being taken off the car thief case.'

'Jon!' said Alice, holding both palms up as if weighing two objects. 'A gang of scrotes nicking cars.' She lowered one hand a couple of inches. 'And SIO on a murder case.' She dropped her other hand so it banged against the sofa. 'Come on.'

Jon nodded. 'I know.'

She settled back into the crook of his arm, head against his chest. 'That's the problem with you. You get your teeth into something and you can't let it go. What's this new case, then?'

Jon leaned over the arm of the sofa and placed the empty plate on the floor. He noticed a strand of saliva set off on a vertical journey from Punch's lower lip and make it to the carpet without breaking. 'A young woman, twenty-two, lived over in Hyde. Someone choked her to death.'

'That's so sad,' Alice murmured. Jon knew she'd be curious to learn more, but she understood that he hated bringing the details of his cases into their home. 'By the way, I heard a bit of gossip in the salon today. That guy you used to play rugby with for Stockport. Married a blonde girl called Charlotte.'

'Tom Benwell?'

'That's him. Have you seen him recently?'

'No. I had two tickets for us to see the rugby sevens at the Commonwealth Games, but he didn't show up. I ended up giving it to a Kiwi then had to sit next to him and watch as his team demolished everyone.'

'That was three months ago, Jon,' said Alice, cutting in

as he was about to start giving a blow-by-blow account of each match.

'Yeah, you're right.' He realized how time had flown by. 'But I tried ringing his mobile a few times. There was never any answer and eventually the line went dead. He must have changed networks.'

'Well, one of the ladies who comes in to get her legs waxed trains at the same gym as that little bimbo he married. She thought Charlotte had walked out on him. Something about him losing his job.'

'Really?'

'Apparently he turned up at the gym searching for her one time. She said he looked a complete wreck.'

'Fuck,' said Jon, feeling guilty. 'We went for a beer once and he told me how he was getting out of the rat race. Said he was selling up and moving to Cornwall, starting a beach cafe or something. I just assumed he'd done it and would ring me when he got the chance.'

'I think you should at least go round and see him, especially after what happened a few years ago.'

'What?' said Jon.

'What?' repeated Alice, rolling her eyes. 'When he got ill, remember? Missed half the season at Stockport?'

Jon frowned. 'That was just some stress thing, wasn't it?'

Alice shook her head. 'Men. What is it with your inability to discuss health problems? According to the gossiping girlfriends at the rugby club, he had a complete breakdown – ended up on the psychiatric wing at Stepping Hill Hospital for two months.'

'Really? He never told me it was that bad.'

'Did you ever ask him?'

'No.'

'Exactly,' said Alice, point made.

Jon sat staring at the TV screen, but uneasiness was now nagging at the back of his mind. He unwrapped his arm from Alice's shoulders.

'What are you doing?' she asked.

'Calling him.'

He got up and retrieved his mobile from the hall. He dialled Tom's mobile, but got the same continuous tone as the last time he'd tried. Scrolling to his phonebook's next entry, he rang Tom's home number. The line was also dead. 'Sounds like both numbers have been disconnected. When did that customer say she'd seen him?'

'About a month ago, I think.'

Worried now, Jon shoved the mobile into his trouser pocket and began pacing back and forth. Punch raised his eyebrows to watch him. 'I'll pop round to his house. It's only five minutes in the car,' Jon announced, looking at Alice for confirmation.

She glanced at the clock on the video. 'At ten forty?'

'I won't start hammering at his door. Just check the house over, see if it's up for sale or if any lights are on.'

#

Jon pulled out of his side street. Soon he crossed Kingsway, a main road leading into the city centre, and headed towards Didsbury. A few turns later and he was on Moorfield Road. He pulled up outside number sixteen and looked at the house. It was dark and deserted, every light turned off.

He got out of the car and glanced around for an estate agent's sign telling him the property was up for sale. Nothing. Walking up the driveway, he noted the absence of any vehicle, then crouched down at the front door. As he lifted the flap of the letter box up, he prepared himself for the buzz of flies and stench of rotting flesh. Pitch blackness greeted him, the temperature inside the house no warmer than the night air outside.

He walked across the lawn to the front window. The main curtains weren't drawn and a chink in the net curtains allowed a strip of light from the street into the room beyond. He saw bare floorboards and no sign of any furniture.

After plunging his hands into his pockets, he walked back down the drive. With each step the sense of being watched grew stronger. At the end of the drive he swivelled round, eyes going straight to the first-floor windows. For an instant he thought something pale shifted behind a dark pane of glass. But focusing on the window, all he could see was dim light from the street lamps reflected there.

Turning the mobile over and over in his pocket, Jon's mind went back to the start of the summer.

Find out more at www.chrissimms.info

Printed in Great Britain
by Amazon